THE
FORGETTING
PLACE

Also by John Burley

The Absence of Mercy

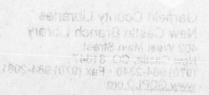

THE
FORGETTING PLACE

JOHN BURLEY

ωM

WILLIAM MORROW

An Imprint of HarperCollins*Publishers*

THE FORGETTING PLACE. Copyright © 2015 by John Burley. All rights reserved. Printed in the United States of America. No part of this book may be used or reproduced in any manner whatsoever without written permission except in the case of brief quotations embodied in critical articles and reviews. For information address HarperCollins Publishers, 195 Broadway, New York, NY 10007.

HarperCollins books may be purchased for educational, business, or sales promotional use. For information please e-mail the Special Markets Department at SPsales@harpercollins.com.

FIRST EDITION

Designed by Diahann Sturge

Library of Congress Cataloging-in-Publication Data has been applied for.

ISBN 978-0-06-222740-9

15 16 17 18 19   OV/RRD   10 9 8 7 6 5 4 3 2 1

For my parents, Dennis and Cari,
who have given me all of themselves, always

THE
FORGETTING PLACE

Part One

Arrival

Chapter 1

Menaker State Hospital is a curse, a refuge, a place of imprisonment, a necessity, a nightmare, a salvation. Originally funded by a philanthropic endowment, the regional psychiatric facility's sprawling, oak-studded campus sits atop a bluff on the eastern bank of the Severn River. From the steps of the hospital's main administration building, the outline of the U.S. Naval Academy can be seen where the river enters the Chesapeake Bay some two and a half miles to the south. There is but one entrance to the facility, and the campus perimeter is demarcated by a wrought-iron fence whose ten-foot spear pickets curve inward at the top. The hospital is not a large central structure as one might imagine, but rather an assortment of redbrick buildings erected at the end of the nineteenth century and disseminated in small clusters across the quiet grounds, as if reflecting the scattered, huddled psyches of the patients themselves. There is a mild sense of neglect to the property. The wooden door frames sag like the spine of an old mare that has been expected to carry too much weight for far too many years. The diligent work of the groundskeeper is no match for the irrepressible thistles that erupt from the earth during the warmer months and lay their barbed tendrils against the base of the edifices, attempting to claim them as their own. The metal railings along the outdoor walkways harbor minute, jagged irregularities on their surfaces that will cut you if you run your fingers along them too quickly.

Twenty-two miles to the north lies the city of Baltimore, its beautiful inner harbor and surrounding crime-ridden streets standing in stark contrast to each other—the ravages of poverty, violence, and drug addiction flowing like a river of human despair into some of the finest medical institutions in the world. Among them is The Johns Hopkins Hospital where I received my medical training. Ironic how, after all these years, the course of my career would take me here, so close to my starting point—as if the distance between those two places was all that was left to show for the totality of so much time, effort, and sacrifice. And why not? At the beginning of our lives the world stretches out before us with infinite possibility—and yet, what is it about the force of nature, or the proclivities within ourselves, that tend to anchor us so steadfastly to our origins? One can travel to the Far East, study particle physics, get married, raise a child, and still . . . in all that time we're never too far from where we first started. We belong to our past, each of us serving it in our own way, and to break the tether between that time and the present is to risk shattering ourselves in the process.

Herein lies the crux of my profession as a psychiatrist. Life takes its toll on the mind as well as the body, and just as the body will react and sometimes succumb to forces acting upon it, so too will the mind. There are countless ways in which it can happen: from chemical imbalances to childhood trauma, from genetic predispositions to the ravages of guilt regarding actions past, from fractures of identity to a general dissociation from the outside world. For most patients, treatment can occur in an outpatient setting—in an office or a clinic—and while it is true that short-term hospitalization is sometimes required, with proper medical management and compliance patients can be expected to function in the community and thereby approach some semblance of stability and normality. This is how it is for the majority—the lucky ones, whose illnesses have not claimed them completely—but it is not the case for the patients here. Too ill to be released into the public, or referred by the judicial system after being found either incompetent to stand trial or not responsible by reason of insanity, Menaker houses the intractably psychiatrically impaired. It is not a forgotten place, but it is a place for forgetting—the crimes committed by its patients settling into the dust like the gradual deterioration of the buildings themselves.

The word *asylum* has long since fallen into disfavor to describe institutions such as this. It conjures up images of patients (there was a time when they were once referred to as *lunatics*) shackled to concrete slabs in small dingy cells, straining at their chains and cackling madly into the darkness. To admit that we once treated those with mental illness in such a way makes all humanity cringe, and therefore one will no longer find "asylums" for such individuals, but rather "hospitals." And yet, for places like Menaker, I've always preferred the original term. For although we attempt to treat the chronically impaired, much of what we offer here is protection—an asylum from the outside world.

Some of this, perhaps, is too bleak—too fatalistic. It discounts the aspirations and capabilities of modern medicine. But it is important to understand from the beginning what I am trying to say. There are individuals here who will never leave—who will never reside outside of these grounds. Their pathology runs too deep. They will never be restored to sanity, will never return to their former lives. And the danger, I am afraid—and the great tragedy for those who love them—is to cling to the hope that they will.

Chapter 2

You've got a visitor," Marjorie said, smiling over at me from the nurses' station.

I glanced toward the intake room. Through the rectangular glass pane in the door I could see Paul, one of the orderlies, ushering in a new patient. *A visitor*, I thought. One of Marjorie's euphemisms.

"Is this going to be one of mine?" I asked, checking the roster board. I hadn't been advised of any new admissions.

Marjorie nodded. "I think you should see this one."

"Did he come with any paperwork?"

"Not that I know of." Marjorie's eyes were back on the chart in front of her, her attention elsewhere.

I sighed. The protocol was that we were to be advised ahead of time regarding any new transfers to the facility, and that those transfers should arrive with the appropriate paperwork, including a patient history and medical clearance assessment. Patients weren't supposed to just show up unannounced, and it irritated me when that happened. Still, one had to keep in mind that we were dealing with a state bureaucracy here. Nothing really surprised me anymore. I decided not to be a hardnose and to let the administrative screwup ride for the moment, although I certainly intended to bring it up with Dr. Wagner later.

Paul had stepped through the door and closed it gently behind him. He motioned me over, and I walked across the room to join him.

"What have we got, Paul?"

"Young man to see you," he said, and we both peered through the glass at the patient seated in the room beyond.

"What's his story?" I wanted to know, but Paul shook his head.

"You'll have to ask him." Apparently, Paul had no more information than Marjorie did.

I pushed through the door. The patient looked up as I entered, smiled tentatively at me. His handsome appearance was the first thing that struck me about him: the eyes pale blue, the face lean but not gaunt. He had the body of a dancer, slight and lithe, and there was a certain gracefulness to his movements that seemed out of place within these walls. A lock of dark black hair fell casually across his face like a shadow. He was, in fact, beautiful in a way that men rarely are, and I felt my breath catch a little as I sat down across from him. I gauged him to be about thirty, although he could've been five years in either direction. Mental illness has a way of altering the normal tempo of aging. I've seen twenty-two-year-olds who look forty, and sixty-year-olds who appear as if they're still trapped in adolescence. Medications have something to do with it, of course, although I think there's more to it than that. In many cases, time simply does not move on for these people, like a skipping record playing the same stanza over and over again. Each year is the same year, and before you know it six decades have gone by.

"I'm Dr. Shields," I said, smiling warmly, my body bent slightly toward him in what I hoped would be perceived as an empathic posture.

"Hello." He returned my smile, although it seemed that even my opening introduction pained him in some way.

"What's your name?" I asked, and again there was that nearly imperceptible flinch in his expression.

"Jason . . . Jason Edwards."

"Okay, Jason." I folded my hands across my lap. "Do you know why you're here?"

He nodded. "I'm here to see you."

"Well . . . me and the rest of your treatment team, yes. But can you tell me a little bit about the events that brought you here?"

His face fell a little at this, as if it were either too taxing or too painful to recount. "I was hoping you'd already know."

"Your records haven't arrived yet," I explained. "But we'll have time to talk about all this later. For right now, I just wanted to introduce myself. Once again, my name is Dr. Shields and I'll be your treating psychiatrist. We'll meet once a day for a session, except on weekends. I'll review your chart and medication list once they arrive. Paul will show you around the unit and will take you to your room. Meanwhile, if there's anything you need or if you have any other questions, you can ask Paul or one of the other orderlies. Or let one of the nurses know. They can all get in touch with me if necessary."

I stood up, but hesitated a moment before leaving. He watched me with an expectant gaze, and despite my better professional judgment, I leaned forward and placed a hand on his shoulder. "It's going to be okay," I told him. "You're in a safe place now."

He seemed to take my words at face value, trusting without question, and in the weeks and months to come I would often look back upon that statement with deep regret, realizing that nothing could have been further from the truth.

Chapter 3

had to ask him for his name, Charles. I don't know the first thing about him." I was in Dr. Wagner's office, trying not to let my irritation get the best of me. It was two days later and the paperwork for the Edwards patient still hadn't arrived.

"Don't worry about the paperwork," he was telling me. "It's not important."

"I don't see how you can say that," I responded. I'd declined to take a seat, and now I shifted my weight to the other foot, struggling to maintain my composure. *Don't worry about the paperwork*, I thought. *He* was the administrator, not me. He should be worried enough for the both of us.

Dr. Wagner had been the chief medical officer at Menaker for as long as I'd been here. He'd hired me right out of residency, although he'd actually suggested during my interview that I consider working elsewhere for my first few years of practice. The conversation we'd had didn't seem that long ago, and standing here today I could picture that younger version of myself sitting in my black skirt and double button jacket—my *interview attire*, as I'd come to see it.

"The job's yours if you want it," he'd told me, "but you should give it some extra thought."

"Why is that?" I'd asked.

He reached forward and slid an index finger along the top of the nameplate near the front edge of his desk, scowled at the dust gathered on the pad of his finger during that single pass. Then he looked at me. "Right now, you want to go out there and make a difference. You're ambitious, enthusiastic, full of energy. You want to use the medical knowledge and skills you've obtained to change people's lives."

"I feel I can do that here," I replied.

He nodded. "Yes, yes. In small, subtle ways, I'm sure you could. But *big* changes, the kind you wrote about in your application to medical school, for example—"

"You read that?" I hadn't included it in my application for this position.

He chuckled and shook his head. "They're all the same," he said, throwing up his hands. "Tell me something." He cocked his right eyebrow and extended his index finger in my direction. The layer of dust still clung to it, displaced from its previous resting place after who knew how many months or even years. "You didn't use the word 'journey' in your essay, did you?"

"Excuse me?"

"Seventy-six percent of medical school application essays have the word 'journey' embedded somewhere in their text. Did you know that?"

"I didn't," I admitted, although I wasn't sure what this had to do with—

"I used to be on the admissions committee at Georgetown,"

he said, "so I should know. I've seen enough essays come across my desk."

"Seventy-six percent, you say?"

"It's a mathematical certainty." He brought the palm of his right hand down on the table with a light smack. "Granted, there's some slight fluctuation from year to year, but on average it's seventy-six percent. The word 'difference' is in *ninety-seven* percent of medical school application essays. *Ninety-seven percent*," he reiterated. "Can you *believe that*?" He chuckled again. "We did a study, tracking the most common word usage in application essays over a ten-year period."

I returned his gaze, not knowing how to respond. The man was eccentric, I had to admit.

"Which means," he continued, "that almost all prospective physicians want to go on a *journey* and to make a *difference*. That's the prevailing dream."

"And?" I prodded, still not clear where he was going with this.

"And you *won't do that* here at Menaker. There is no journey. Patients are here for the long haul and, for the most part, they're not going anywhere. And although you might make a small difference in the lives of some of these patients, that difference will be played out slowly over the course of ten or twenty years. It's not something you'll notice from month to month, or even from year to year. Young doctors come here because the place has a reputation of housing the sickest of the sick. I get that. I can understand the allure. But within a short time, most of them move on—because this is not what they wanted. Not really."

"Some of them must want it," I countered.

He only sighed. "A few, yes. But most don't. I've read enough essays to know."

I'd gone home that night and managed to unearth my own medical school application essay from eight years before, and goddammit if he wasn't right. I'd used the word *difference* twice, and the essay's last sentence read, *I look forward to the journey on which I am about to embark. Pathetic*, I thought, standing there in my kitchen. But at the time I'd written it I'd meant every word. The next morning I called him up to accept the position. Maybe my expectations had changed since applying to medical school. Maybe I just wanted to prove Wagner wrong.

"Did you look?" he asked, and we both knew what he was referring to.

"Yes," I admitted.

"And?"

"And I must be in the minority," I lied. "When would you like me to start?"

That was five years ago, and despite his predictions at the time, I've been relatively happy here. The nursing and support staff at Menaker are dedicated, and the faces of those I work with seldom change. There is a sense of family, and for someone like myself whose real family has been splintered in numerous ways, there is a certain nurturing reassurance in that stability. Wagner had also been right about the patients, who are clearly in it for the long haul. Practicing psychiatry in a place like this is like standing on a glacier and trying to influence the direction it will travel. It's difficult, to say the least. But sometimes, despite all the forces working against us, we are able to effect a change—subtle, but real—and the victory can be more gratifying than one can possibly imagine. But all jobs entail occasional days when you feel like banging your head against the wall, and for me today seemed to be one of them.

"Am I *missing* something here, Charles?" I asked. The volume of my voice had ratcheted up a notch. I made myself take a breath and exhale slowly before continuing. "We cannot admit a patient involuntarily to this institution with no court order and no patient records. It's false imprisonment, tantamount to kidnapping."

If Wagner was concerned, he didn't show it. "I think you should leave the legalities to me," he advised. "Focus on the individual before you, not his paper trail. *Talk* to him."

"I've *been* talking to him. For two days now. He doesn't say much—doesn't seem to know *what* to say."

"It can be difficult."

"It's frustrating. I have no patient history or prior assessments to help me here. I don't even have a list of his current medications."

Wagner smiled through his goatee. It was a look, I suppose, that was meant to be disarming. "I think you have everything that you need right now. Talking to him is the most important thing. Everything else is secondary."

I turned and left the office without a retort, deciding that whatever response I might muster wasn't worth the price of my job.

Chapter 4

W hy don't you tell me a little bit about your childhood," I suggested. We were walking across the hospital grounds, an environment I felt was more conducive to psychotherapy than sitting in a small office as my patient and I stared at each other. Something about the outdoors opens people up— frees them, in a way.

He gave me a pitying, incredulous look—one I'd already become accustomed to receiving from him. I never would figure out where that look came from, but I began to recognize it as his default expression. It was the look I imagined parents of teenagers received with regular frequency. *I'm embarrassed for you because of how clueless you really are*, it seemed to say, except with teenagers there was usually an added dose of resentment, and I never got that from him. Rather, Jason's expressions were touched with empathy—something about the depth of those eyes, perhaps— almost as if he were here to help me, instead of the other way around.

"On the surface, I was part of what you might call a traditional family. We lived in a middle-class suburban neighborhood in Columbia."

"Columbia, Maryland," I clarified, and he nodded. It was located in Howard County, about a thirty-minute drive to the west of us.

"Dad was a police officer," he continued. "Mom used to be a teacher, but when the kids were born, she took several years off to run a part-time day care out of our house. It allowed her to stay home with us during those first couple of years."

"You say 'us.' You had siblings?"

"A sister."

"Where is she now?"

He sighed, as if he'd explained this all a thousand times before. I wondered how many psychiatrists he'd been through before me.

"Your sister," I prodded, waiting for him to answer my question, but he was silent, looking down at the Severn River below us.

"Is she older or younger?"

"She was three years older," he said, and his use of the past tense was not lost on me.

"Is she still alive?"

He shook his head. "I don't know. I haven't spoken with her in a long time."

"You had a disagreement? A falling-out?"

"No," he said. His face struggled for a moment. Beyond the iron pickets, a seagull spread its wings and left the cliff, gliding out into the vacant space some eighty feet above the water.

I put a hand on his shoulder. I wasn't supposed to do that, I knew. There are rules of engagement to psychiatry, and maintaining appropriate boundaries—physical and otherwise—is one of them. What may seem like a compassionate gesture can be misconstrued. Extending a casual touch, or revealing too much personal information, for example, puts the psychiatrist at risk of being perceived by the patient as someone other than his doctor. The relationship of doctor and patient becomes less clear, and the patient's sense of safety within that relationship can suffer. And yet, here I was with my hand resting on my patient's shoulder for the second time this week. I found it unsettling, for I was doing it without thinking, almost as a reflex, and I didn't understand where it was coming from. *Was I attracted to him?* I must admit I did feel something personal in his presence, a certain . . . *pull*. But it was hard to define, difficult to categorize. But *dangerous*, yes . . . I recognized that it had the potential to be dangerous for us both.

"What happened to your sister?" I asked, withdrawing my hand and clasping both behind my back.

"Gone," he said, following the flight of the gull before it disappeared around the bend. He turned his eyes toward mine, and the hopelessness I saw there nearly broke my heart. "She's been gone for five years now, and alive or dead, I don't think she's ever coming back."

Chapter 5

The evening group session I ran in the Hinsdale Building on Tuesdays and Thursdays finished on time, but I had paperwork that I'd been putting off, and by the time I finally put that to rest it was almost 8 P.M. Full dark had settled across the campus, and although the hospital does a pretty good job with exterior lighting, the footprint of the place is still over twelve acres and unavoidably prone to large swaths of shadows. It's for this reason that I don't like leaving after dark. It's not the patients I'm afraid of, although we house more murderers per capita at Menaker than they do at the closest prison, Brockbridge Correctional Facility in Jessup. And, yes, we've had our share of attacks—something the visitor brochures about this place will never mention. An experienced nurse was once killed here during the night shift, struck by a large television (this was before the days of flat screens) hurled at her by a patient while her back was turned. She'd fallen forward, the TV's trajectory matching the arc of her fall, and the second impact had crushed her skull between the old Sony and the tiled floor. There are inherent dangers in working with people—many of them with a history of violence—whose self-control is tenuous at best.

But no, it's not the patients I'm afraid of, but rather the *dark itself* that I find menacing. It's been that way for as long as I can remember, and I can't help but think that it has something to do with *him*, the way his mind turned the final corner that night when I was eight years old, the way I had to go looking for him, terrified that I was already too late.

The wide brick walkway from the physician offices to the front gate was well lit, but I could hear the April night breeze pushing past the oaks on either side, making their newly budding limbs shift and sway as if finally awakening from a long sleep and realizing they had someplace better to go. I could hear the trees whisper to one another, spiteful old men with malevolence in their hearts, the shadowy expanse of the grounds providing complicit cover for their furtive movements. A finger of one of the branches dipped down to graze my shoulder as I passed, catching on the slick fabric of my windbreaker, and for a moment I felt that it did not want to let go.

"Out for a walk, Lise?" Tony Perkins called out to me from the watchman's booth near the gate, and the sound of his voice made me jump.

"Goin' home, Tony," I replied, but he held up a hand for me to stop a second.

"Let me get someone to escort you. Make sure you get there safe."

I live in an apartment less than a quarter mile from the hospital, which enables me to commute by foot in all but the most inclement weather. Security here doesn't like me to walk home at night unattended, and they often have someone accompany me on the trek if I'm leaving after dark. It's sweet of them and reminds me how Menaker, for all its notoriety, can sometimes feel more like a close-knit community than a hospital for the criminally insane.

Tony spoke into his radio, listened to the response. "Matt will take you," he advised me.

I only had to wait a minute.

"Headin' home late, Dr. Shields?" Matt Kavinson emerged from a side path, flashlight in hand.

"Working hard, Matt," I answered.

"You always do. You mind a little company on your walk?" he asked, and I smiled, telling him I was glad to have it.

We bid Tony a good night and left the front gate behind us, the stern silhouette of the hospital lifting its head into the night sky to watch as we descended the hill. The wind picked up and buffeted us from behind, making me wish I'd selected a heavier jacket this morning. It's hard to know in April, as the cold gray tomb of March slams shut for another year and the hot, oppressively humid days of summer begin to rise like swarms of locusts from the Maryland marshes.

"How was your day, Dr. Shields?" Matt asked as we rounded the last corner and my apartment complex came into view. He was good company—quiet and unobtrusive—but there were times when you could almost forget he was standing beside you.

The image of Jason Edwards rose in my mind, those dark eyes looking out over the water below us, our mutual gaze following the gull as it disappeared around the bluff. *Gone*, I could hear him say . . . *for five years now . . .*

"One of my patients . . ." I replied, hesitating, as I stopped now at the entrance to my building. What more could I share? Confidentiality prevented me from discussing such things. It's what makes psychiatry such a lonely profession.

Matt waited for me to go on. He turned slightly away, regarding the hedges hunkered like sentries along the front of the building. "You think you can help him?" he asked, articulating the question in my own mind, and I realized that I wasn't sure if I could. There was something in the way Jason had looked at me today, his expression hopeless, his face defeated from the very beginning—as if I had already failed him, as if everything I had to offer was on the table, and in a cursory glance he could see there was nothing there to save him.

"I don't know," I answered honestly, wishing I felt more confident in my abilities. I certainly *wanted* to help him, but wanting and doing are two roads that may never merge. A gust of wind snatched at the words as they left my mouth, carrying them off into the night.

Matt was quiet for a moment. He clicked off the flashlight, now unnecessary as we stood beneath the glow of the streetlamps. "You'll do what you can," he said. "He believes in you."

I looked at him, wondering whether there was any truth to what he'd said, and found it unlikely that he could know such a thing. "Does he?"

Matt nodded, his face a little sad, but he made an effort to smile nonetheless. "Of course," he responded, turning to go. "You're all he has left."

Chapter 6

lay awake that night thinking about Jason. Matt's words—*He believes in you . . . You're all he has left*—had struck a chord with me, and I kept mulling them over in my mind. It was an odd thing for him to say. His role at the hospital would not grant him access to the background information of our patients. And yet, human relationships trump legal and professional boundaries all the time. If he was dating a nurse who'd been there during Jason's intake, or even knew someone who worked at Jason's prior institution, there was a possibility that Matt knew more than I did about my own patient. That bothered me, but his words weighed on me for another reason as well. It's the nature of psychiatry—the role we've chosen to play. So often we are the only tangible thing anchoring our patients to their delicate perch above the abyss. It keeps me awake at night, contemplating that relationship, and when I close my eyes in the dark, edging carefully toward the elusive precipice of sleep, I can sometimes feel them slipping from my grasp—all of them. I startle awake, reaching out for a better hold, but find myself alone in the room with nothing but black and empty space above me.

I hadn't commented on it today during our session, but it

turns out that Jason and I grew up in the same community—
Columbia, Maryland—although I can't recall having ever run
into him in those earlier years. It didn't surprise me. I've made a
concerted effort to distance myself from that time in my life, as
if there's still a danger of sliding backward into that lanky prepu-
bescent body and the years of emotional abandonment that have
prevented me, even now, from mustering the courage and vulner-
ability to maintain an intimate personal relationship.

I was a child of distractible parents who occupied their
thoughts with practical matters: their jobs and daily errands, relationships with friends and acquaintances, the maintenance of a
house that was more a physical structure than a place of refuge,
the anxiety of never having enough money to feel truly secure. I
remember watching them as we sat around our kitchen table at
dinner, my father's eyes often distant with worry, my mother's
hands straightening her silverware over and over again, as if it
might have moved when she wasn't looking. My brother and I
used to horse around, make faces at each other over the evening
meal, converse in our Donald Duck voices until one of us in-
evitably knocked something over or snorted milk out our nose.
We did it because we were children and that's what children do,
but there was also a certain desperation in that interplay, our
eyes darting in the direction of our parents' faces as we tried to
get them to laugh or smile and shake their heads, their attention
returning to the family in front of them. I remember that I had
the foolish idea that we could somehow change them—awaken
them—and one of my life's greatest disappointments was discov-
ering that we could not.

The worst kind of loneliness, I think, is to be in the presence
of those you love and have them treat you like you aren't there.

To this day, when I picture the face of my mother, it is always in profile, her eyes studying something in the room that is not me. There was so much worry, so much preoccupation in that expression, and because she never talked about the things that troubled her, I was left to imagine the worst. "What's wrong, Momma?" I would ask, but she wouldn't answer, or would respond with, "Hmmm?"—like I'd just disturbed her from a light snooze. Sometimes, if she was sitting still, I would slide up beside her and put my head on her lap. On good days, her fingers would absently stroke the hair on the side of my head, looping a blond lock around the soft curve of my ear, and during those moments I would feel that we were somehow closer. But just as often her hand would lie motionless in her lap, as if the weight of my head on her thigh was causing her some unseen discomfort that she was too stoic to mention, and after a while I would move away, ashamed of my own neediness, and leave her to her thoughts, the retreating tread of my footsteps nearly silent on the thick carpeting of our lifeless house. I would don my sneakers and ease out the front door, closing it gently behind me as if somewhere in the house lay a sleeping infant who must not be roused. I would go down to the creek, picking my way through the twist of underbrush, the sticker bushes slashing at the tan flesh of my calves and ankles, leaving bloody scratches that I wouldn't notice until my evening bath. And when I'd come to my private spot in the woods, I would throw jagged little stones at the trees until my arm ached with the repetitive effort and the hollow place inside of me hurt just a little less.

Chapter 7

The next morning, the earth was strewn with debris from the windstorm the night before. An audience of trees looked down on severed limbs cast about the ground, their hunched and beaten postures reminding me of a congregation of amputees gathered in the wake of a war.

I usually stop at Allison's Bakery for a cup of coffee on my way to work. It's along my walking route and the place always smells like a blend of coffee beans and cinnamon. They offer an assortment of fresh baked muffins and pastries as well, but lately I've been sticking to just coffee. I'm thirty-three, and my body hasn't yet begun the first turn of its downward spiral, but I can feel it wanting to, feel my metabolism beginning to slow, my joints becoming less limber than they once were. I was too thin in college, and the five pounds I've put on since then suits me well, but I wouldn't want it to go any further. The body will take certain liberties if it thinks no one is watching.

"Morning, Lise," Amber greeted me as I stepped to the counter. She was the proprietor's niece and had been working there as long as I'd been coming. Her hair, long and straight, reflected the morning sunlight streaming through the shop's large front window, which I noted had sustained an unsightly crack in the left upper corner since the day before.

I tilted my head toward the window. "Looks like you took on some damage last night."

Amber nodded. "Something big must've hit it." She turned to pull a cup from the stack behind her and began filling it with my usual. "Glad it didn't shatter completely."

"Insurance should cover it, I'd imagine." I wrapped my palms around the outside of the brown paper cup she placed on the counter in front of me, indulging myself in its warmth. Two men in suits, occupying one of the shop's few tables, glanced at us over their morning newspapers.

"I guess," Amber replied. "I haven't called Allison about it yet. Figure I'll let her sleep another hour before giving her the bad news." She produced a small paper cup from behind the counter. "Here, try these," she said. "We just got them in last week."

Inside were two chocolate-covered almonds. I tilted the cup to my lips and let one slide into my mouth. "Why do you tempt me with these things?" I asked, shaking my head. Amber smiled and gave me a wink as she watched me down the second one.

I heard a bell chime, and three more people entered through the front door. They looked haggard, caffeine junkies here for their fix.

"Have a good one," I said, handing the small paper cup back to Amber, who dropped it into the recycling bin behind her. I turned and went to the counter along the far wall, adding skim milk to the coffee and furtively spitting the chocolate almonds into a napkin that I tossed into the garbage. It was a deceitful thing to do, I realize, but there is a ledge one walks between the realms of politeness and self-discipline, and to lean too far in either direction is to risk losing contact with the other. One of the businessmen—young, good-looking, but with an air of being wound a little tight—caught me doing it. He offered me a thin conspiratorial smile, and I returned it before squeezing past the patrons toward the door.

Outside the world was waking up, the people moving along with greater purpose than they had when I'd exited my apartment fifteen minutes before. I could hear the sound of passing traffic along the main thoroughfare a few blocks away, but like myself, many of the local commuters traveled by foot. It was one of the things I loved about this neighborhood—that feel of a close-knit community, something that's become more elusive as the world continues to grow and the distance between each of us presses outward. There was once a time in America when it was considered normal to know everyone on your block. Now, it's different. We guard ourselves more closely, suspicious of unsolicited kindness. We've grown up, lost our innocence, realizing too late that it was the best part of us and that it's never coming back.

Two blocks ahead, behind wrought-iron pickets, the hospital's brick architecture rose up like a mirage against the sky—something ethereal—a place guarded from the outside world, and the world from it. The people living on either side of that fence existed in their own separate realities, aware of one another's presence only in the vaguest sense, as an abstraction, as if the human lives on the other side of that demarcation were a backdrop, an inconsequential part of the scenery. *And where do I fit in?* I wondered, moving back and forth between those two worlds, but not truly belonging to either. I brought the coffee to my lips, took a careful sip, wondering—not for the first time—which population posed the greater risk. The muscles in my legs burned as I climbed the steep hill toward the facility, stopping at the gate to rest and look back upon the town below. The two businessmen had left the coffeehouse, and I caught their eye as they stood on the sidewalk preparing themselves for the day. I lifted my hand in a half wave, feeling suddenly that it was my duty to narrow the gap between us all.

They regarded me coolly, and neither returned the gesture.

Chapter 8

May 12, 2010

When he thought of that evening, what his mind kept returning to was the blood. There had been *so much* of it—an *impossible* amount—more than the human body should contain. It had seeped from the hole between the ribs, pooled beneath the body, congealing into something that was no longer liquid but rather a cooling gelatinous mass on the hardwood. The sole of his shoe brushed it as Jason sank to the floor beside the body for the second time, causing the coagulated puddle to jiggle like a dark lake of Jell-O.

He'd been upstairs in the bedroom when it started, watching a repeat episode from the third season of *Mad Men*. If the doorbell had rung or if she'd knocked, he hadn't heard it. What he *did* hear eventually was the sound of arguing from the floor below. At the outset, Amir's voice had been calm, reasonable, placating. But as the discussion continued his tone took on a sharper edge, becoming defensive, even angry. Jason recognized the female voice as well, and he'd gotten up, deciding he should go downstairs to intervene.

Then a scuffle—noisy at first, but then quiet and focused. He'd never noticed that before, how a physical altercation becomes progressively quieter as the struggle intensifies. Words turned to muted grunts. Halfway down the stairs, Jason could hear the unmistakable sound of a body striking the wall, the clatter of a picture frame falling to the floor.

That got him running, moving quickly through the living room and into the short hallway leading to the front door.

He saw them go down together, arms clasped around each other in what could've been misconstrued, under different circumstances, as a lovers' embrace. Amir landed on top of her, the air from their lungs making an *umph* sound as it was simultaneously forced from their bodies. She arched her back, dug for something attached to her belt, and a second later she was driving a clenched fist into the left side of his rib cage. A single strike and Amir lay still—odd, Jason thought, because she hadn't hit him that hard—and he had time to wonder if maybe Amir had struck his head on the way down, had knocked himself out when they'd contacted the floor. Then she was pushing herself out from under him, was getting to her feet, and there was blood on her hands—too much of it *already*—bright red and dripping from one fingertip onto the blue jeans of the inert body at her feet.

His eyes fell to Amir, to the area where she'd struck him, only now he could see the blood pumping from a wound on the left side of his torso, the knife lying next to him on the floor. Jason dropped to his knees, stuck his fingers into the hole in the shirt left by the knife, and tore the fabric apart to get to the wound. *"Help me hold pressure!"* he pleaded, placing a hand over the site, the blood spilling through the small spaces between his fingers. It was everywhere now: on his hands, arms, and clothing. Days later, he'd notice faint crusted remnants clinging to the underside of his fingernails.

She knelt down beside him, taking hold of his forearms as she shook her head slowly from one side to the other.

"He's gone, Jason."

"*No. He's not gone. Help me move him to the couch. We've got to—*"

"He's dead," she said, letting the words fill the hallway, the town house, the crater of irrevocable absence above which the two of them now perched.

Not dead, not dead, he thought, for the person lying here had been alive and well ten minutes before, had sat at the bistro table and eaten dinner two hours ago in the kitchen behind them. *How can he be dead when the blood is still warm?* he wanted to argue, but he realized that was no longer true. The blood—inert and useless now—had already started to cool.

"*What have you done? WHAT HAVE YOU DONE?!*" he cried out, his words filling the hallway, racing through every room of the town house and back again. But, of course, he knew what she had done. She had come here to protect him—just as he'd known she would. Just as she always had.

She stood, fished a cell phone from her pocket, dialed a number.

"Are you calling an ambulance?" he asked, as if this were a situation that might still be salvaged—might still be undone.

"No," she said. "I'm calling my field office. We'll need a cleaner."

Chapter 9

Let's go back to your relationship with your sister. What was she like?" I asked as we passed Morgan Hall—the main administration building—on what had become our routine walking route across campus. The brick exterior of the building was chipped and scratched beneath the windows, as if something roaming the grounds at night had done its best to claw its way inside.

Jason offered me that half smile of his—ironic and sad, but not completely devoid of hope.

"She always looked out for me, protected me. It's what I remember most about our relationship."

"What sort of things did she protect you from?" I asked, and he was silent for a while, as if the conjuring of those memories required a force of will, a certain mental preparation.

"I tend to think of my early childhood as being fairly happy, although I wonder if I was just too young to know any different. It wasn't until I was about fourteen, though, when things really started to change for me."

We'd come to a stop near the east end of the perimeter. There was a small gate built into the fence here. From the looks of its rusted hinges and neglected condition, I guessed it had been pad-locked shut for the past twenty years, maybe longer. I'd forgotten it was here, and it occurred to me now that so much of Menaker was like that. It lay quiet and unobtrusive, like a water moccasin sunning itself on the trunk of a fallen tree along the riverbank. There are parts of this place that you can almost forget exist until you stumble upon them and they strike out at you from the high grass. I glanced over at Jason, who was looking out past the fence at the tree line beyond, his expression lost in recollection. I said nothing, only waited for him to continue.

"Fourteen is a . . . turbulent age. I think we were all redis-covering girls back then. I still remember how strange and ter-rifying and wonderful that was. It was like we'd known them as one thing our whole lives but were encountering them for the first time as something other than what we'd established them to be. Part of it was their physical development. Their bodies were changing—maturing and becoming different from ours in obvi-ous ways that could no longer be ignored. Part of it was our own hormones kicking in, awakening from over a decade of dormancy and demanding to be dealt with.

"I had this friend, Michael. I guess you could say he was my best friend. He lived a block over from me, used to stop by every day after school—you know: hang out, ride bikes, toss the foot-ball around, that sort of thing. We'd both been living in the same neighborhood since we were born, had grown up together. Our families sometimes even spent vacations with each other, rent-ing out a beach house for a week or driving up to Pennsylvania for a few days of skiing. We were pretty close, and I valued that friendship—relied on it, I suppose—in a way that I didn't fully understand or have the ability to articulate."

The wind moved through his hair—tussled it almost—making him look much younger. I could imagine him as an adolescent.

"Our best friends are those we make in childhood," he said, his eyes clearing for a moment as he looked over at me. "Do you ever notice that? You can live to be a hundred and meet all kinds of interesting characters along the way . . . but our *best* friends are the ones we had as children."

He turned his face away from me, absently brushed a lock of dark hair back from his brow. "Michael and I were in the same grade at school and shared several classes—used to even copy each other's homework from time to time." He smiled. "There was this girl in our English class—Alexandra Cantrell, I still remember her name—who joined us midyear when her parents relocated to Maryland from somewhere in the Midwest, maybe North Dakota." He paused for a moment, then continued. "*Man*, she was beautiful. Long blond hair that she liked to wear pulled back into a French braid; tall and thin with a slightly athletic build; light blue eyes that reminded me of the way the sky looked just before dawn. She was smart, too— easily one of the brightest students in our class—and had this sort of innocent kindness about her that made you just want to be around her, even if you were only in the periphery of her circle of friends."

"She must have been pretty popular," I commented, and he nodded.

"All the guys went crazy when she got there. Most of them were too chickenshit to do anything about it, but the way they used to talk about her . . ." He grinned. "The general consensus was that she was untouchable, out of our league, although I don't recall wondering whose league she might've been in."

"Girls like that," I said, "spend a lot of Saturday nights at home without a date."

"I know that now, but I didn't back then." He shrugged. "It didn't matter, though. I was less intimidated by her popularity than most of my peers. I hung out with her because she was a nice person and fun to be around. Michael, too. The three of us spent a lot of time together that year."

"So there was you, and your best friend, and this beautiful girl," I summarized. It wasn't difficult to see where this story was heading.

"Right," he said. "There were other kids, of course. Like I said, lots of people liked to be around her. But for the life of me, I can't remember who they were. In my mind, what it came down to was the three of us."

"Three is an unstable number," I commented, and he nodded his agreement.

"There was a pond close to our house that would freeze over in the wintertime. We used to go there to skate and play hockey. I remember telling Alex about it one day after school, and her eyes lit up like a Christmas tree. 'Take me there,' she said, and so I did, neither of us bothering to stop home on the way. I don't know where Michael was at the time, why he wasn't with us that day, but he wasn't. We took the school bus, Alex getting off at my stop instead of hers, and we walked two blocks down the street and cut left through the woods to the pond. It had snowed lightly the night before, and we walked mostly in silence, listening to the soft crunch of wet powder beneath the soles of our shoes.

"I remember how, when we came to the edge, she dropped her book bag on the ground and just charged out onto the ice without testing it first, trusting that it was thick enough to hold her weight because I said it was. And of course I ran out after her, planting my feet when I was three-quarters of the way across and sliding the remaining distance to the opposite side. I could hear the ice cracking and settling beneath us—we both could—but she never paused, never cast an uncertain look down. I gathered a snowball and lobbed it out toward the center of the pond where she was standing. It missed her by a good two feet, but she grabbed her chest and fell to the ice like a wounded soldier, lying with her face turned up at the sky, her arms and legs fanned out as if she were in the midst of making a snow angel. I went back out onto the pond, dropping down on one hip and using my momentum to slide into her. We bumped and our bodies did a half turn on the ice, coming to rest with our heads together, our torsos angled slightly away from each other. Laughing, I started to get up, but she reached over and put her hand on my arm. 'Wait,' she said, and so I lay there in the quiet of the afternoon, looking up at the blanket of gray above us. I could hear the steady beat of my heart in my ears, and I wondered if it was loud enough for her to hear as well. I began to say something, but she said, 'Shhh,' and so we lay there together in silence as the wind moved through the trees and the ice buckled and cracked beneath us.

"That was when I started to wonder just how strong that ice was. There'd been a warm spell the week before, and I counted in my mind the number of days since then that the temperature had hovered around freezing. *Five—no, four days*, I realized, and I wondered if that was enough. I could feel the chill of the frozen surface biting through my jeans, imagined the paralyzing temperature of the water just beneath, and considered the thin barrier that lay between. In my mind, I could suddenly see it giving way, the two of us plunging downward, the startled expression on our faces as our heads disappeared below the surface. I could see us reaching up to clutch at the edge of the hole, the ice there breaking away as we attempted to hoist ourselves out. I could feel the shocking chill turn to numbness, our bodies becoming slow and lethargic, the white plume of our breath dissipating over the minutes that followed until at last . . . there was nothing.

"'We should go,' I told her. 'The ice is thinner than I thought. I don't trust it.'

"She turned her body to look at me. 'It'll hold,' she said, and put her right arm across my chest, resting her head on my shoulder.

"Suddenly, I was sure that it wouldn't, that we were lying out there on borrowed time already, that it was prone to give way at any moment. I heard it shift again beneath us, and this time it sounded like the last warning. 'Get up,' I said. 'We've got to go.'

"I remember her looking at me with a wounded expression as I nudged her off me so I could stand, like I was rejecting *her* instead of trying to keep both of us from harm. 'What's your *problem?*' she said. 'What's *wrong* with you?' I don't think she was intending for her words to come out so accusatory, so sharp, but they sliced into me before either of us knew it was going to happen, and once they had there was no taking them back.

"'Nothing,' I replied, backing away from her. 'Nothing's wrong with me.'

"I turned my back on her then, not caring if she fell through the goddamn ice or not, and walked off and left her there. I could hear her calling out to me as I trudged up the hill through the light snow—*Jason, I'm sorry. Whatever it is, I'm sorry*—but I pretended I didn't hear her, pretended it was anger I felt instead of something else.

"After that, we didn't see much of each other for a while. She called me on the phone once, tried to apologize, but it was clear she didn't know what she was apologizing for, and there was nothing I could say to explain it to her. Michael, of course, asked me about it, told me I was acting like a jerk and ought to get over it. But I just couldn't. I'd close my eyes and think about the two of us lying there, one of her arms wrapped casually around me, and the ice suddenly breaking away beneath us, our muted screams for help tapering away into silence. 'What's *wrong* with you?' she asked over and over in my head, and I couldn't look at it. All I could do was back away."

I stood there at the institution's fence and watched Jason struggle. I wanted to reach out to him but reminded myself of the boundaries between doctor and patient, how they needed to be respected.

"Triangles are curious things," he said. "You can't change the relationship between any two points without affecting at least one of the other two relationships. Michael and I had known each other our whole lives, but we'd known Alex for only a few months. I took it for granted that what we shared between the two of us would remain unaffected. But that didn't happen. Maybe it was because of the way I'd treated her, which was unfair. In our small court of public opinion, the verdict was that *she* was the victim, not me, and until I could come up with a reasonable explanation for my actions I was on the outs with both of them. I told myself that it didn't matter, that I didn't care, but of course that wasn't true. I was losing him; that was obvious. What was less obvious was what to do about it.

"Finally, I decided to make amends. And so I rode my bike over to Alex's house the next Saturday afternoon. I'd been there a few times before, and her mother recognized me when I knocked on the door. 'Hi, Jason,' she said. 'Alexandra's playing out back with Michael.' I almost left then, feeling more like an outsider than ever, but then I decided no, I was coming to apologize, and so I walked around to the backyard expecting to find them. When I got there, the yard was empty, although Michael's bike was leaning against the house. I looked around for a moment and, figuring they must have headed up the block, was about to leave when I noticed the opening to a narrow trail at the edge of the woods that bordered the far end of the yard. I trotted across the grass and entered the woods, following the path for about fifty yards until it started sloping downward toward the chuckling sound of a stream below. The earth was a little loose here, and I had to hold on to the trunks of trees as I descended. I was mostly looking down at my footing instead of focusing on the bank of the stream below me, so I was near the bottom before I saw them. I remember how the trees seemed to shift, to open up slightly so that I suddenly had a clearer view—and that was when I noticed them, standing on the opposite side of the stream with their arms locked around each other, kissing softly, almost gingerly, as if they were each afraid of hurting the other. I stood motionless on the hillside, watching from above, realizing that I was already too late, that the nature of their relationship had changed when I wasn't looking, and that what they had now excluded me almost entirely. A barrage of emotions struck me then—anger, resentment, betrayal, isolation, jealousy—but I remember that what I felt most of all was a sense of shame. I was ashamed to be surreptitiously encroaching on this moment between them, ashamed to be thinking that I longed for it to be me wrapped in that embrace. I stood there, wrestling with my anguish, for a few more seconds before quietly turning to go. But the root my right foot was resting on gave way unexpectedly as I shifted my weight. There was a snap and I cried out in surprise, grasping at a tree limb that broke off in my hand. My left knee struck the ground and the earth there crumbled away, sending me sliding down the remainder of the embankment with an accompaniment of pebbles and debris.

"'Jason,' Michael said, letting go of her, but I was seeing him only in my peripheral vision. I couldn't look at them directly, couldn't bear the humiliation, and so I leaped to my feet and scampered back up the hill as fast as I could. By the time I got to the top, I realized there was something wrong with my ankle. It had begun to throb with every step. I didn't run—couldn't really—but I made my way as quickly as possible along the path, limping across Alex's backyard when I got to it and, retrieving my bike from the front of her house, pedaling home as furiously as my wounded body would allow.

"I awoke the next morning to find my right ankle swollen to twice its normal size, and I couldn't bear weight on it. It was Sunday and my mother, realizing that our doctor's office was closed, took me to the ER for X-rays. I was fortunate that I hadn't broken it, the doctor told us, but I'd suffered a bad sprain and was reliant on crutches for the next two weeks.

"When we got home from the hospital, I expected to see Michael sitting on our front steps waiting for me. But he didn't stop by that day or the next. In fact, a week went by and I saw very little of either of them. At school we would catch each other's eye for a moment in the hallway before pretending we hadn't noticed. In class, we'd sit in our assigned seats, keeping our eyes focused on the teacher or on the pages of our respective books. In my mind, I was convinced they were either angry with me or embarrassed *for* me, and that either way I was the cause of all that had gone wrong between us.

"I don't know how much time would have elapsed before we spoke to each other if it hadn't been for an art project I decided to take home from school one day. It was a framed painting I'd made the week before. I'd gotten it back that day with a note from the teacher that read, 'Great use of contrast. This shows real promise.' At a time in my life when I wasn't feeling very happy with myself, I grasped that small piece of praise like a life preserver and held on to it. I wrapped it up in a plastic bag to protect it from the rain and hobbled on my crutches to the waiting school bus. It was awkward to carry, too big to fit into my backpack and tricky to hold on to with my hands occupied with the crutches. I laid it along the outside of my right crutch and held it there with my forearm. It was slow going, and I almost missed the bus, but the driver saw me coming and held the painting for me while I lurched up the steps and into a seat. *So I'd made it halfway*, I thought, *which was good*. But the distance between the bus stop and my house was three blocks off the main road, perpendicular to the route the driver normally took. I disembarked ten minutes later, and I guess I must've looked pretty pathetic working my way down the street because I heard Michael call out to me, 'Yo, Jason. Wait up,' and a few seconds later I could hear his shoes slapping along the wet sidewalk as he came up behind me.

"'Here, give me that, you moron,' he said, and I handed him the plastic-bundled painting so I could use my crutches more effectively. He didn't say anything else, just walked beside me in the rain, the two of us looking down at the asphalt, our shoulders hunched slightly against the weather. When we got to my house I opened the door and we stepped inside. I rested my crutches against the wall and unslung my backpack, dropping it beside me. My parents were both at work and the house was silent except for the sound of our jackets dripping onto the tile floor. We stood there facing each other, neither of us speaking. His eyes met mine only briefly, and then he sort of shrugged and moved toward the door. 'I'll see ya,' he said, and I panicked, knowing that this was the moment for me to say something, to do what I could to make things right between us.

"'I'm sorry,' I blurted out, and he paused with his hand on the doorknob.

"'Yeah, it's okay,' he replied. He took a breath, his left hand raking back the wet brown hair from his forehead. He smiled a little, his hazel eyes regarding me in a way that told me we were still friends, that we'd both been acting like idiots but now all was forgiven. I thought about the years we'd spent together growing up, about the secrets we held on to for each other, about the loyalty that had been built brick by brick like a fortress around us. I wanted to tell him that it was still there, that fortress, and that all we had to do was step inside once again.

"'I'm sorry I didn't recognize it,' he said, 'what was developing between us.' I wanted to tell him it didn't matter, that I had recognized it for both of us. 'Sometimes two people just . . . connect, you know?' he tried to explain, and I nodded. 'I mean, it's like it's not there one day and the next day it is.' He shifted his stance so that his body was turned more fully in my direction, and I took a half step forward.

"'The thing is . . . I think I love her,' he said, and I froze, my mouth going dry. 'Yeah,' he said, more confidently now. 'I love her, dude. I just didn't know you felt the same.'

"I looked away from him, focusing on the stairs leading up

to our living room. I could feel myself tearing up, could feel my throat getting tight. 'I don't,' I told him, but he scoffed a little.

"'It's obvious,' he said. 'I've seen the way you look at us.'

"I shook my head, remained silent, knowing my voice would betray me.

"'Just because I'm spending time with her doesn't mean I can't also hang out with you,' he reminded me. 'We've been friends a long—'

"Without thinking, I leaned forward and wrapped my arms around him, burying my face against his shoulder. I could feel his chest rise and fall against me, could feel the warmth of his body beneath the damp bulk of his jacket. He did nothing for the span of a few seconds, just stood there and let me hold on to him. And then his voice—alarmed, and too loud within the confines of the foyer—was in my ear.

"'What are you doing?' he asked. 'Jason, get off me.' He pushed me away with his hands, and I had to step back onto my sprained ankle to keep from falling. I kept my eyes on his this time, and I think I was crying but I'm not sure. He looked at me in disbelief. 'What's *wrong* with you,' he said, and it wasn't a question but an accusation. In my mind, I could hear Alex asking me the same thing, bewildered by the sudden panic that had taken hold of me as we lay there together on the ice, her arm wrapped around my chest. 'I've seen the way you look at us,' Michael had said, assuming that the hurt and yearning in my eyes was directed at her, not him. Suddenly, the realization dawned on him, and his face changed as if he'd unexpectedly come across something pungent and revolting.

"That's when he struck me, his arm flashing out so quickly that I think it surprised even him. I took the blow in the left temple, my head rocking back and to the right as my vision became a kaleidoscope of images in front of me. The house was quiet except for the sound of our breathing, and standing there—blinded by my tears—I remember wondering whether he would hit me again. My arms hung loosely at my sides, refusing to defend me, and I stood there waiting for it—that second blow—and however many more would follow. Instead, I heard something worse: the sound of the door opening and closing as he left. And it was only then that I allowed myself to crumple to the floor, the sobs ripping through me like bullets, the self-loathing rising in a great wave, and a vague awareness that I had uncovered something in myself that I did not want to deal with. I wanted it to disappear for a while inside me, to come out different or not at all.

"The house stood still around me—silent and watchful—and I remember feeling alone in a way I had never experienced before. I did not think about the ramifications of what I'd done, did not consider the price I would pay in the weeks ahead. That would come later. For the time being, I only sat there with my discovery, not knowing what to do with it. The palm of one hand went to my face to wipe away the tears, and when I looked down I noticed a streak of blood crossing the lifeline. I stood up on my one good leg and, situating my crutches beneath my arms, lurched to the bathroom where I inspected myself in the mirror. There was a gash just beneath my left temple—here." He pointed to the remnants of a faint scar I hadn't noticed before.

"My mom took me back to the hospital to get stitches, and I saw the same doctor who'd treated me for my ankle a week and a half before. When he asked me how it had happened, I gave him some lie about tripping on my crutches, striking my head on the counter. He must not have believed me because he cleared everyone else out of the exam room, asked me if someone had done this to me, if anyone was hitting me at home. I could feel my face flush at the response—a liar's face—as I told him, 'No, it was my own fault. I wasn't being careful. I did this to myself.' He studied me for a moment, then pulled out his pen and jotted something down on the chart. I remember wanting to look at what he'd written, convinced that the final diagnosis would not be 'fall' or 'laceration,' but rather the same accusatory question that had been posed to me twice over the past month. 'What's *wrong* with you?' it would say, and for the first time I had an answer.

"I winced when the pinch of the needle entered my body. The burn of the Novocain ebbed into a strange numbness. *What's* wrong *with you?* I thought over and over again as the sutures pulled the edges of my wound together, their futile attempt to return me into something whole. And when I began to cry, Mother squeezed my hand and whispered her own false reassurance—that it would be over soon, that I just had to be brave a few minutes longer."

Chapter 10

I want to know what he did," I told Wagner, cornering him near the nurses' station.

"Who?" he asked, glancing uncomfortably at the patients around us and signaling to me, perhaps, that it was inappropriate for us to be seen interacting like this.

I didn't care.

"Jason Edwards," I said. "My patient—the one who showed up with no court order, no medical records, no written documentation of any kind. I want to know his psychiatric history, his family background, whether he's ever been hospitalized before . . . and I want to know about the events that landed him here—what crime he was charged with."

"We've been through this before," Wagner reminded me. "I don't have any more information than you do."

"*Bullshit,*" I replied. A few heads turned in our direction and I lowered my voice. "You wouldn't have accepted him here otherwise. You can't commit a patient to a state psychiatric hospital without a court order, and you know it. Now, there's *something* you're not telling me about this case, and I want to know what it is."

He sighed, as if what I was demanding wasn't relevant to my patient's treatment, as if we'd been through this charade a thousand times before. He glanced down at his watch. "I have a meeting in half an hour."

"Well then," I pressed, "you've got twenty-five minutes to talk to me."

Wagner appeared to consider his options. He'd been avoiding me lately; I was almost certain of it. I watched him deliberate a moment longer, then he shook his head with an air of resignation. "Fine," he said. "You want some background on this case? Come with me."

I followed him down the hall, feeling the eyes of patients and staff upon us as we exited the dayroom. It irritated me, those stares. I wanted to turn around and tell them to mind their own damn business, that *I* was the only one acting responsibly here. Instead, I focused my attention on the back of Wagner's sport coat, something beige and polyester that made a soft swishing noise with the pendulum movement of his arms as he walked.

When we were both inside his office, he shut the door and went around his large oak desk to a tall wooden cabinet against the far wall. He pulled open the top drawer and fingered his way through a series of files before finding the right one. I took a seat, inwardly reflecting on how ugly this office was with its rigid, unyielding furniture, its decrepit gray carpet, its complete lack of any natural light, its pretentious but cheaply framed diplomas hanging slightly askew on sickly yellow walls. I wondered how he could stand it, or whether he even noticed.

"The case surrounding Mr. Edwards's presence at Menaker involves the death of an individual named Amir Massoud," he said.

I waited for him to go on, but he seemed to need further prod-
ding. "They knew each other?"

"They were in a relationship," Wagner replied, tossing a newspaper article on the desktop in front of me. I bent to study it.

MAN STABBED TO DEATH IN SILVER SPRING TOWN HOUSE the
headline said. My eyes scanned the lines of text, taking in the
story.

> Twenty-five-year-old Amir Massoud was fatally
> stabbed within his Silver Spring townhome in Mont-
> gomery County, Maryland, on the evening of May 12.
> Police report no signs of forced entry. The victim's
> domestic partner, 25-year-old Jason Edwards, was
> taken into custody for questioning, as the incident
> is suspected to have been the result of a possible
> domestic dispute. Mr. Massoud was a graduate stu-
> dent in civil engineering at University of Maryland.
> He is survived by his father and two siblings. Fu-
> neral services are scheduled to be held at National
> Memorial Park in Falls Church, Virginia.

"He was convicted?" I asked Wagner, picturing the quiet,
thoughtful face of the patient I'd been interacting with over
the past several weeks. We all have the potential for violence,
I know—particularly when it comes to crimes of passion—
but I was having difficulty imagining Jason wielding a knife
in a homicidal rage. It didn't coincide with the impression I'd
formed of him.

Charles studied me from across the desk. "Not exactly."

Of course not, I realized. Jason was in the same category as most of the other patients here—either deemed psychologically incompetent to stand trial, or the more difficult to obtain judicial finding: not criminally responsible by reason of insanity.

"Did he come to us directly from the court system, or was he transferred here after spending time at another facility?"

"Lise," he began, "there's more to this case than you're prepared to handle."

"What do you mean?" I asked. His denigrating tone annoyed the hell out of me, but I tried not to give him the satisfaction of showing it.

"Simply that there are broader forces at work here than you can imagine. Suffice it to say that Jason is only tangentially involved."

"I don't understand."

"I know," he replied. "But unfortunately any further information I provide would be difficult to integrate with what you already know."

He talks like a true administrator, I thought, *constructing his sentences with the careful design of conveying as little useful information as possible.* I scowled at him. "What in the hell does *that* mean?"

He shook his head. "I know this puts you in an awkward situation."

"It puts me in an *impossible* situation," I corrected him. "I mean"—I raised an exasperated hand into the air and let it fall like dead weight into my lap—"what am I not understanding here, Charles? Is this political? Are you protecting someone? *Jesus,* we have a responsibility—a professional and moral duty—to act in the best interest of our patients."

"I feel that I'm doing that."

"*Do you? Do you really?*" I asked.

He regarded me impassively, his features unyielding. "I'm sorry I can't tell you more."

"One thing is becoming clear to me," I said, standing to go. "You're allowing yourself to be manipulated by outside influences that have *nothing* to do with the medical management of this patient." I went to the door, put my hand on the knob, but turned back to look at him one last time before I left. "Your judgment is compromised," I told him.

He had the audacity to turn those words back on me, as if somehow *he* were the righteous one. "So is y—" he started to respond, but I slipped into the hallway and shut the door behind me before he could finish.

Chapter 11

That night I couldn't sleep. I lay in bed staring at the wall, the images of newspaper articles I'd tracked down online that evening popping into my head like the small explosions of flashbulbs from a 1930s-era camera. For hours I'd hunched in front of my PC's monitor, the index finger of my right hand clicking away, moving up and down along the mouse's roller as my eyes darted back and forth across the paragraphs. It had been hard to concentrate. At the far end of the hall outside my apartment someone was yelling—the person's voice wild, hysterical, chaotic. I was reminded yet again of the thin artificial separation between institutions like Menaker and the vast, untethered world beyond, and wondered how many souls had been misassigned to each. I got up, paced the room, considered calling the police. But already I could hear other voices—calm and authoritative—in the hallway, and I realized that someone must have beaten me to it. The yelling escalated for a moment, followed by the ensuing sounds of a brief struggle. Others in the complex—my neighbors—might be opening their apartment doors and poking their heads through the thresholds for a quick peek at the action. But not me. I saw enough of this type of thing at work. My days were filled with it. I had no desire to witness it here, in the ostensible shelter of my personal life.

After the noise abated, I went to my computer again and sat down. Amir Massoud had indeed died on the night of May 12, 2010—stabbed to death in the front hallway of his townhome. He'd died at the feet of his domestic partner, Jason Edwards. The knife, bearing Jason's fingerprints, had been lying on the floor next to the body when police arrived. I could imagine the blood on Jason's shirt, his pants, his palms, already beginning to dry into something lifeless and irreparable. I could imagine the first arriving officers taking in the scene in a glance and, with hardened faces and practiced efficiency, pulling their weapons and ordering Jason to show them his hands, to move away from the body and to lie facedown on the floor while they pinned him down with a knee to the back of the neck. His arms would have been twisted behind him, his wrists ensnared in the uncompromising steel of the cuffs. In my mind, I could see him being led out to the street, the officer grunting, "Watch your head," as Jason lowered himself into the back of the vehicle. I could envision him sitting at some table amid lime-green walls in the station's interrogation room, could hear him being grilled by the detectives, could even imagine him breaking down under the emotional strain and confessing to it all. I could envision all that, but what I could not picture was the actual murder. I could not imagine the hand of my patient wrapped around that knife as he plunged it into his lover's chest. I closed my eyes, concentrated on forming that image, but it simply wouldn't develop. What appeared instead was the expression on his face the first day I'd met him.

During my medical training, I'd seen that look from time to time. It was in the faces of some of the terminally ill cancer patients I'd treated as an intern: a surrender, an overwhelming fatigue, a desire to let go, to be done with it all, and yet the realization that there was something beyond their control that was holding them here still. They resented it, I knew, the indignity of that lingering existence. Jason had borne that look the first time I met him, and there were days when I noticed it still, as if he were stuck in some purgatory from which he might never be released.

I switched off the computer and went to the bathroom, studying my reflection in the mirror. There were dark lines beneath my eyes and the corners of my mouth seemed to droop into an unhappy countenance. My face looked puffy and swollen, like I'd been crying, although I had not. The water was cold as I splashed it on my face with cupped hands filled from the faucet, harboring the hope that when I returned my gaze to the mirror I'd look different—somehow refreshed and unburdened.

I did not.

I climbed back into bed and lay there in the dark. An argument in the apartment next to mine could be heard through the thin walls. I sandwiched my head between two pillows, tried to ignore it, and felt like I was eight years old again, listening to my parents bicker in the other room.

"He's got no place else to go," I could hear my mother saying, her voice low and meek in response to my father's domineering presence. He was a man used to exerting his will over others, and it infuriated him when he perceived resistance to a course of action on which he'd already decided.

"Well, *living with us is not the answer!*" he exploded, and I could hear something strike the common wall shared by our adjacent bedrooms. A shoe, I thought. It was just a shoe—not my mother's head.

There was silence in the house, and despite my fear I pulled back the covers, crossed the room, and padded out into the hallway. The brass knob of my parents' closed bedroom door was cold in my hand.

A quick sound of footsteps on the other side, and suddenly the door was yanked open, the doorknob wrenched from my grasp. My father stood in the threshold, glaring down at me. "What do *you* want?" he demanded, the sentence feeling more like an allegation than a question. Beyond him, I could see my mother sitting on the side of the bed, a forgotten article of clothing folded in her lap.

"I . . . I heard something hit the wall," I replied, too stunned to try for anything but the truth. "I just wanted to make sure you and Mom were okay."

"We're fine," he told me. "We were just having a little discussion about your uncle Jim. Your mother thinks it's a good idea for him to come live with us."

"I like Uncle Jim," I said.

My father got down on one knee in front of me, looked me straight in the eye. "Let me tell you something about your uncle Jim that your mother is too chickenshit to mention. Your uncle Jim is crazy. He's been in and out of institutions for years now, had his brain poked and prodded by all those quacks over at the psych hospitals in Baltimore, Springfield, and Ellicott City. *And what good has it done him?*" he asked, casting a challenging look over his shoulder at my mother. "He's still as crazy as the first day I laid eyes on him. And now"—he turned his smoldering gaze back on me—"she wants him to come live with us. You think that's a good idea, Lise? Do you?"

I stood there, a deer in the headlights, not knowing how to respond.

"Leave her alone," my mother told him from where she sat on the bed. "She hasn't done anything. You don't need to yell at her, too."

"I'm not yelling," my father said, standing up and turning away from me. He raked a hand through his thinning hair. "I'm just trying to be the voice of reason here." He crossed the room, put his hand on the nightstand. "He attacked a lady. Did you know that, Lise?" I shook my head, but he went on without waiting for a reply. "He attacked a lady in broad daylight. And now he's got criminal charges against him."

"That they dropped," my mother said, "because he's ill, not dangerous. And they're willing to release him if there's someplace willing and able to take him in."

"Why does it have to be us?"

"Because we're the best place for him," she replied. "The half-way houses, the hospitals, the board-and-care facilities—he doesn't do well in those other settings. He needs familiar surroundings, people who truly care about him and who will make sure he takes his medications."

"A fat lot of good they've been doing him," my father said, un-snapping the watch from his wrist, winding it, and placing it on the nightstand.

"The medications help. But he has to take them, Roger. They don't always make sure he does that at those other places."

"And you will?" he asked.

"He's my brother," she said. "I want to see him well."

My father put his face in his hands, sighing his resignation. He dropped them to his waist, placing them on his hips as he considered the two of us for a moment. "This is a bad idea," he said. "I'm telling you that now, and I want the both of you to remember this conversation when things go poorly. Because when that happens, it will be your responsibility, not mine."

"I love him," my mother said, "and he needs us."

There was a shrug of the shoulders as my father walked into the bathroom and shut the door behind him. I could hear the click of the latch, and that was the end of the conversation. But he'd given in to her, I realized, and more than anything else, *that* was what surprised me. It was the only time in my life I'd seen my mother stand up to him. And despite how it all turned out— how my father's admonition proved accurate—I really wish she had stood up to him more, that she had found her voice instead of curling deeper into herself over the years, becoming someone I could barely recognize and almost never reach.

TWENTY-FIVE YEARS LATER, I was thinking about it still. And behind some closed apartment door in the hallway beyond, I could hear the muffled cries of the screamer begin again. The police hadn't taken him away after all, I realized. They'd merely returned him to the confines of his domicile, instructing him to keep quiet and to stop bothering his neighbors. Perhaps this was where he belonged then—with his family—not yet broken enough to be removed from society's midst. I turned onto my side and pulled the covers up over my head, but sleep was a long time coming.

Chapter 12

"Good morning," I greeted Amber, stepping to the counter at Allison's Bakery for my usual cup of joe. She smiled widely as she poured and, sliding the beverage across the counter, selected a few small confections and popped them into a sample cup for me to try. I picked one up between my thumb and forefinger, raising an eyebrow.

"Cinnamon apple crunch," she said, "with just a touch of hazelnut."

I took a sip of coffee, forgetting to blow on it first, and almost burned my lip.

"Be careful," Amber warned, but I held up a hand, accepting the blame. I knew better. The coffee here was hot. You had to give it a minute.

"Don't forget these," she said, tapping the cup of apple crunch. I picked it up and took it with me as I crossed the bakery, stopping to add some milk to my coffee and to toss the sweets in the trash before temptation got the best of me. I waved to Amber as I exited the shop, heading in to work a little earlier than usual in order to review some charts and catch up on paperwork.

I was thinking about the day ahead of me when a screech of

brakes brought me around to the present, my body flinching as a dark Chevy sedan came to an abrupt stop at the crosswalk, its bumper only a foot and a half from my lower leg. My heart, responding to the threat after it was over, doubled its pace in the space of a few seconds.

"Sorry," I called out, shamefaced, realizing I hadn't checked for traffic before stepping into the street. I stepped back onto the sidewalk, motioned for him to proceed. The car idled for a good ten seconds, enough time for people behind it to start tapping their horns. I wondered whether he wanted me to cross, but I couldn't make out the driver through the glint of sun coming off the windshield. I decided to hold my ground, indicating again that he should go. The car sat idling for another few seconds, then lurched forward and passed me, hurtling down the street and hooking a right at the next intersection.

I'd barely had a second to look through the side window at the occupants, but I'd taken in as much as I could. The faces of the driver and passenger had been turned in my direction, contemplating me with their slate-faced stares. It was the two businessmen I'd noticed in the coffee shop the week before, on the day after the storm. My mind moved from day to day since then, realizing their consistent lingering presence in the background of my commute: at the bakery that first day, in the doorway of the flower shop perusing the day's offerings, at the newspaper stand a half block from here, on the park bench across the street, and now . . .

I walked quickly up the hill toward the hospital, checking over my shoulder several times along the way. *I'm just spooked by the near miss*, I told myself, *that's all. Of course* I had seen them many times before on my way to work. They were on their *own* way to work, weren't they? There was nothing more to it than that. *But always lingering*, a small voice inside my head interjected. *Never in a hurry. Never actually going anywhere. Until . . .*

Until today. *And what's different about today?* Well, I was heading in earlier, that was one thing. Perhaps I'd caught them off guard, thrown off their schedule. But there was something else that was different as well. I thought of my confrontation with Dr. Wagner the day before. *There's more to this case than you're prepared to handle*, he'd advised me, but I had bulldozed ahead anyway, pushing him for answers that he was either unable or unwilling to give. In doing so, I'd raised my head above the water, called attention to myself as a possible threat to whatever or whomever he was protecting. In response, the incident today had been . . . what? An escalation? A warning?

I passed through Menaker's guarded gates with a palpable sense of relief. For the first time, I felt the full weight of the protection it had to offer—not to the patients hospitalized here or to the outside world, but to me personally. I looked back toward the fence, the iron posts standing shoulder to shoulder like sentinels.

There are broader forces at work here than you can imagine, Wagner's voice echoed inside my head. *Suffice it to say that Jason is only tangentially involved.*

Perhaps, I thought, *but he is involved. And now . . . so am I.*

I've mentioned before that, in the best sense of the word, Menaker is an asylum. It is about safety. But lately, it seemed, Menaker was also about secrets. Was it really possible that Dr. Wagner had been compromised, infected by whatever *broader forces* he was referring to? Could I no longer trust him? As I looked around once more—at the security cameras perched strategically near the corners of the buildings, at the two nurses engaged in hushed conversation as they shuffled along the walk-way to my right, at the guard observing me with an innocuous smile from the booth near the facility's front entrance—I began to wonder how far such an infection might spread, about how far it may have *already* spread.

There was no way of knowing for sure, so I lowered my eyes to the concrete walk in front of me and headed inside.

Chapter 13

You were telling me about your conflict with Michael," I reminded him. We were near the northern perimeter of the property, and as we talked I found myself frequently looking past the fence at the streets beyond, my eyes searching for idling cars, for the two men who'd nearly run me down earlier today. A few people shuffled by on the sidewalk, glancing toward us with interest, curiosity, or vague indifference—I wasn't sure. I had the persistent feeling of being watched, although there wasn't much to be done about it. The perception, I knew, might not even be accurate. Most likely, it would pass.

Jason's eyes were focused on our shuffling feet. The spring breeze lifted a finger of dark hair from his forehead, and I could see the hint of a scar—like a reverse comma—on his left temple. It actually added to his appeal, giving his youthful face a touch of maturity. Maybe it was simply the intimacy of knowing his secret, of having been trusted with a view at the portions of the wound that ran much deeper than skin.

"I don't know if I lost Michael's friendship completely that day—the day he struck me. But what I did lose was his willingness to express that friendship, to try to understand what I was going through. He told people what had happened. To this day, I can't bring myself to believe it was something he did out of maliciousness. Maybe he was confused or hurt. He probably felt betrayed in a way—like everything we'd shared up to that point had been a lie. If he'd realized that I'd been as surprised by my actions as he was, that if this was an ambush it had been sprung on both of us . . . He would have scoffed, I'm sure. But it was true. Still, it didn't matter. He told people, I think, because it was impossible for him not to. There are some things you can't carry around on your own for very long. I don't blame him. But once it was something beyond the two of us, there was really no stopping it."

"You were fourteen," I said. "The fallout must have been—"

"It was mild to begin with," Jason said. "Michael wasn't at our bus stop the next morning, and so I lurched up the bus's steps by myself, crutches tucked into my armpits like two shotguns I was afraid might go off at any moment. I took an empty seat near the front, propped my head against the window, tried to make myself invisible.

"It must've worked because at the next stop Michael and Alexandra climbed aboard and walked right past me like I wasn't there. I kept my eyes out the window, watching the rain spatter the surface of puddles along the sidewalk. The remainder of the ride to school was uneventful, and as we came to a stop in the parking lot and Mr. Gavin engaged the wheezy pop of the air brake and swung the doors wide, I sat still in my seat and let the other kids get off before me, not wanting to hold up the line with my awkward three-legged descent. 'You be careful now, Jason,' Mr. Gavin warned me halfway down. He must've been referring to my crutches, but I took it more as an admonition for the days ahead."

I nodded. Beyond the fence where we were now standing, a squirrel darted across the street and was nearly struck by a passing car. I winced, but the tires missed its fragile body by a few inches. It reached the other side and scampered up a tree where I lost sight of it amid the leaves.

"People talk about the calm before the storm," he continued, "and that's how it felt to me during those first few days. In the Emergency Department, the doctor told us that the stitches in my face would need to be removed in five days, and I used that time as a barometer. I told myself that if I made it that long without hearing anything from Michael or the rest of my peers, then there was a good chance the whole thing would just . . . blow over. It was flawed reasoning, I knew, but it gave me something to hold on to, something to set my sights on. *Five days*, I told myself. *Just five days.*"

Jason paused, placing one hand on the iron rail. "I made it three."

His image seemed to fade a bit as I watched, as if he were being pulled—physically as well as mentally—into his own recollection. I could almost see him, not as he was now but as he might have looked back then: the uncertain countenance and boyish face of an adolescent, the scar along his left temple red and puckered beneath the stiches, the greatest losses of his life still ahead of him.

He started walking again, slowly, his eyes scanning the buildings to our right. I matched his pace, wondering if he was seeing those buildings for what they really were, or if, in his mind, he was fourteen once more and on his way to school.

"I was limping down the hall toward my locker," he said. "My ankle had healed enough that I could finally walk on it, and I'd decided to leave my crutches at home that morning. So there I was hobbling along, still favoring my right ankle and keeping close to the wall so that I could lean against it for support if necessary. We had six minutes between classes, and the hall was full of conversations, laughter, the flow of student foot traffic. I stopped at the water fountain for a drink, and as I was bent forward I felt someone give me a light smack on the butt as they passed. I stood up quickly, looked around, but no one looked back at me, no one snickered—in fact, no one appeared the least interested in my response.

"*Something harmless*, I told myself. *Just a friend messing with me.* It was certainly possible. Problem was, I didn't have that many friends—except for Michael and Alex, and I had the feeling they'd fallen irrevocably off the list recently. And neither of them was in the hallway; I would've recognized them, even from behind. So I made a decision that it was nothing. I went to my locker, changed out my books, and headed off to science. I remember we were diagramming the GI tract of an earthworm that day—mouth, pharynx, esophagus, crop, gizzard, intestine—and all the while I kept feeling that light smack on my butt in the hallway. A scrunch-faced pimply boy named Bret Forester leaned over to study my drawing. 'Don't forget the anus,' he whispered, just loud enough for a few others around us to hear, and a twitter of muffled laughter wound its way around the room as my ears turned red and miniature beads of sweat popped out on my neck and upper back. 'Quiet,' the teacher ordered, and the room filled with a heavy silence—the deadly, expectant communal anticipation of a crowd come to witness the offering of a human sacrifice. *It's nothing*, I told myself, focusing my eyes on the surface of the teacher's desktop two rows ahead, looking at no one, my ears still blazing, the sharpened pencil forgotten in my hand. *It's nothing,* I thought again, the phrase repeating itself like a mantra until the overhead tone sounded, marking the end of class. 'Nothing,' I mumbled softly to myself as we filed through the open door. But of course I was wrong.

"'Hey, Jason. How 'bout a kiss?' Bret Forester quipped somewhere off to my right. 'I hear you like boys,' he said, and there was no mistaking the motive behind *that* jab.

"I didn't think, didn't deliberate. I responded out of pure self-preservation because to *not* respond—to continue to ignore it—would only make matters worse.

"I dropped my books and swung. I wasn't a fighter, wasn't big or particularly athletic, but I had the advantage of surprise—and fury—on my side. My clenched fist struck him directly in the nose, making that scrunched-up face of his fold in on itself even more. He fell backward against the wall, his small ugly mouth forming a perfect circle of astonishment. And suddenly the blood began to flow—a startling amount for the single shot he'd taken. His nose was broken. I could see its crooked angle through the splay of fingers pressed against his face. I said nothing, just stood there and stared him down, waiting to see if he would come for me, ready to go to the ground with him if necessary. But bullies are really cowards, and all it takes is the proper show of force to back them down—at least temporarily."

Jason glanced at me then, and I could see a furrowing in his brow that hadn't been there before. "But bullies can also be dangerous when crossed. And they have friends. So I stood there and did the math in my head, totaling the reinforcements on both sides of the equation. On my side, of course, it was just me. There was no one else I could count on, and I realized then and there that I would take a beating for this. They would gather their forces and come for me. I would be ready for them—expecting it—but I knew I couldn't win. Not on my own. And even through the blood and pain, the cold, hateful look in Bret Forester's eyes told me that he knew it, too."

Chapter 14

I allot a certain amount of time each day to talk with my patients, and my session with Jason had already run over, but I couldn't leave it at that. "Eventually, they caught up with you," I surmised, and he nodded.

"I couldn't outrun them—not with my ankle the way it was—and so the first time they came for me I simply stood my ground."

"How badly were you injured?" I asked.

Jason shrugged. "Not as badly as I'd anticipated. Black eye. Cut lip. Once I went down, I was able to get my arms up over my head and face, but they kept kicking me and managed to break a few ribs and bruise both of my kidneys in the process. The ribs took six weeks to heal, and there was blood in my piss for three days after the assault. But all things considered, I counted myself pretty lucky. Mostly, I was just glad it was over."

I waited for him to continue.

"Except, of course, it wasn't over. With guys like that, it's never really over, is it? Once they set their sights on you, it becomes a compulsion, like a patch of dry skin they just can't scratch to their satisfaction. And even though you're cracked and bleeding—and on some level they must realize that they've gone too far—they simply can't stop until something irreparable happens, until the wound is too macerated and ruined to tolerate anything further.

"The second time they came for me was in the school bathroom. I fought back hard that time—hit one of the boys, Tim Maddox, in the windpipe, putting him out of commission. Clayton Flynn took a kick to the knee that I hope he *still* feels on rainy days, and I kept swinging at Bret Forester's pimply, bulldog face, trying to break his nose for the second time. But there was a fourth boy, Billy Myers, who was mean, quiet, and probably the only one of them with true lethal potential. He's locked up in a maximum-security prison somewhere right now, I just know it, but on that day he snuck up behind me while most of my attention was on Bret and he hit me in the back of the head with something hard and metal, and that's all I remember of the fight until I woke up to a small crowd of students around me, some teacher's voice calling my name, and my head resting on the lower lip of a urinal.

"They took me to the hospital—my fourth visit in two months—only this time the ER doctor was a woman who made small noises I couldn't interpret and shook her head as she examined me. They did a CT scan of my brain, which was thankfully normal, kept me overnight for observation, and discharged me the next morning with a diagnosis of concussion."

Jason's eyes cleared for a moment. "My sister came to visit me in the hospital," he recounted. "She sat at my bedside and studied me, saying very little. I had other visitors, of course, but it was *her* presence that I remember the most. We must've spoken to each other during that visit, but the only thing I remember was what she said to me just before leaving. She walked over to the bed, leaned forward, and planted a kiss on my forehead—which was pretty unusual behavior for her. She drew back a bit, observed me with a calculating look. I thought she was going to give me a brief lecture, tell me something useless like how I needed to stop fighting and just stay away from those kids. But what she instead said was 'This will not happen again.' Then she turned and left, leaving me to wonder how she could promise a thing like that. Yet, somehow, I believed her, and a half hour later I pulled the string to shut off the fluorescent light above my bed, closed my eyes, and slept better than I had in weeks."

"Was she right?" I asked.

"In a way," Jason replied, and he smiled as if I'd said something funny.

About fifty feet from where we stood, Menaker's grounds-keeper, Kendrick Jones, spotted us and lifted an arthritic hand in our direction. His forearm was a tapestry of scratches, his face stained and weathered by the relentless sun. He tried to stand fully erect, but could not—his back permanently stooped from all those years tending the yard. I could see the dull, sightless opaqueness of his right eye, the result of being jabbed four years ago by the sharp end of a branch he'd been trimming. I tried to imagine how Kendrick might've looked his first day on the job, and whether he would've taken the position at all if he real-ized how the hospital would latch itself on to him like a parasite, sucking the youth and vigor from his body until he was nothing but a brittle, pathetic shell. I raised my hand to return his ges-ture, but his good eye had spied a wayward thistle near the fence. He frowned and scuttled after it, leaving the two of us alone once again.

"Three weeks went by before they came for me again," Jason told me. "I can't say I was surprised. I knew they would come, knew they weren't finished with me yet, especially since I'd gotten in a couple of good shots the last time. They wanted a decisive victory, wanted to humiliate me completely. I realized there was trouble as soon as I got off the bus that afternoon. The neighborhood was too quiet, the streets emptier than they should've been. Right away I got that fluttery feeling in my stomach, like I wanted to giggle and throw up at the same time. I'd only covered a half block, walking fast, when Tim Maddox stepped out from the bushes onto the sidewalk ahead of me. He smiled, but there was no humor in it, and as he started walking toward me I broke to the right, running but not all-out yet, saving my wind for when I'd really need it.

"Bret lived three blocks away, and as I ran down the sidewalk he and Clayton stepped off his front lawn and into the street. Clayton had a bat in one hand, its thick end resting on his shoulder, and he looked eager to use it. I hooked left into the woods, moving through the trees until I came to the lip of a gulley. I could hear them entering the woods behind me, taunting me, calling out, 'Wait up, we just wanna talk to ya.' And all the while I kept thinking, *Where's Billy Myers?* The stealthy one. The meanest of the four. The only one with murder in his eyes.

"I ran along the edge of the gulley, my ankle beginning to ache. The path of my flight was looping around toward home. *If I can get inside the house, lock the doors,* I thought, *then maybe I'll be okay.* They were chasing me through the brush, shouting to one another: 'There he is!' 'Up ahead!' 'Get him!' But I was getting close to the house, could recognize the thatch of trees that bordered our street, and even with my messed-up ankle, they were lagging behind, out of breath, all words and no steam. I remember thinking that my escape was almost too easy. It didn't make sense that

I was outdistancing them like this. And on the heels of that I kept thinking, *Where's Billy?*"

"It was a trap, wasn't it? They were flushing you toward him."

Jason nodded. "Billy stood waiting for me at the edge of the woods. I was pretty winded by then, and as he came hurtling toward me down the slight hill there was no chance of dodging him. He meant to tackle me head-on, but I saw it coming and at the last second dropped to one knee and his forward momentum allowed me to take him out at the legs. He hurtled over me, somersaulting once in the air, and before I heard his body crunch against the ground behind me I was back on my feet and moving up the hill.

"But he was fast, so fast, and I felt him snag my ankle from behind, bringing me to the ground. I kicked out with my other foot, caught him in the face with the sole of my shoe, but that only seemed to anger him. The others were bullies and opportunists, but Billy Myers was crazy—*and he will kill me*, I thought as he clawed his way up my body, pinning me to the ground, his eyes wild, spittle flying off his lower lip.

"'You're gonna get what's comin' to ya, faggot,' he hissed in my face, and he wasn't talking about another beating this time, because he reached into the back pocket of his jeans, pulled out a black-handled thing that he dangled in front of my face, and with the flick of a spring-loaded switch, a six-inch blade shot out from one of its ends.

"I was plenty scared then because—like I said—the look in Billy Myers's eyes told me he had every intention of using that thing. I started bucking and thrashing beneath him, trying to throw him off me, but by then his reinforcements had arrived and they piled on top of me, too, holding down my arms and legs.

"'*Hold him still, goddammit!*' Billy instructed as he yanked up my shirt and placed the cold point of the blade against my stomach.

"'Hey, Billy,' Tim Maddox whispered, as if the rest of us couldn't hear him, 'you're not gonna really cut him, right? You're just messin' with him.' There was a pleading tremor in his voice, and I realized that he, too, was scared of Billy—of what he was, and what he was capable of doing.

"'Just shut up and hold him,' Billy said. He looked calm now—tranquil even—as if a thin curtain had fallen across his face, leaving him devoid of emotion. Only his eyes betrayed him, revealing the nastiness beneath, and I stopped wondering if he was going to cut me and braced myself for the silent punch of steel through the flesh of my abdomen.

"'Excuse me,' a female voice interjected, and I watched as all four of their faces looked up in unison. It was almost comical, the synchronized upswing of their heads, their jaws dropping open slightly. In the next second there was a whooshing noise as something cut through the air and connected with Billy's forearm. I heard a resounding crack as the bat made contact. Billy screamed and rolled backward, clutching an arm that now hung at a grotesque angle from his elbow. The knife fell with a soft plop onto my stomach, and I looked down to see a single bead of blood welling up where the point had pressed against my skin. Billy's arm had taken most of the bat's force, but the follow-through of my sister's swing caught Tim Maddox in the temple, sending him flying backward—ironic, since he'd been the one who'd brought the Louisville Slugger to the ambush in the first place but had tossed it onto the ground in order to get a better hold of me. If the bat hadn't struck Billy first, if the bones in his arm hadn't absorbed a good portion of the force of that swing, I'm fairly certain the direct impact to Tim's head would've killed him.

"Bret made a half lunge for the Slugger, but she brought it down in an ax chop onto his outstretched hand, and there was another crunch of bone and a howl of pain. She turned to Clayton next, who was scuttling away from her in a crab walk across the ground. She was three years older than all of us, but moved like an apparition, the bat rising above her head once more as she readied herself for the next swing. *She's going to kill them*, I thought. *She's going to keep swinging that thing until they're all stone quiet and dead.* I called out her name, but she didn't seem to hear me. She brought the bat down as hard as she could, and Clayton—*thank God*—rolled to the left so the fat wood slammed into the earth instead of his face, and then he was on his feet and running, blubbering, slipping down the embankment in a wake of sobs and ratcheting, gasping breaths. I got up and ran to her, the knife slipping from my belly and landing, forgotten, in the leaves. I put my arms on her shoulders just as she was turning her attention back to Billy. She spun around to face me, and her eyes were just . . . vacant . . . not registering me at all. I remember looking right into that face and not recognizing her, either, wondering to myself, *Who is this person?* And there was . . . I don't know, a moment . . . during which I thought she was about to turn that bat on me. Because she didn't know me, you see? She was just . . . gone."

He looked at me beseechingly, implored me to understand. I swallowed once and nodded.

"I screamed her name, screamed it right into her face. I'd forgotten about Billy Myers and the rest of his pathetic band of delinquents. I'd forgotten that, less than a minute before, he'd pressed a knife against the skin of my belly, threatened to carve into me. All I could think about was that empty, shapeless space between my sister and me. It was like she had taken an unsuspecting step backward off a precipice, and I was standing there watching her body plummet downward, her upturned face becoming smaller and smaller until I could no longer make out her features. She could have been *anyone*—or no one—and *that* scared me more than anything that had come before.

"I kept yelling her name, shook her a bit, and at last her eyes seemed to focus. She blinked and looked at me—*finally*—like I was someone she knew. The other boys were gone, scattered like roaches beneath the threat of her merciless foot. I took the bat from her hands, let it clunk to the ground, and we stood there in the woods—just the two of us—for a long time. 'You okay?' I asked, and I guess it was strange that *I* was the one doing the asking, but she seemed to understand what I was talking about and nodded back at me. 'Yeah,' she said, 'I'm good.'

"That was the most we ever talked about it—that day. I asked if she was okay, and she answered, 'Yeah, I'm good.' And that was the end of it. Billy Myers was absent from school for a week, and when he showed up again his right arm was in a cast and cradled in a sling. He didn't look at me, didn't say anything to me when I spotted him in the hall. None of them did. They averted their eyes when we passed one another, flinched away from me as if I were something venomous that might strike out at them again. I suppose I should've taken some satisfaction in that. But I didn't. Instead, I felt sick, the nausea rolling over me in waves, my body lifting and falling in its surf. All I could think about when I saw them was the *whoosh* of wood through the air, the splintering crack of bone, and Clayton rolling to the left as the bat buried itself in the earth where his head had been lying a split second before.

"And the vacant expression in my sister's eyes as she turned in my direction. That I thought of most of all."

Part Two

Protection

Chapter 15

Marj's Kitchen is a culinary and social mecca for locals in my town. The front entrance is so slight and unassuming that, if you arrived by car, you could easily miss it during your first lap around the block. Inside, however, the lights are turned up and the large dining area is typically awash in laughter and boisterous conversation. One interesting aspect of the place—and a likely deterrent for out-of-towners—is the communal dining. A vast wooden table stretches its massive torso from one end of the room to the other. Its flanks are lined with chairs, like ribs spreading to the floor. If you want to eat in *this* restaurant, you select an open spot along the rib cage of the beast and become part of the organism. The relationships among the patrons have the ease and familiarity of family. If you don't know the person you're sitting next to, you will soon. And because of its somewhat bohemian atmosphere, the joint self-selects for some of the town's more colorful characters. In this way, it reminds me a bit of Menaker: a heaving band of outcasts brought together under a common roof, and somehow—almost predictably—finding friendship, or at least camaraderie, within their midst.

The food, I must admit, is mediocre. It's simple, reliable, warm, and filling—what you'd call *comfort food*, I suppose. Nothing fancy or decorative, the offerings are brought to the table by the proprietor, Marj herself, in heaping bowls to be scooped onto plates and passed around in a clockwise fashion. You take as much as you want, eat what you take, make no special requests, and bring your plate, cup, and utensils to the counter for the dishwasher when you're through. But, for most of its patrons, the food isn't the main attraction. People come here to talk, to listen, to argue, to be welcomed, to immerse themselves in cheerful infectious animation. To be counted among the living.

To say that I'm a regular at Marj's is a bit of an understatement. Fact is, I eat here most nights. I realize that sounds extreme, but the place simply suits my needs. I work long hours and live alone. I know how to cook, but it seems like a lot of effort to concoct a meal that will only be eaten by me. Because of patient confidentiality, I have a job I can't talk about, and close, intimate relationships have always been difficult for me. The problem stems from the environment in which I grew up, I suppose—offspring to an emotionally absent mother and a belittling, verbally abusive father. I realize that people have to take responsibility for themselves—to resist blaming the past for their shortcomings—but honestly, who comes out of a childhood like that completely intact? So I've learned to rely on myself, to go it alone rather than depend too heavily on others. But there are times when I do seek social interaction, and Marj's Kitchen is filled with people I know who will not ask for more than I can give.

I pulled up a chair between Manny Linwood and Tim Barrens. Tim was diving into a mound of mac and cheese like he hadn't eaten in weeks, although I'd seen him polish off a similar-looking plate two days ago.

"The good doctor arrives," he commented, his words slightly muffled by the napkin he was swiping across his mouth.

"A lady of questionable credentials, blown in from the night wind," Manny said, and gave me a wink.

"Hello, boys," I greeted them, offering a smile, the strain of the day slipping from my body like a river of dirt beneath a hot shower. "Can a lady get a salad around here?"

Across the table, Rob Friedlander peered at me over the slick yellow top of a piece of corn bread. "Chunka iceberg lettuce and a single tomato, maybe," he said. "Marj don't specialize in salads."

A heavy hand fell on my shoulder as the subject of discussion—Marj, not the salad—materialized from the kitchen. "Don't listen to him, honey," she said, populating the space in front of me with a clean plate and utensils. Her voice was deep and full, her forearm thick and strong, the way a restaurant proprietor's should be. She smelled vaguely of olive oil and freshly baked bread. "Salads are our specialty."

At that, Rob seemed to choke a bit on his corn bread, but he said nothing, dropping his eyes to the tabletop.

"A chunk of lettuce and a tomato for the doctor," Manny ordered, as Marj filled my cup with iced tea from a tall glass pitcher.

"You could use a salad yourself, Mr. Linwood," she said, but Manny just shook his head.

"I'm allergic to anything green," he advised her.

Tim retrieved a basket of corn bread from the center of the table and offered it to me, but I declined, not feeling particularly hungry this evening. Jason's story today had upset me. In my mind, I kept hearing the soft, lethal *whoosh* of the bat slicing the air, kept picturing the unnatural angle of Billy Myers's splintered arm as he clutched it against his body, his eyes wide and full of terror. I imagined—could almost feel—the bat striking the earth, the shudder of the impact ascending into the handle. I'd come here to be in the presence of others, hoping the lights and chatter would drown out those other thoughts. I did not want to be alone in my apartment tonight until it was absolutely necessary.

I looked along the length of the table at my haphazard collection of companions, and my eyes made contact with the pinched, mousy face of Janet Windsor. She glanced back at me, attempted a half smile, then let it fall away with a sigh, like a dress she kept in her closet because she thought it was pretty but never had the confidence to wear in public. I nodded to her, feeling a certain kinship in our individual struggles, but she looked away quickly.

The night drew on. A few stragglers arrived after I did. But by now it was getting late and people were standing up and finding their way to the door—to whatever evening activities awaited them beyond the confines of this place. Manny produced a ragged deck of cards from one pocket and dealt them out to Tim and me, and we played for a bit, none of us really wanting to go home. Marj stood in the doorway leading to the kitchen, her broad shoulder resting against the frame, and watched us for a while with maternal interest—a mother presiding over her children after dinner, during the final hour before bed.

Eventually, Marj dimmed the lights, signaling to us that it was time to go. We left together, but quickly split off as we continued down our separate avenues. I walked briskly, the night breeze ruffling my shoulder-length hair and sending a fleeting chill down the back of my neck as I turned the corner. I fished my keys from my pocket and let myself in through the building's front door, crossing the lobby, taking the elevator to the third floor, then heading down the hall to my apartment and slipping inside. I was breathing quickly, trembling a bit, my heart thudding dutifully inside my chest. I went to the window and parted the curtain with one hand, looked down at the street below.

I'd felt his presence during the final two blocks. He'd been following me, pacing me, watching me in the slim light of a quarter-moon. He stood now on the sidewalk on the opposing side of the street, beneath the pale yellow cone of a streetlamp.

I couldn't discern much about the man's features from this angle. He wore a beige overcoat that drooped straight down from his shoulders like a wet sheet, and the fedora on his head sat at a slight angle, casting a shadow across his face. It was as if he'd stepped right off the screen from a film noir crime drama, a cigarette burning in one hand. Its glow intensified as he raised it to his lips for a final drag, then dropped it onto the sidewalk and used the toe of one shoe to crush it out. He looked up at my window, studying the crack in the curtain through which I peered. I hadn't turned on the lights, and I didn't think he could see me. Still, I could *feel* him staring, could feel his eyes moving over me like beetles.

I pulled away from the window and stood in the darkness of my apartment, trying to control my breathing. Five steps across the room took me to my desk, where I picked up the cordless phone, my hand shaking so much I thought I might drop it. I punched a button, heard a tone, and dialed 9-1- . . .

By this time I was back at the window, and when I looked down there was only an empty sidewalk. My finger hovered over the 1 on the phone's dial pad, debating whether to call the police anyway. *I should at least make a report,* I told myself. *He followed me. He knows where I live.* But something made me hesitate, and after a few seconds more I hung up the phone without dialing that final number. Because he had disappeared into the night and there was absolutely no sign of him. And because he'd been careful, so careful, that even the cigarette—the one he'd crushed into the sidewalk—was gone.

Chapter 16

Jason shifted his position on the concrete bench in Kogan Plaza. The last remnants of winter had yielded to spring in the nation's capital, the cherry blossoms decorating George Washington University's Foggy Bottom campus in broad swaths of pink. A chickadee flitted down from a tree branch to the walkway near his left foot. Its head darted at the cement path, snatching into its beak a small shard of pizza crust. A second later, with a quick spasm of the wings, the bird was off with its prize.

Jason watched as it disappeared around the near corner of Lisner Auditorium. He smiled, enjoying the warmth of the sun filtering through the cherry blossoms, the soft chatter of students, and the smell of spring being carried across the campus in the arms of an April breeze. The thought occurred to him—briefly and without much conviction—that he ought to be in the library finishing up an English paper on the modernist era in European literature, but his brain was fried from a political science exam he'd taken earlier that morning. It wouldn't hurt, he decided, to linger here a bit longer.

He leaned back, closed his eyes, and rested the palms of his hands behind him on the bench. The newspaper in his lap was filled with an amalgam of the old and the new. Pope John Paul II had died five days earlier at the age of eighty-four. The Iraq conflict continued to drag on with no clear end in sight and no sign thus far of the weapons of mass destruction that had led to the war in the first place. In Afghanistan yesterday a U.S. military helicopter had gone down, killing at least sixteen people. CNN's website had reported this morning that a Palestinian-fired rocket had struck an Israeli cemetery, a reminder that even the dead are burdened with the price of our basic human inability to get along. He found himself stirred by such accounts, felt the desire to become more deeply involved in what was happening around the world. He was here pursuing a career in journalism and wondered where such a career would take him, whether his ideals would yield over the years to more pragmatic considerations. But on a day like today the chaos and disarray of the world seemed far away, like the vague recollection of a dream that had all but dissipated in the morning light. It—

The force of the impact struck him in the left temple. He startled, his eyelids snapping open, his body coming to attention. There was the plastic clatter of something falling to the concrete, and when he looked down he saw the underside of a purple disc. A Frisbee, he realized, bending at the waist to scoop it up.

"Man, I'm *really* sorry about that," a voice sounded to his left.

Jason turned his head, squinting into the sun. The Frisbee's owner dropped to one knee, making it easier for Jason to look at him. He was slim and darkly complected. His short black hair was thick, wavy at the top, capping a face that seemed almost too young for college. But there was a sharp intelligence in the brown eyes studying him now with their own quiet confidence.

"You're bleeding," the guy said. His right hand reached out and wiped at the side of Jason's face where a trickle of blood was working its way down from where he'd been struck. "Just a small abrasion. Nothing that needs stitches or anything." He shook his head. "I'm *really* sorry about that," he repeated. "It was a bad throw, but still . . . I should've caught that one."

"You okay?" a girl asked, trotting over to join them.

The Frisbee owner turned to her. "You hit him in the head, Allison. Nice going."

"No, I'm . . . I'm fine," Jason assured them. "I mean, it was just a Frisbee. It's made of plastic."

"You see, Amir?" the girl said. "He's fine."

"He's bleeding," the other commented.

"Where?" she asked, bending at the waist to get a better look.

"Right there," he said, pointing. "I already wiped most of it away."

Jason looked from one face to the next.

"You mean that little red mark?" She shook her head. "It's nothing."

"Says the premed who already thinks she's a doctor," Amir remarked to Jason. He offered him a hand, and Jason took it, rising to his feet. "Your assailant here is Allison," he continued. "She's got some work to do on her Frisbee-chucking skills."

"It was a perfect throw," Allison insisted. "He just missed it."

"Don't worry about it," Jason said, introducing himself.

Amir clapped him on the shoulder. "Well, the premed says you're fine, but I think we should keep an eye on you for a while—

make sure you don't lapse into a coma or anything. How 'bout joining us for some pizza at Vacarro's?"

"Yeah." Jason nodded. "Pizza sounds good." He slung his backpack over one shoulder, and the three of them headed off toward the eastern border of campus where I Street intersected Pennsylvania Avenue. He handed the Frisbee back to Amir, who put a hand on his arm—the fourth time, Jason noticed, that he'd touched him in the last three minutes—and leaned in close before whispering, *"Trust me. It was a bad throw."*

Chapter 17

"Good morning, Amber."

"Morning, Lise." She turned and snatched a paper cup from atop its patient stack of brothers and let the coffee flow. "Running late this morning," she observed, fitting the beverage with a top and placing it on the counter. She selected a few chocolate-covered walnuts from behind the glass display window and plunked them into a sample cup for me to try. I offered her a weary smile, knowing she wouldn't accept "No, thank you" for an answer.

"I didn't sleep too well last night," I admitted. After my unwelcome visitor, I hadn't been able to settle down and rest until about three in the morning. I'd circled the cramped confines of my modest living room—around and around the couch I went—debating whether I'd been right to not call the police. *Someone ought to know about the incident,* I told myself. But what information could I really offer? I hadn't gotten a look at his face, and the trench coat had masked much of his frame. He hadn't accosted me or done anything overtly threatening. So . . . what? Was it a crime to walk the public streets at night, to stand on the sidewalk near the park and smoke a cigarette? Technically, he hadn't even littered, since he'd taken the cigarette butt with him. I could imagine the bored, placating expression on the officer's face as he stood in my apartment, taking the report. *We'll keep an eye out, ma'am*, he would say. *In the meantime, it might be a good idea to have someone walk you home if you're heading back late at night.* I'd nod, forcing a tight smile of appreciation for this condescending piece of paternalistic advice. *Yeah, thanks*, I'd think. *Thanks for nothing.*

Amber gave me a discerning once-over. "Well, you look like shit," she said.

"Thanks." I smiled, tucking a few wayward strands of hair behind my right ear. "I'm glad you like the new me."

Amber looked doubtful. She gestured to my coffee. "You want a shot or two of espresso in that?"

I raised my eyebrows. "And take a nosedive in about three hours?"

"Just offering."

"I know," I said. "I appreciate that." I started to turn away from the counter, but then paused and turned back.

"Reconsidering that espresso?" she asked.

I shook my head, glancing around the shop for a moment. It was only the two of us, but I leaned in across the counter just the same. "I don't know if this would be something you'd remember," I started, "but about a week and a half ago there were two guys sitting at that table"—I pointed behind me—"one day when I walked in."

"Two guys, sitting at a table," she said, and I realized how stupid it all sounded.

"It was the day after the storm," I prodded her. "The store's front window had been cracked the night before. I came in here to get my coffee as usual," I continued, "but there were these two guys—dressed in, you know, business attire and reading the paper—that I hadn't seen here before. They were sitting right at that table over there." I gestured again. "I haven't seen them in here since then, but the other day on the street . . . I stepped off the sidewalk and they almost ran me over with their car."

"Wow," she said, looking alarmed.

"I wasn't hit, but it was pretty close. It scared me."

"I'll bet."

"Anyway"—I shrugged—"I was just wondering if you might remember them from the day they were in here."

"You wanna report them?" she asked.

"No," I replied. "It's just that, well, in your line of work you see a lot of people walk in and out of those doors—most of them locals. And I figured, you know, maybe you knew them."

Amber gave it some thought, but a few seconds later she was shaking her head. "Sorry, honey. I can't picture them."

"No," I said. "I didn't expect you to." I let out a small sigh, wondering if I should tell her about the guy who'd followed me home the night before. But what was the point of upsetting her when there was nothing she could do about it? I gave her a nod. "Thanks for the coffee."

Her brow furrowed a bit, and she tucked the right side of her lower lip in as she watched me. "You okay, sweetheart?"

"Yeah," I responded. "Fine." I gave her a tight, self-assured smile and left the shop with a half wave, forgetting the dash of milk I usually added to my drink as part of my morning ritual.

And maybe it was just that, but I didn't feel right the rest of the day.

Chapter 18

How was your relationship with your sister," I asked Jason, "following the incident in the woods?"

"Mostly, it was unchanged." He wiped at his nose with the back of one hand. He seemed to be coming down with a cold. I offered him a tissue and he took it, but he held it absently in his hand, working it with his fingers. We'd elected to stay inside that day. "You must understand that she's *always* been protective of me, even when I was a little kid. I never really understood it, but she used to take the blame for things that I did, just so I wouldn't get in trouble."

"Like what?"

He shrugged. "Like whatever. We'd be horsing around, throwing a Nerf basketball in the dining room, and I'd knock over something fragile—one of our mom's figurines she used to display on our windowsills—and my sister would walk right over to it and sit down next to the shards on the floor like she'd knocked it over and not me. One of our parents would come in, and she'd fess up immediately. She'd get sent to her room or sometimes even take a spanking, and all the while I'm just standing there knowing it was me who knocked the thing over." Jason gave me a half smile, but it didn't sit comfortably on his face. "Looking back on it now, I think things would've turned out better for both of us if she would've let me take some of those punishments for myself. But it was in her nature to protect me. It was almost a compulsion. You understand?"

"How did you get along with your parents?"

He shrugged. "Okay, I guess. Dad, you know, was a cop. He worked odd hours and often wasn't home in the evenings. Mom was a teacher. She took a few years off from work when we were younger but went back to work when I started kindergarten. She didn't seem very happy about it, but I think we needed the money. I remember her and Dad arguing about that—her need to work full-time, how we were spending more as a family than we were bringing in, and how that kind of life led to trouble sooner or later. So when I broke something, even something small and stupid like one of those figurines, I always thought, *Mom and Dad worked hard to pay for that.* It represented a piece of themselves, a span of time they'd sacrificed in order to afford it, and I was sorry as hell to have wasted it with my recklessness. I would often cry over stuff like that, and Dad would look at me with a touch of disgust on his face, scrunch up his nose, and tell me not to be such a goddamn baby all the time." Jason took a deep breath and let it out. "I don't think he ever realized I was crying for him."

"How much does your family know about your sexual orientation?" I asked.

"You mean, do they know I'm gay?"

I nodded.

"My sister knows," he said. "Or she used to know." He shook his head. "She's been gone for so long now . . ."

"And your parents?"

"My mother accepts it, but we don't talk about it much. My father . . ." Jason grinned. "I think he still hopes it's a phase I'll grow out of one day. Like skateboarding when I was younger."

"How's *that* working out for the two of you?"

"I turned thirty last November," he said.

"So it's a brief thirty-year phase."

"And counting," he agreed.

We were quiet for a while, watching patients mill about in the dayroom.

"Would it be fair to say that your sister took on a somewhat paternal role in your relationship?"

"I suppose."

"Jason," I said, feeling my heartbeat kick up a notch, "what happened to your sister?"

He shot me a look that I couldn't quite interpret. I could see alarm in his eyes, and . . . *was it fear?* This was uncomfortable territory for him, I realized, and I was pushing him into it. It struck me as I asked the question that it might be too soon. We were forming our therapeutic alliance, but it was still tenuous. If I leaned on him too hard, our relationship and everything I'd worked toward thus far could crumble. Still . . . here was a big piece of the puzzle that hung in the space between us, and I reached out for it, the edge of the thing brushing against my fingertips.

Jason's lips tightened, his blue eyes turning to slate. I could feel him pulling back, could feel the chasm opening up between us. I allowed the silence to sit fat and bloated between us for a full minute, then tried a different approach.

"Do you know why you're here?"

He looked at me, his eyes searching for how to proceed, as if the answer had been weighing upon him for many years and he wanted nothing more than to lay it at my feet so he could rest at last. For a moment, I was afraid. Of all the patients I'd sat with over the years—of all the secrets I'd heard, the demons I'd brought to the surface and helped my patients to confront— there was something hidden here that I did not want to know. I didn't understand why I felt this way, an unexplainable conviction that this thing he was carrying—this thing that continued to consume him like an infection—was somehow contagious and would consume me, too, if I let it. I wanted to stand up, to walk away and never look back. But it was too late for that now. Because already a door had been partially opened, and although I was afraid, I also needed to know what lay behind it.

This, I realize, so often leads to our downfall. We press forward not because we want to know, but because we *must* know. It doesn't matter how terrible that knowledge is, or what price must be paid for it. And it is not until the moment of revelation that we scurry back in horror and dismay, attempting to eradicate the image from our brain, to step back in time so that we might turn away from the door before it is fully opened, wishing—seconds too late—for the opportunity to walk away intact.

"I'm here because a man is dead," he told me. "It was someone I cared about very much, someone I loved." He put a hand to the side of his face, then dropped it back into his lap. "I can't change that now, although I wish to hell that I could."

His eyes turned away from me, searched the corner of the room for a moment. When he looked back at me, his expression had softened.

"I lost her too that night," he said, "only I didn't realize it at the time. I had no way of knowing she would disappear so completely. I was too distracted by my own grief."

"Where did she go?" I asked.

"She went away. I . . . I don't know." He sighed, struggling with his answer. "I'm here because one day she may come back, and until then it's *my* job to protect *her* for a while." He brought his hands together, fingers interlaced in a gesture both desperate and familiar. "I have to believe that, you know—that she may come back. I have to trust that one day she'll find her way back. I can't lose both of them."

"Are you helping her by being here? Is that part of how you're protecting her?"

"*God*, I hope so," he said. "I don't know what else to do."

Chapter 19

I sat in my office, moving sheets of paper from one pile to the next. My right hand opened the upper drawer of my desk, removed a notepad, and placed it on the wooden surface in front of me—but when I picked up a pen, the tip poised above the blank page, I couldn't remember what I'd been so intent on jotting down just a few seconds before. Instead, I allowed myself to doodle, my thoughts focused elsewhere, and when I returned my attention to the page I was surprised to see that I had written a name: Uncle Jim.

I mouthed the words, my tongue and teeth sliding forward in rapid succession, and then the press of my lips together at its final syllable. I did this without making a sound, like a child who is convinced that uttering the name of the bogeyman in the still of the night will somehow summon him.

But he wasn't the bogeyman, I reminded myself. He was only my uncle, someone who'd been quirky and funny, cool to hang out with—someone who'd paid attention to me, who'd listened to what I had to say. In many ways, he was the antithesis of my parents.

"You and I got a lot in common, Lise," he'd often told me, wrapping an arm around my shoulders and looking down at me with a sly wink. "We see things differently than other people."

"We do?" I'd ask, and that really got him laughing. Me, too. When Uncle Jim started laughing, it was impossible for me not to join him.

"*Helllll, yes,*" he'd say. "What d'ya think this is, some dog and pony show?"

"Well, I've never seen a dog and pony show," I told him earnestly, "but I really want to." And at that he would just about split a gut, slapping his thigh with his free hand and clapping me on the back with the other.

"*Oooh, boy, you're a funny one.* Never seen a dog and pony show."

"But I really want to," I interjected once again, and that sent him peeling off into another fit. How the tears used to roll down his face as he bent over holding his gut from the strain of laughing so hard. It sort of became a routine between us during the three months he lived with my family. We'd go through that same bit of dialogue, him telling me how we had so much in common, how we saw things differently than other people, and when I'd feign surprise he'd tell me *helllll, yes,* and *what'd I think this is, some dog and pony show?* He'd look down at me, putting on a serious face for a second, but by then we both knew what I was going to say and, more often than not, one of us would already be giggling.

I remember feeling truly happy during those early weeks. For the first time in my life, maybe, I had someone to talk to, someone who seemed to understand me. I could feel myself opening up, feel the tightness I'd grown accustomed to loosening more each day, until I began to . . . well . . . until I began to forget what it had been like before. And in some ways, I think it might have been the same for Uncle Jim. Because when you're feeling good you start to forget the darker times in your life. Maybe it's because they seem less significant, because the power they once held over you has dissipated. You want to believe that those days were an anomaly, that they're never coming back. But it's a mistake to think that way. I recognize that now. Because the minute you lose respect for those days is the minute you start to slide back toward them.

Much of the problem lies with medication compliance. Patients with psychiatric conditions may stop taking their medications for many reasons, but three of the most important are lack of insight, side effects, and what I call the *blind spot*.

Mental illness impairs many things, and one of them is the insight that one has a mental illness to begin with. Patients with schizophrenia, for example, may not have insight into their disease. It can be difficult to convince them of the diagnosis, and many will be resistant to taking medication for a disease they do not believe they have.

Side effects become a factor for many: dry mouth, sedation, weight gain, tics and movement disorders, disturbance of sexual function, to name a few. In some cases, patients may feel that they lose touch with the essence of who they are. I've had patients tell me, *When I'm on that medication, I'm not myself anymore*, and if *that's* not an obstacle to medication compliance I don't know what is.

Then there's the *blind spot*. I equate it with that large space just a little behind the driver and to either side of a car, where big things that we don't see can hide. It's like that with mental illness.

Patients may know that if they don't take their medication, they have a tendency to become psychotic. They've been hospitalized several times before. But they're having a good month—a good year, even—and to stick with the analogy for a moment, the road ahead looks beautiful: just one straight open highway. They check their mirrors, see nothing but vacant blacktop behind them, and figure why not switch things up a bit—get off the meds and get over into the fast lane for a while where they can really open her up. So they let the car start to slide over a lane or two. But they forget to do a head check, and what they don't see is that last case of psychosis—the one that put them in the trauma center for a month because they thought they could fly—right next to them, just a little back and to the left, sitting there in their blind spot and ready to mess them up good this time. Maybe even kill them.

Looking back on it, I don't think it was lack of insight or side effects that made Uncle Jim stop taking his medication. I think it was the blind spot. He either didn't see it or refused to see it. But I did. I watched it bear down on him, overtake him. Still, I said nothing—and the guilt of being a part of what happened next may go a long way in explaining my choice of professions. But maybe in the end it was no choice at all. Maybe it was just part of my penance. And if all those years of training have taught me anything, it's that there are some things you can never undo, can never make better. Sometimes you have to allow yourself to forget.

Sometimes . . . it's the only way.

Chapter 20

That afternoon I went for a run, which I occasionally do over my lunch break. When the weather is nice, I prefer to run outside, listening to my iPod or the familiar, soft bustle of the town moving through its daily routines. My usual route takes me down Macarthur Street, past Marj's Kitchen. I hook a left at the chipped pillars of the city's sagging courthouse, circle the children's playground to the north, then merge with the Kermen A. Woods Trail that runs parallel to the Severn, the path winding through a loose splay of birch and American elm, offering both modest solitude and unfettered views of the river below. I like to feel the impact of my rubber-soled cross-trainers slapping the packed soil. I like to feel the wind on my face with its hollow promise of freedom and the conviction that if I can just generate enough speed I could take to the air and finally rise above it all: this town; the looming presence of Menaker and its inescapable shadow on my life; the maddening, quiet predictability of my own mortality. I run and run, focusing only on the burn of muscle and the rhythmic pull of ribs working in concert with my own quick respirations. I concentrate only on the path ahead, stretched long and lean above the Severn, my legs pistoning beneath me. There is the mounting tension, the plateau of fatigue rising up from the water to meet me—then the euphoric release, the letting go as the body takes over. I hold on to it for as long as possible before finally coasting downward along its inevitable ebb as the world slides back into focus.

Others use this trail, of course. It's very popular among the locals, and most of the faces I encounter plodding along the path nod to me with familiar recognition. Still, there is something sacred in a run—a patch of time sequestered only for oneself— and it should go without saying that, unless stipulated otherwise, people want to be left alone. Which is why it surprised me on my return trip to hear someone call out my name.

I'd been slowing anyway, at least—coasting the ebb—and turned and let my legs pedal backward a few paces as I waited for the man approaching from behind. He was tall and trim, his brown hair cut short along the sides and back—good-looking in a college-boy sort of way, although I guessed from the slightly weathered look of his face that he was closer to my age than that of the undergraduate peers I'd left behind ten years ago. He wore navy running shorts and a gray T-shirt with the word ARMY in black lettering across the front. It went well with the quasi-military look of his haircut, although the crop of hair at the top of his head was long enough to suggest that if he *had* been in the army, he was no longer active duty.

In the wake of the stalking behavior I'd been subjected to recently, I'd be both foolish and naive to say I didn't feel a twinge of unease roll up my spine as he approached, but the portion of the trail we were now traversing was well traveled, and the disarming smile he offered helped to allay the worst of my fears for the moment.

"I'm sorry, do I know you?" I asked, falling back into a medium-paced jog beside him.

"Special Agent Daryl Linder," he introduced himself, the name spilling out as effortlessly as if he were reclining in an easy chair, taking in the last of a televised ball game.

"Special agent," I said, letting the words fall between us with a plop.

"I'm with the FBI," he said.

I stopped running, looked at him to see if he was joking. He returned my gaze blandly, reached into the back right pocket of his shorts, pulled out a worn leather flip wallet, and showed me the badge and ID to back his claim.

I must've still looked skeptical because he added, "You're welcome to call the local bureau office in Baltimore to verify my identity if you like, Dr. Shields."

"How do you know my name?" I asked, irritated by the implied intrusion into my privacy.

"I don't mean for this to upset you," he said, "but my partner and I have had you under surveillance for the past few weeks." Holding up a hand before I could voice my indignation, he assured me, "Don't worry, you haven't done anything wrong."

"If I haven't done anything wrong, then why have you had me under surveillance?"

"I wonder," he said, looking around, "if you'd mind accompanying me back to our office for a few minutes."

"Why?" I asked.

He smiled, trying to put me at ease. "We can talk more freely there. It's . . . a bit more private." He waved to a middle-aged man as he passed us heading in the opposite direction.

"Am I under arrest?"

"No, no. Of course not," he responded. "As I said, you've done nothing wrong." We were reaching the end of the trail where it merged with the asphalt sidewalk of the neighborhood. The tree cover had thinned considerably and Special Agent Linder took me gently by the upper arm.

"It's best if we're not seen together on the streets."

"Best for whom?" I asked.

"Best for you," he said, "and for your patient Jason Edwards."

I felt my anger rise. "That's confidential information."

"Actually, it's a matter of public record. Jason was adjudicated to your facility."

I pulled my arm from his light grasp, squaring off with him. "What do you know about him?"

He seemed indifferent to the aggressive tone of my voice. To this six-foot-two federal agent, I posed no physical threat whatsoever. Still, my hackles were up, my first instinct to protect my patient with the ferocity of a mother bear protecting her cub.

Linder let my question linger in the air for a moment before responding. "We know quite a bit, actually. Much more than you do, in fact. We'd like to help, if you'll let us."

"What could the FBI possibly want with him?"

"It's a bit of a story," he advised me. "Not one I can tell you here."

"Well, then, I'll take you back to my office at the hospital."

"No." He shook his head. "That's not a good idea. It would put you and Jason in further jeopardy."

"Are you implying that Menaker's not safe?" I asked.

"I'm *telling* you it's not," he said, and despite meeting him for the first time today, something in his tone convinced me that he believed this to be true. "It's not safe for either of you there. Not anymore."

Chapter 21

May 19, 2005

Jason did not consider himself superstitious, only forewarned by events from his earlier life. He told himself that six years had gone by since the event with Michael and Alexandra, that he had reinvented himself and was no longer the fourteen-year-old boy who'd been pursued through the woods by Billy Myers and his band of bullies. And although there was some truth to that, the logic rang false. It was hard to get his heart around it, to feel bolstered by the conviction of those arguments. Because the mistakes and terrors of one's past are never truly forgotten. The best we can hope to do, he realized, is to compensate for them and move onward, so that when the past comes around again we can approach it differently, trying for a better outcome.

Once again, there were three of them, and three is an unstable number. In many ways, Allison reminded him of Alex. She was beautiful, popular, smart—genuinely kind in a way that made people want to be around her. She expressed interest early on, taking the lead in their relationship by assuming certain physical liberties. One night when they'd all gone to a midnight movie, she reached out in the darkness and took his hand, resting her head on his shoulder. Amir was sitting on the other side of Jason, and never let on that he'd noticed, never mentioned it. But Jason could feel him sliding away, could once again feel the ice cracking and buckling from below, as if he'd never left that frozen pond six years ago.

Part of him wanted to respond to Allison's not-so-subtle advances—not because he was physically attracted to her, but because it would have been so much easier. He could live a normal life, would not have to spend the rest of his days looking over his shoulder for Billy Myers or someone like him. She did kiss him once—Allison—at a party toward the end of the semester when they were both a little drunk. He kissed her back, wrapped a hand around her waist and pulled the firmness of her twenty-year-old body against him. He felt . . . nothing. No, check that. It was actually a feeling worse than nothing. He felt like a fraud.

She'd pulled back, looked at him with that sharp, inquisitive way of hers. She didn't appear hurt—more like she was trying to decide if she should be or not. "What is it?" she asked.

He couldn't answer, tried to look away, and in that moment he spotted Amir watching them from the far corner of the crowded room.

She put a finger on his chin and turned his face back to her. "You either don't like girls or you don't like me, Jason. Be fair to both of us and tell me which it is."

"No," he replied, not sure what was going to come out of his mouth. "It's just . . ." But his throat tightened and the words wouldn't come. He could feel his face going red—something he hated about himself, that quick blush response that betrayed him every time.

She watched him for a moment, then reached up and placed her palm on the side of his face, and on the other cheek she planted a soft kiss. "You should've told me sooner," she said, and was gone, twisting her way through the crowd, out the door, and into the night.

He followed her out onto Twenty-Third Street and saw her turn the corner at G. He had to run to catch up, and when he put a hand on her shoulder, she turned quickly, angry now.

"You should've told me," she said again, her eyes glistening with tears that she refused to wipe away. "I mean"—she looked at him, shaking her head—"we're *friends*, right? You consider me a friend, don't you?"

"Yes. Of course."

"Then you could've told me. You can tell me something like that, you know."

He nodded.

"Because it hurts like hell to take a chance—to reach out to someone you really like—and be rejected. You know what that's like?"

"Yeah," he replied, the wind whipping through campus catching his words, trying to pull them away. "I do."

She was silent for a while, staring at the sidewalk. When she looked back up at him, her face had softened. "You should tell him."

"Who?"

She gave him a thin incredulous smile. A bus passed by along G Street, and she waited until it had turned the corner, until she didn't have to compete with the growl of its diesel engine. "Who do you think?"

He said nothing.

"He likes you, Jason. But he's scared too."

"You sure about that?"

"No," she replied, glancing past him for a moment before adding, "Guess you'll have to ask him."

He turned, and there was Amir crossing the street in the direction of his dormitory: head down, shoulders hunched, hands jammed into his pockets. Jason turned back to Allison, but she was walking away, the soles of her sneakers soundless against the concrete.

So he jogged to catch up—not to the beautiful girl who'd uncovered him in the flat, empty space of a kiss—but in the direction of his own fear and uncertainty. He caught up to Amir near the Episcopal church, asked him to take a walk with him. Opening that part of himself was like stepping into Michael's arms in the foyer of his house six years ago. He said what needed to be said, readied himself for the crack of a fist against his temple—not painful, really; just . . . shaming. And when that didn't come— when it was only a light touch against the skin of his forearm and the words *Okay, then*—he allowed himself to see that things could be different, that no imprisonment lasts forever, and that hiding is only a prelude to showing yourself once again.

Chapter 22

As much as Marj's Kitchen is a hot spot for locals in the evenings, during the afternoon, when people are at work, it typically boasts all the activity of an abandoned nuclear test site. I honestly don't know why she keeps the place open for lunch, except maybe for the same reason my mother keeps my childhood bedroom ready and waiting for me although I haven't lived in that house for sixteen years.

That being said, I do occasionally stop by the place on my lunch break to chat it up with the town's matriarch. Marj is easy that way: she listens like the stuff coming out of my mouth really matters. Despite my professional affiliations, I've never been under the care of a psychiatrist myself, but the random hours I spend at Marj's carry with them the general *feel* of psychotherapy, although without the usual insurance copay.

I'd agreed to meet Special Agent Linder and his partner here because I figured it would offer me a certain home field advantage and because, statistically speaking, we were likely to have the place to ourselves. Daryl Linder and his shorter, somewhat stouter colleague, Special Agent Aaron Remy, placed their orders and sipped their beverages as I tried to adjust to the day's surreal turn of events. To Marj, I'd introduced the two of them as fellow psychiatrists—Dr. Linder and Dr. Remy, the two of them exchanging almost comical glances—who'd come to tour Menaker in the interest of joining our clinical staff. Marj gave me a quizzical look, but she agreed with my assertion that Menaker had an excellent reputation in this region (she said it with a straight face, as if she would know about such things) and added that no one had ever gotten food poisoning at *her* restaurant—a claim, she sadly confided, that could not be made by any of the other so-called dining establishments in the area. She left us to ponder that, humming softly to herself, while she retrieved our orders of chicken casserole.

"So," Agent Remy began. He picked up his fork, inspected it, then scowled and wiped at it with his napkin. "Let's start with what you know about Jason Edwards, and we can go from there."

I shook my head. "I can't divulge any patient information. You know that."

"The fact is," Linder interjected, "you don't have much to divulge. He came to your facility with no paperwork, is that correct?"

I looked at them, knowing I could give them nothing without a court subpoena, and even then . . .

"During his medical intake," Remy said, "I assume you weren't provided with the courtesy of any prior psychiatric diagnoses? A list of any medical conditions or allergies Mr. Edwards may have? His prior medications?" He paused, turned to his partner, and held up his fork. "Does this look clean to you?"

Linder smiled behind the back of his hand.

Remy put down the utensil and focused his eyes on me from across the table. "Have you even *seen* a copy of the court order remanding your patient to a long-term psychiatric facility?" he asked. "Surely, you've seen that."

"There's been a delay in his paperwork," I replied, but the excuse sounded pathetic, even in my own ears. It didn't matter that I'd pointed this out to Wagner for weeks. When push came to shove, *I* was Jason's physician and the responsibility—and liability for such an egregious break from hospital policy—still rested squarely on my shoulders.

"A delay," Remy echoed, letting the words fall onto the table for all three of us to consider. "A man is held against his will at a state psychiatric hospital with no legal documentation to support such a confinement, and the best you can offer me is that there's been a delay in his paperwork?"

I studied the table in front of me, unable to meet their eyes. I didn't like the way this interview was going. The two of them were supposed to be providing *me* with information, not levying an interrogation regarding aspects over which I had little control. "Should I have a lawyer present for this meeting, gentlemen?" I asked.

"No, you don't need a lawyer," Remy responded. "I'm just trying to demonstrate how people can be pushed to do things they don't feel comfortable with. We know you raised a stink about this with Dr. Wagner when Jason arrived."

I shook my head in disbelief. "How do you know that?"

Linder leaned forward, resting his muscular forearms on the table. "Dr. Shields—"

"Lise," I interrupted him. "Please, call me Lise."

"Okay, Lise." He took a breath. "You imagine Menaker to be

a confidential environment in which you and your patients can interact."

"Something like that," I said.

"It's not," he told me flatly. "Since the arrival of Jason Edwards, that confidentiality has been compromised. For the time being, you should assume that everything you do, any conversations you have at that facility, are being monitored."

"How?" I asked, not wanting to believe him.

"As we've already established," Remy reminded me, "with the proper motivation even good people can be pushed to do things they wouldn't ordinarily do. You've been treating this patient—holding him at Menaker—without proper consent from either the patient or the state. You've been doing this because you think it's the right thing to do, not because you're confused about the legal requirements of court-mandated psychiatric institutionalization, correct?"

"I don't feel like I've had much of a choice." I was angry and embarrassed, feeling as though I'd been tricked, but having no idea by whom or for what possible reason.

"Exactly," Remy replied. "You don't feel like you've had much of a choice. And neither do any of the other reluctant participants at Menaker. But they play along because someone has figured out how to access the right pressure points, no?"

I looked at Linder, and he gave me a sympathetic smile. "The people pulling the strings here are very good at what they do. Believe me, neither you nor the rest of the staff at Menaker ever stood a chance."

"So who's pulling the strings?"

The two agents looked at each other, gauging how best to proceed.

"During your sessions, did Jason mention his sister?" Remy asked.

I sighed, running a hand through my hair. "Again, I really can't divulge—"

"Doesn't matter. I withdraw the question," Remy said. "I will stop asking and simply tell you how it is. But I'm going to preface this by warning you that some of what we're about to tell you may sound somewhat . . ."

"Implausible," Linder finished for him.

"Right," Remy agreed. "Implausible is a good word. But I want you to understand, Dr. Sh—I want you to understand, Lise, that implausible is quite different from impossible. *That's* the thing to keep in mind here."

"Okay." I nodded. "I'm all ears."

Marj appeared suddenly through the kitchen doorway, sauntered to the table—still humming—and set the communal meal in front of us. "You'll enjoy this very much," she commented.

"Thank you," Linder said, smiling warmly—the expression one of his specialties, it seemed.

"I'll be in the back," Marj advised me. "Give me a holler if you need anything."

I assured her that we would, and she shuffled away, leaving us to our lunch.

"I should've asked for another fork," Remy lamented when she was gone. Agent Linder reached to his left, snatched up the instrument, and replaced it with his own. "Happy?" he asked.

Remy shrugged.

"Trust me," Linder said, turning to me. "We've been working together for six years now." He gave his partner a sideways slant of the eyes. "He's never happy."

I said nothing. Remy forked a piece of chicken into his mouth without letting it cool—a rookie mistake. He winced and reached for his soda.

"You were going to tell me about Jason's sister," I prodded.

"Jason Edwards grew up in Columbia, Maryland—not too far from here," Linder began. "He had one sibling, a sister, who completed high school a year early, attended college at Johns Hopkins, graduating summa cum laude with a dual major in biochemistry and international studies, and was recruited directly into the Central Intelligence Agency at the age of twenty-one. The details of her career with the agency are classified, but we do know she served as a staff operations officer for the National Clandestine Service's counterterrorism division from 2005 through 2008."

"If the details of her career are classified, how do you—"

"The FBI works closely with the CIA's counterterrorism division regarding matters of domestic terrorism—that is, terrorist acts occurring on U.S. soil," Remy explained. "The bureau coordinated several operations and investigations with Ms. Edwards over that time period. From what we've gathered, her reputation was a good one."

"What does this have to do with Jason?" I asked.

"Nothing, at first," Remy answered. "Jason Edwards lived a much more conventional life than his sister. Following high school, he attended George Washington University in D.C., where he met Amir Massoud, a civil engineering major who took an interest in student-led political activism. Mr. Massoud was born to Lebanese parents. His father was a diplomat who worked at the Lebanese embassy in Northwest D.C. He and his wife were living in the United States at the time their son was born. Amir grew up in the District, attended public high school there, and received an academic scholarship to G.W. He and Jason met during their sophomore year, developed a romantic relationship, and became involved in the university's LGBT chapter. They took up residence together a year later and graduated in 2007, moving to Silver Spring, Maryland. Amir went on to pursue a graduate degree at the University of Maryland, while Jason worked as a freelance journalist."

"A promising start," I commented.

Linder laced his fingers in front of him on the table. "How familiar are you with the 2006 Lebanon War?"

"I don't recall specifics," I admitted.

"Well, here are the basics," Remy chimed in. "On July 12, 2006, a group of Hezbollah militants fired rockets at several Israeli border towns and ambushed a cluster of soldiers patrolling the Israeli side of the border. Israel launched a ground invasion and countered with airstrikes on Lebanese civilian infrastructure targets, including the international airport in Beirut. Hezbollah responded by launching additional missiles into Israel. A ceasefire was brokered by mid-August, but not before the conflict killed some twelve hundred Lebanese citizens and more than a hundred fifty Israelis.

"The usual polarities came into play. Hezbollah received support from Iran and several other Middle Eastern countries, while the United States backed Israel's right to self-defense. More generally, however, the fighting was met with widespread international protests, and there was particular outrage over Israel's targeting of civilian sites."

"What was somewhat surprising," Linder said, "was that the United States was quick to fulfill requests from Israel for military weaponry in the form of satellite and laser-guided bombs that were later used on Lebanese civilian targets. In fact, the Bush administration rejected calls for a cease-fire during the early days of the conflict.

"Many Lebanese Americans were angered by the U.S.'s willingness to support the apparent targeting of Lebanese civilians. There were protest demonstrations in Washington, although small and not highly publicized. But the military conflict ended relatively quickly—the thirty-four-day war, they called it—and, for most people, life returned to normal."

"But not for Amir Massoud," I said, hazarding a guess.

"No," Remy responded. "Because his mother, who'd returned to Lebanon several years before, was among the civilian casualties."

Linder shook his head. "The loss of a loved one is never easy," he said. "But the loss of a loved one at the hands of a government that you've adopted as your own . . ."

"Such motivations are the building blocks of revenge," Remy observed. He lifted his cup toward his lips, but paused to regard me before taking a sip. "You think something like that is easily forgiven, Dr. Shields?"

"No," I answered, allowing my gaze to fall to the table. From the back of the restaurant, I could hear the clink of silverware being unloaded from the dishwasher.

"Planning an act of revenge on the U.S. government and its people takes time, intelligence, coordination, and patience," Linder said. "The big things—bombings and the like—often require funding and support, and for that Amir Massoud turned to a small terrorist cell here in the United States who call themselves Al-Termir."

"I wouldn't imagine they'd be too thrilled with his sexual orientation," I noted. "Isn't homosexuality a capital offense in many Arab nations?"

"Technically," Remy advised me, "he wouldn't have been considered Arab. Amir was born in the United States and was a U.S. citizen. He wasn't even Muslim. But even if he was, he'd expressed hostility toward the United States and a willingness to act on it. He would have been seen as an ally to be exploited for a greater good."

"So he made contact with this organization," I said, "and then?"

"And then he waited," Linder replied, "and planned."

Remy shifted in his seat. "During that time, Amir graduated from G.W. and pursued graduate training in civil engineering, which means he understood how to design and build large structures, but also knew the critical points in which—with the right impetus—they would fail. The goals of a domestic terrorist attack are to maximize casualties, to make the rescue of survivors difficult, and to make some sort of political statement. He lived close to D.C., and selecting any public or government target would have fulfilled the third objective. Satisfying the first two objectives, however, are a little more difficult. People move from place to place, which makes timing tricky. Large events bring lots of people together, but security is tight and rescue personnel are nearby. Duffel bags and backpacks are checked at the gates, and getting something—an explosive device, for example—into position and then getting out of there before the thing goes off poses certain technical challenges.

"So what you're looking for is a highly trafficked area with easy access and egress, lots of commotion to obscure any conspicuous activity and to contribute to the ensuing panic, and the type of structure that will fail so catastrophically that emergency rescue providers will encounter monumental obstacles in the process of finding and rescuing any survivors."

"Terrorism 101," I commented, and felt a chill slide down my spine.

"The Washington Metro is the second-busiest rapid public transportation system in the United States, second only to New York City's subway. On any given weekday, it moves almost three-quarters of a million passengers and has numerous strategic stops throughout the nation's capital. The busiest stop, with almost thirty-three thousand passengers per day, is Union Station along the Red Line. The subterranean portion of the facility is two levels housing twenty-nine tracks shared by Amtrak, MARC train, and Virginia Railway Express. The station itself houses shops, restaurants, and eateries and is a major tourist destination. The U.S. Supreme Court Building is less than a mile away."

I could feel my stomach sinking at the thought of it—all those people moving about the station. An elderly couple on their first trip to the District, a class of fourth graders arriving on a field trip, mothers pushing infants in strollers . . .

"Now, cases regarding acts of domestic terrorism are the FBI's jurisdiction," Remy said, "but intelligence and data gathering, identifying threats and tracking them—that's the CIA's strong suit. And Jason Edwards's sister spearheaded that investigation."

"It was clearly a conflict of interest," Linder pointed out. "Once they uncovered Amir's ties to Al-Termir and identified him as a potential threat, she should've bowed out. Because she was compromised—too close to it—and that's when mistakes get made."

Remy toyed with his napkin for a moment, sliding the material between his thumb and index finger. "CIA agents, by and large, are conspiracy theorists at heart. It's part of their training, their culture. And once they latch on to something, it's hard for them to let go. They want to see it through to the end." He glanced at his partner, then turned his attention back to me. "Some of us in the bureau—myself included—had the feeling she was becoming a liability. I find it difficult to believe she never divulged information to her brother. From what I understand of their relationship, she was very protective of him."

I thought of Jason's sister at the age of seventeen, stepping forward defiantly amid the small gang of her brother's tormentors, the heavy whisper of the bat beginning its swing.

"Yes," I said. "I think she was."

"I can imagine the conversation, though," Linder said, leaning forward. "Jason's sister comes to him with something like that, with allegations against his domestic partner. I can imagine the resistance, the denial, even the anger Jason must have felt. How receptive do you think he was to those accusations?"

"Not very," I replied, and Linder nodded his agreement.

"You know, I think you're right," he said. "I think he probably stood up for Amir, told her to back off, to leave them alone, to go sniff up some other tree."

"And what do you think Ms. Edwards said to that?" Remy asked.

I considered it. "I don't know for sure, but my gut tells me she was not the type of person to be easily dissuaded."

"Your gut is correct," Linder responded. He looked up toward the door of the restaurant, as if he'd heard a noise and expected someone to walk in, to intrude on our privacy. No one did.

"It's unclear whether Jason told Amir about his conversation with his sister, although I suspect that he did. You cannot make those types of remarks to one person in a relationship without the other finding out. If he did, it's also unclear whether Amir would have disclosed that information to the extremist group he was working with. They would've dropped him, I'm sure—abandoned the entire plan and scattered like bits of ash in the wind. They might have even killed him, since he'd be perceived as a loose end who might cooperate with the CIA and FBI in exchange for his freedom. While they were at it, they probably would have gone for Jason, too. They would've assumed that Jason knew what Amir knew, and that was too much information to risk surrendering to the hands of the U.S. government."

"Are you sure he was guilty?" I asked. "You know this for a fact?"

"He was guilty, yes," Remy told me. "Guilty of conspiracy to commit murder—to perpetrate a terrorist act on the United States. According to Ms. Edwards, Amir Massoud admitted as much to her in the doorway of his town house on the evening of May 12, 2010." Special Agent Remy paused for the span of a single heartbeat—I felt it go *clunk* in my chest—before adding, "Just before she killed him."

Chapter 23

I sat in my apartment that night, my mind turning over the rest of our conversation again and again like a flat stone in my hand. With each turn the surface appeared both familiar and alien. I could understand the basic facts of the story as Linder and Remy had presented them, but I couldn't make sense of what they meant, or how to proceed from here. *There was a struggle between Amir and Agent Edwards,* Remy had told me, *accusations and denials building toward violence. We've been able to piece together details of that night from interviews with those involved.*

Amir had grabbed her, the report stated, his fingertips digging into the sinewy base of her neck just above the collarbones. She'd been caught off guard, stumbling and falling backward as the two of them crashed to the floor in their locked embrace, the full force of the man's weight landing on top of her and punching the breath from her lungs. She'd tried to go for her service weapon, slung high in its shoulder holster under her left arm, but couldn't get to it, couldn't bring her right arm across her body with his weight on top of her. The world around her began to blanch, she'd said in her statement, the man's clenched, livid face floating above her like a balloon tethered to his shoulders, and she'd realized she was on the brink of unconsciousness. But there was a tactical knife she carried in a sheath affixed to her belt. She'd been able to arch her torso slightly, to work her right arm into the space created by the curve of her spine. Her fingers had found the small dark handle and she'd delivered the knife from its leather casing, her arm completing a half circle and driving the weapon home between the fifth and sixth ribs.

The fingers had loosened their hold, Amir's body going limp on top of her, and she'd lain there taking deep whooping gasps of air as the color of the room fell back into place, and with it, the image of her brother—the ovals of his eyes and mouth wide with horror, his clawed hands filling the slim hollows of his cheeks, the silent scream only she could hear—looking down on the two of them. As gently as she was able, she'd pushed Amir's body off her and to the side. She stood up, still gasping for breath and leaning over at the waist, a bloody palm leaving its mark on the right leg of her jeans as she braced herself with her hands. Jason fell to his knees, turning the man over in his arms. He grasped the tiny hole in the fabric of Amir's shirt and tore open the blood-matted clothing, pressed his hands against the wound. *"Help me hold pressure!"* he pleaded, but his sister knelt down beside him, taking hold of Jason's forearms as she shook her head slowly from one side to the other.

"He's gone, Jason."

"No. He's not gone. Help me move him to the couch. We've got to—"

"He's dead," she said, the words tasting like cardboard in her mouth. Amir Massoud had conspired to carry out a terrorist attack on American citizens. Hundreds of innocent people would have died, their bodies blown apart or crushed beneath tons of rubble, bloody hands sticking out from the debris. She had tracked him, photographed him in D.C.'s Dupont Circle conversing with two militant extremists from Al-Termir, and when she had finally confronted him with the accusation, Amir had tried to kill her. And if he'd been successful, what would he have done with Jason? Would he have killed him, too? Yes, she thought. There would have been no other choice.

"*What have you done? WHAT HAVE YOU DONE?!*" Jason cried out, his face turned away from her. And the answer to that question, of course, was that she had managed to save herself and, in doing so, to save the life of her brother and countless others. And now one person lay dead in this room instead of two. She'd admitted in her formal report of the incident that she did not regret the action she'd been forced to take in order to remain on the living side of *that* equation. And yet . . .

And yet her brother had loved him. He'd trusted him, confided in him, had established a life with him. And now . . . now Jason would mourn him. And for that—for the suffering Jason would endure in sporadic waves over the many years ahead—she was intensely sorry.

She'd fished her cell phone from her pocket, dialed a number.

"Are you calling an ambulance?" he'd asked, his face puffy but still hopeful, and the innocence of his question must have broken her heart.

"No," she said. "I'm calling my field office. We'll need a cleaner."

"A cleaner?"

"Someone to . . . yes, this is Edwards," she said into the phone, her voice becoming more formal as she rattled off her ID number. The conversation lasted less than thirty seconds, and when she was done she turned to study him, to gauge how quickly he was adjusting to the situation.

"We should call for an ambulance," Jason reiterated.

"No," she said. "We stand right here and wait. Don't touch anything."

He got to his feet and they stood facing each other, hands hanging limply at their sides as the minutes ticked away. Outside, the night was quiet, except for the usual sounds of the city: a car passing by along the residential street; a dog barking; a siren somewhere far off in the distance.

"I'm sorry, Jason," she said. "I really am."

He nodded slightly—a subtle downward tilt of his chin as he stood there reeling in the shock of the past few minutes—signaling his acknowledgment of what she'd said, but not his forgiveness. Perhaps never his forgiveness.

Twenty minutes later, a car and a dark van pulled up out front, the wheels barely rolling to a stop before their drivers were out of the vehicles and walking up the front steps. The front door opened and they walked in—no knock, no introductions.

"Twenty-eight minutes ago," she advised the men.

The cleaner—a short, neatly dressed man whose thinning hair was combed straight back from his forehead—stood perfectly still, his eyes taking in the scene in one brief sweep and then focusing on the larger man with whom he'd arrived.

"Options," the big man said, his voice deep and stern.

"We call this in to local authorities, reporting it just as it happened," Jason's sister replied, her words crisp and disciplined, as if she were reciting the answer to a homework assignment to her teacher. In a way, perhaps she was.

"No," the man said. "Any word that a CIA agent was involved will blow this entire investigation wide open. Al-Termir will disappear without a trace, and the agent we have on the inside will need to be pulled immediately. We're talking years of wasted work."

"Second option," she said, not bothering to explain or justify the unauthorized confrontation. She would be grilled about the incident later, but for now time was short and decisions had to be made. "The suspect disappears. No explanation to his partner or contact with his family—just picks up and leaves town. Maybe he wants out. Maybe he goes into the witness protection program. For our purposes, it doesn't matter. He disappears and is never heard from again."

"Third option," the man said, wanting everything on the table.

"This was a home invasion. A struggle. Mr. Massoud was killed. The perpetrator got away."

"Both the second and third options will involve investigations by local PD. They'll suspect Mr. Edwards." He pointed to her brother. "They'll push him hard, try to get him to crack. You think he can hold up to that and keep his story straight?"

All three of them looked at Jason, measuring him with their eyes. It was the first time the two men had acknowledged his presence. Jason met their gaze with resentment and indignation—the three of them standing in *his* house, deciding what should be done, as if the matter barely concerned him.

"Fourth option," Jason said. "I tell the police I killed him."

"No," his sister replied at once. "Absolutely not."

The big man held up a hand, silencing her. "Wait," he said. "I want to hear what Mr. Edwards has to say."

Jason's face was pale and shell-shocked. His hands and clothes were caked with blood, his knees slouching inward, threatening to buckle beneath him. He was bent forward slightly at the waist, as if he'd been kicked hard in the crotch and was standing there during that split second it took for his brain to register what his body already knew. He had the look of a beaten man, one who realizes that nothing he does from this moment onward will ever change that. Only his eyes were alive, peering out at the three of them with sufficient intelligence to demonstrate that he was still present in the moment, that he was still capable of understanding the choices in front of him. The voice that spoke up now came from that part of him. It was quiet and wavered a bit. But it was there in the room and it wanted to be heard.

"It's what the police will suspect happened regardless of what I tell them," he said.

"And you go to prison for the next couple of decades," his sister responded. "No, Jason. It's not an option."

The cleaner stared blankly at his superior, awaiting the man's direction. Neither spoke, but in the brief silence that followed it seemed they had completed the calculations and arrived at the same irrefutable conclusion.

"You're not seriously considering this," she protested, taking a step toward her boss.

"Yes, I am," the man said. "He's right. It's the option with the least number of moving parts—the simplest and most likely scenario. It's the most believable explanation."

"I won't agree to it," she said.

"You'll agree to whatever I decide, Agent Edwards." His voice remained calm, but contained an inherent menace, the tone of a man who *will not* be crossed. He turned back to Jason. "We could offer you certain immunity. In some ways, the judicial system can be easier to manipulate than local law enforcement—*if* we want to keep our heads down. Once an investigation is completed, once an individual is convicted, the public's interest is, for the most part, satiated." The big man nodded to himself, even smiled a bit although it never touched his eyes. "I could get you released within a few years, have your record expunged as if it never happened. We've negotiated similar arrangements many times before. If all goes well"—he shrugged, as if it were the simplest of matters—"we could offer you employment with the agency."

Jason's eyes were on the floor now, considering. He would later tell me there had been a fluid quality to the room, the walls disappearing for a moment and giving way to the brown limbs of the forest, his back pressed flat against the earth, the face of Billy Myers peering down at him, wild-eyed, the cold steel of the blade pressed against his stomach. He could feel his intestines squirm away from that blade, could picture that single drop of blood welling up on his belly where the knife's tip penetrated the skin by a single millimeter. And then he could hear the cut of the bat through the air, Billy's arm becoming a useless, crippled thing, the rest of them scattering like rodents. *And here she is again*, he thought, looking up at his sister as the walls fell back into place around them, leaving only the lingering smell of the woods in his nostrils.

"Was he really guilty of what you said he was?" he asked, and the pinched expression on her face was answer enough.

"I'm sorry, Jason," she said again. "I'm so very sorry."

Jason was silent for a few seconds longer. When he looked up at the other men, they could see that his eyes had gone dull and beaten like the rest of him. "I'll do it," he said without purpose or conviction. He sat down on the floor next to Amir and placed a hand on the dead man's shoulder. "Now leave us alone," he told them, and they at least had the decency to do *that*. His sister located Jason's cell phone and placed it beside him on the floor before she departed. Forty minutes later he used it to dial 911. The conversation with the emergency operator was brief. After he'd hung up, Jason closed his eyes, rested his head against the wall, and listened to his own breathing until it was drowned out by the sound of approaching sirens.

Chapter 24

I took the following day off, called in sick with a flulike illness. It wasn't far from the truth, either. I'd been up for a good portion of the night, tossing in bed as the scene Linder and Remy had recounted played out in my mind. When I allowed my eyelids to slide closed, the images were like those from a feverish dream: vibrant, manic, and full of too much color. I could see the knife slipping effortlessly between Amir's ribs, his body going first rigid, then heavy and lifeless above an expanding maroon blemish—like a rapidly dividing birthmark—on the hardwood floor. I could see Jason's mouth opening in a silent scream, his fingers digging into the flesh and late-evening stubble of his cheeks, his eyes becoming two dark pebbles sunk deep into his face, the reflection of his partner's crumpled body swimming across their smooth black surfaces. I could also imagine the two other men deliberating over how the situation should be handled, although I had difficulty picturing them in my mind. All I could see clearly was Jason and Amir and the knife protruding like a vestigial appendage from between the man's ribs, and with those images came the conviction that all this could have somehow been prevented.

I awoke to rays of sunlight bleeding through the slatted shades that hung like closely gathered ribs across my bedroom window. I lifted my head from a pillowcase that felt damp with sweat, the fabric creased and bunched from the previous night's struggle. The fitted sheet had freed itself from one of the mattress's corners, and I left it that way as I climbed out of bed and made my way to the bathroom, feeling light-headed, nauseated, and more fatigued than I'd been the night before.

In the bathroom, after I'd urinated, I splashed some cold water on my face and checked my reflection in the mirror. Lingering drops of water congregated at the tip of my nose and along the lower edge of my chin, a few of them letting go as I watched, casting their rotund bodies into the pale blue sink below. My hair was a rat's nest of twisted strands, and dark semicircles puffed out the skin beneath my eyes like small translucent bowls of black broth.

I'd agreed to meet with Agents Linder and Remy again today, this time at the hotel restaurant located in the Westin on Porter Street. We'd decided to meet at 10 A.M. when it would be mostly empty. There was more to discuss, they'd said, but it had been clear from my reaction the day before that I'd needed time to process. Time seemed to be a concern for them, and there'd been a brief discussion as to whether they could afford waiting the extra day. I'd encouraged them to tell me the rest right then and there, but Linder had shaken his head no. "Tomorrow," he'd said. "It can wait until then."

I showered and dressed, popping a few Advil for the headache that tracked me down during the first half hour after rolling out of bed. The invisible viselike hand squeezing my temples relented a bit by the time I left my apartment, but my muscles felt stiff and heavy as I trundled down the sidewalk.

The Westin was once a posh hotel overlooking the Severn River. It serviced clientele from Annapolis and visitors to the Naval Academy who did not wish to stay in the city proper. But traffic into Annapolis had become congested over the years and parking difficult, making the short commute into the state's capital increasingly tedious. When a newer branch of the hotel chain opened up near the Academy, the one in my town became obsolete almost overnight, and although it remained open for business, coming here was like visiting an athlete long past his prime. The building was maintained and serviced out of a lingering need for its facilities. But its floors would never again see the shine they once held, and its carpets endured the stains of time with as much dignity as they could muster against the embarrassing backdrop of their own implacable decay.

The two of them were already occupying a corner table, and I waved away the greeter—a young girl of about twenty-three whose bored eyes never met my face—as I crossed the restaurant to join them. I took a seat and nodded when Linder pointed to a pot of coffee resting on the table, allowing him to fill my cup.

"Sleep well?" Remy inquired.

"What do *you* think?" I asked, and the man shook his head.

"It's a lot to take in," he said, lifting his own cup to his lips.

The waitress came by to take our orders. Remy asked for a bowl of oatmeal with brown sugar, Linder a fruit plate. Feeling like I should order *something*, I requested toast and jam, knowing I'd touch none of it.

We sat there for a minute or two sipping our coffee, Linder making a few forays into small talk that I batted away with single-word answers. Finally, Remy—whose bluntness I'd developed an appreciation for over the past twenty-four hours—started on what we'd come there to discuss.

"I think you got a pretty good picture yesterday of the circumstances leading up to the arrest of Jason Edwards for second-degree murder."

I nodded. "I imagine he was never convicted."

"No," Remy replied. "A conviction would have meant prison. Jason's defense attorney was able to successfully convince the judge assigned to the case that his client was not guilty by reason of insanity."

"How did he manage to do that? If Jason had no prior psychiatric history . . ."

"Suffice it to say that the agency was able to utilize its resources and to exert its considerable influence over that matter. We're talking about the CIA here. A single conversation is all it would've taken."

"Why Menaker? Why not some other facility?"

"He wasn't sent to Menaker initially," Remy replied. "Jason was arrested in May of 2010. It takes time to move through the court system. Even for cases where defendants are found not guilty by reason of insanity—I believe you use the acronym NGI?" he asked, and I nodded, although in Maryland the legal term was "not criminally responsible by reason of insanity." "Even for those defendants, the process takes time."

"Generally, a defendant would receive two independent psychiatric evaluations," I said.

"Right. And the courts move slowly—too many criminal cases being ground through the mill. You know?"

"Yeah."

"So he was out on bond awaiting a decision for almost a year,"

Remy said. "He wasn't finally remanded to a state psychiatric hospital until April of 2011. Initially, he was sent to Eastern State Hospital in Williamsburg, Virginia. And he stayed there for four years before being transferred to Menaker."

"Why was he transferred?"

Linder's face became somber. "The CIA took a loss."

"A loss—what do you mean?"

"Two of their agents were murdered. One of them was the undercover agent who'd infiltrated Al-Termir. The other was an operative who'd worked his way into the ranks of a similar extremist group based out of Los Angeles. Both of them were executed on the same day, and the most likely explanation was that the identity of the men had been leaked to the groups by someone within the CIA itself."

"Jesus," I said, and Linder nodded.

"During the Cold War, we'd become accustomed to the idea of spies within our midst siphoning military and state intelligence to our enemies. But the war on terror is a different type of battleground, isn't it? The stakes seem less global, more personal. The enemy is invisible, can't be negotiated with, and has nothing to lose. The attacks come from within and can happen at any moment. And a mole inside the CIA releasing information to these ultraviolent factions . . ." He trailed off, and the only sound came from the light traffic along Porter Street just outside.

"The agency took what precautions it could," Remy said. "Agents who'd investigated either of the two groups were strongly cautioned and often reassigned, and any likely civilian targets were offered protective custody. Your patient Jason Edwards was transferred to Menaker immediately. No chart, no paper trail— just moved."

The table fell silent for a full minute as they allowed me time to adjust to the reality of the situation. It was ironic in a way. After treating Jason as my patient for the past few weeks, I'd developed the distinct sense that we were making progress. We were uncovering things, I thought, strengthening our therapeutic relationship. But now they were telling me that Jason Edwards was not a patient at all. He was a boarder, a tenant, and to him Menaker was nothing more than a place of refuge—a cage to keep him safe from an extremist group that would do him harm if it could.

"Why tell me any of this?" I asked. "Most of this information, I would imagine, is confidential."

Neither of the men said anything. A moment later our breakfasts appeared on the table and they busied themselves with their food. For something to do, I poured myself another cup of coffee.

"Do you wonder," Agent Linder finally responded, "why the FBI is involved in this? Since it's mostly a CIA matter."

I shrugged. "Cases of domestic terrorism, you said, are FBI jurisdiction."

"But nothing happened," he reminded me. "There *was* no bombing, at least nothing linked to Amir Massoud. Agent Edwards's confrontation with Amir aborted any event that might have otherwise occurred."

I touched the tips of my fingers to my right temple, feeling the return of my earlier headache.

"We're here," Linder went on, "because Jason's sister came to the FBI for assistance. She'd lost trust in the agency and the people she was working under. She didn't know who else to turn to. But that's not why she came to us."

"No?"

"No," Remy said. "She came to us because she was afraid."

"For Jason?" I asked.

He nodded. "And for herself."

"A week and a half ago," Linder advised me, "someone deleted the report of the incident from her office computer's hard drive and external backup system. Her supervisor—a man who'd been stationed in the D.C. area for most of his career—was reassigned to a foreign field office. On her first trip to Menaker, Jason's sister was tailed and had to abandon the visit. Last weekend, someone gained entrance to her house while she was at work."

"The place wasn't ransacked," Remy told me. "There was no forcible entry. But she could tell that several items around her desk and cabinets were disturbed, as if someone was looking for something. They'd also successfully logged in to her home computer—which was password protected, by the way."

"A professional job," Linder remarked.

I frowned. "What did she think they were looking for?"

"Copies of the incident report, maybe," Remy said, "or information regarding Jason's new location."

I looked down at my uneaten toast. "Right now, she's his only ally."

"Except for you," Remy said. He finished the last of his oatmeal, placed the spoon in the bowl, and wiped at the corner of his mouth with his napkin.

"They should put him into protective custody," I said. "He'd be safer there than at Menaker."

"I don't know if that's true," Linder replied. "Right now, he's hiding in plain sight. Sometimes that's the last place people look."

"But at the moment the agency has other concerns," Remy advised me, "because they've lost another one."

"Another agent?" I asked, and he nodded, rubbing the right side of his face with the meaty palm of his hand. He looked weary and a little beaten, like a boxer whose years in the ring have finally caught up with him.

"Jason's sister," he said, his dark eyes meeting mine from across the table. "She disappeared three days ago."

Chapter 25

The remainder of the day was spent moving from one activity to the next, driven by the need to occupy myself with something purposeful but finding nothing to quell my inner restlessness. I wandered the streets for a while, taking in the fastidious bustle of the town's businesses and patrons, but found the noise and commotion agitating. Eventually, I made my way to the outskirts of the town and the entrance to the jogging path along which I'd met Agent Linder. *Where I'd been tracked down by Agent Linder,* I corrected myself. My running shoes were at home, so I chose to walk instead, turning my face to catch the irregular breeze. Linder had recommended I stay away from the trail for the time being, since the location was somewhat isolated, but I refused to be cowed by a predicament that was no fault of my own. "Am I to be afraid now?" I'd asked him at the hotel. "Am I to behave like a frightened rabbit in my own neighborhood?"

"I'm just suggesting that you take precautions," he said, "until we have a better idea of how this is going to unfold."

I replayed his words, considering their implications. They'd filled me in on what they knew. From here on out, we were all sprinting in the dark.

"A few nights ago," I said, "someone followed me home from Marj's Kitchen. Was that one of you?"

Linder and Remy looked at each other, and the expression that passed between them did nothing to reassure me. "That was earlier this week?" Remy asked.

I nodded. "Monday night," I said, and I told them about the man who'd followed me to my apartment, who'd stood there on the sidewalk looking up at me. Linder shook his head. "This is what I'm talking about, Lise. We don't know *who* that was, but it wasn't either of us. And until we have a better picture of what's going on here—"

"*And when will that be?*" I demanded.

The two of them just looked at me from across the table.

"Until that time," I said, placing my coffee cup on the table with a bang, "I'm supposed to . . . to do *what?*"

"Sit tight," Remy said. "Keep a low profile. Don't do anything to attract attention. Continue treating Jason in the same manner as before."

"They'll get the information out of her," I told them. "It won't be long until they know where he is."

"We shouldn't jump to conclusions," Linder replied. "We don't know what happened to Agent Edwards. She may have gone into hiding." He slid a cell phone and small charger across the table. "Keep this on you. It has our numbers programmed into its contacts, plus a GPS so we'll know where you are. We'd like you to be our eyes and ears inside Menaker, to keep us advised of any unusual developments."

"Like what?" I asked.

Linder shrugged. "You know that facility, the people there. We don't."

"You'll know if something's about to go down," Remy said, "and if or when that time comes . . ."

"You call us," Linder finished.

"And you'll be there?" I asked. "If I need you?"

They both looked back at me, their faces solemn and protective.

"We're not going anywhere," Remy said. "You call one of the two numbers on that phone, and we'll come running."

"We're staying local," Linder advised me. "If you call, we can be anywhere in this town in less than five minutes."

Less than five minutes, I thought, looking out over the Severn River. In my pants pocket I ran a fingertip over the phone's hard plastic casing, then pulled it out, familiarizing myself with its buttons and small touch screen. *Less than five minutes*, they had told me. *You call . . . and we'll come running.* There was some reassurance in that, but it felt false—a feather to cling to as I plummeted from a cliff. If the men who'd taken Jason's sister decided to come for him—or for me—then five minutes later there would be nothing left but the empty space where we'd once stood. There would be no finding us. *That* was the truth. And phone or no phone, there was nothing Linder or Remy could do to stop it.

Chapter 26

August 25, 2006

They sat in silence in the backseat as the cab merged onto the G.W. Parkway and wound its way through the midday traffic toward Reagan National Airport. The temperature had already reached 98 degrees today, and Jason was sweating, the taxi's lackluster air-conditioning offering much noise but little respite from the metropolitan area's notorious summer humidity. Their driver chattered away on his cell phone in a language Jason didn't recognize, and next to him Amir sat with his face turned toward the closed window and the Arlington National Cemetery beyond. It was an hour-and-forty-minute flight to Montreal, then almost seven hours overnight to London and another four and a half to Beirut. Amir would be gone for two weeks, attending his mother's funeral and spending time with relatives he'd never met—but there was something ominous in his silence, and Jason couldn't help but wonder if he would ever come back.

Jason had tried to comfort him, to be present during his grief, but the body he'd held seemed very distant from the person within. And why not? To lose one's mother was a devastating thing, but for her to die on the other side of the world in a country ravaged by war was something else entirely. "I should've been there," Amir had whispered last night in the darkness of their bedroom. In his mind, Jason pictured the missile descending from the sky, the deafening explosion and *whomp* of the blast as the concrete building where she'd lived was reduced to fire, rubble, and the unrecognizable remnants of what had been scores of human beings a moment before.

"If you'd been there," Jason responded, "you would have died as well."

"Yes," he replied, the inflection of his voice acknowledging the fact but not retreating from his assertion.

"You're returning on the eighth?" Jason asked now as the driver took the exit for the airport.

Amir glanced over at him. "Yeah," he said before turning his attention back to the window. There was little reassurance in the answer.

A minute later the cabbie eased the car up to the curb near a sign designating departures for Air Canada. Amir pulled the latch and was out the door before the vehicle came to a complete stop. Jason and the driver followed suit, staying close to the car to accommodate the line of traffic squeezing by on their left. *Too many people*, Jason thought randomly as he stepped to the curb, joining Amir. The cabbie popped the trunk to retrieve the suitcase.

Jason placed a hand on his partner's forearm. "I'm so sorry."

Amir turned his face to study him. There was a hardness in his eyes that Jason had never seen before. "It's part of life there," he said, "something my people are forced to endure. Living here in this country, you will never know what that's like."

"No, I . . . I suppose not."

The driver placed the luggage on the curb beside them, then turned and got back into the car.

"Are you sure you don't want me to come with you?" Jason asked. "I could—"

"No." Amir reached down for the suitcase's handle, brought it up in a snap.

"Are you angry with me?" Jason asked. "Have I done something to—"

"No," he said, and his face softened then, his features transitioning back into the person Jason loved. "You haven't done anything wrong, and I'm not angry with you. It's just that . . ." He swiveled his head to look at the people moving all around them. Then his eyes were back on Jason. "It's just that I have to go bury my mother now."

"Okay," Jason said, and leaned into him, wrapping his arms around him for a moment before letting go. "Come back safe."

Amir nodded. "I'll try." He turned and walked through the gaping mouth of the terminal's sliding glass doors.

Jason watched until the doors closed once again.

Chapter 27

When I returned to work the next day, my perception of Menaker and the people there had taken on a surreal quality, as if I were an actress in a play where everyone knew their lines but me. The groundskeeper, Kendrick Jones, gave me a smile and a wink with his good eye as I made my way up the front walkway. "Dr. Shields," he greeted me. His expression was friendly—amicable—and yet I had the feeling he was recalling an inside joke between the two of us, one I'd long since forgotten. I wanted to stop and ask why he was smiling like that, to have him chuckle as he recounted some humorous interaction we'd once shared. But I was afraid my question would be met with only a perplexed look. "Jus' sayin' good morning, Dr. Shields," he would tell me, and I would feel like a fool for asking.

Across the open stretch of grass to my left, I caught a glimpse of Dr. Wagner heading up the front steps of the administrative building about two hundred yards away. He turned his head as he reached the top, glancing back across the yard. I wasn't certain if he saw me or not, but his head quickly whipped back around as he pushed open the front door and disappeared inside.

I continued up the walkway and entered the main clini-

cal building, whose egg-white walls had long since faded to the
stained yellow of an old man's teeth. In the hallway leading to the
activity room, I encountered Paul Drevel, one of the orderlies.
He acknowledged me with a nod. "Beautiful morning, isn't it?"
he offered, and I agreed with him in a voice that sounded a bit
forced and wooden, even to my own ears. "Anything special on
the agenda today?" I asked him, but he shook his head *nah, same
old, same old*.

I've always liked Paul. His casual, unassuming demeanor puts
the patients at ease. On weekends, when things are slow at the
hospital, he often brings in his guitar and plays in the common
area, his soft, steady voice filling the room until the walls seem to
melt away into the background. During the space of that time, it's
easy to forget that we're all here in Menaker, serving our own private sentences. In the wake of all I'd learned over the past forty-
eight hours, I felt that I needed someone I could trust—someone
on the inside—who could look out for Jason and watch my back
as well. If there was anyone here who could not be compromised,
it was Paul.

I stopped in the hallway and put a hand on his elbow. "Can I
talk to you for a moment?"

Paul looked down at my hand. When his eyes rose to meet
mine, he did not look surprised—almost as if he'd been waiting
for me to ask.

I led him back down the hall, turned left at the next intersection, continuing until we came to the closed door of a conference
room used for evening rounds. It would be empty now and a reasonable place for us to speak in private, but when I placed a hand
on the knob it was locked.

"Do you mind?" I asked, gesturing at the door, knowing Paul

had a key to the room. He wasn't supposed to, but he did. Except for the physician offices—and maybe even those—there wasn't a locked room at Menaker that Paul did not have access to. It was a little project he'd been working on over the years, amassing those keys, and we all pretended we didn't know about it, although everyone on the medical staff did. I don't know why he started the collection in the first place. Perhaps he figured he might need it someday. Or maybe it was something he did for his own amusement and satisfaction—a little defiance in the face of strict policies and procedures. But mostly I think it was about control, an illusion we all like to cling to when we can.

Paul reached into his pocket, brought out a set of colored keys, pausing only long enough to glance over his shoulder to ensure we were alone, and had the door open in less time than it would've taken for me to recite my own name. As soon as we were through its threshold, he flipped on the light and closed the door behind us.

I let out a breath, enjoying the quiet privacy of the room. For the moment, as far as I could tell, we were not being watched.

I took a seat at the long table in the center of the room, inviting him to do the same. "How long have we known each other, Paul?"

"Long enough, Lise," he said, lowering himself into a chair. "What's troubling you?"

"You know I've been treating Jason Edwards."

He nodded, but his eyes looked wary.

"Dr. Wagner ever mention him to you? Ever bring him up in conversation?"

Paul shifted in his seat, running his fingers along the smooth contour of the table. "What do you mean?"

"He tell you why Jason's here?"

"I'm not involved in those types of conversations," Paul replied.

"But you know this place and the patients here better than any of us." I tried to catch his eyes, but he was looking down at his hands now. "And yet you don't know much about Jason Edwards, do you?"

He shook his head.

"Does that strike you as odd?"

He said nothing—still wouldn't look at me. *Was I making a mistake in coming to him, making myself more vulnerable instead of less?* Still, who else could I trust?

"I'm going to tell you something," I pressed on, "that I want you to keep between the two of us. Do you think you can do that?"

"Depends on what it is," he replied. "I could get in trouble just for letting you in here. I'm not supposed to—"

"You're not supposed to have keys to every locked door in this facility. I know. But I don't care about that. None of us do. What I care about is the safety of these patients, and I know you do, too. That's why I'm confiding in you. Because I trust that your heart's in the right place."

He looked up at me, finally. His face was guarded, but there was something in his eyes—*Was it empathy? Pity?*—that tipped the scales, convinced me I could trust him. I took a breath and told him as much as I dared.

"Jason doesn't belong here," I said. "Believe me when I tell you the circumstances are complicated, but in a way it doesn't matter. Because right now what he needs most is protection. There are certain people—dangerous individuals—who may be coming for him."

"You should talk to Dr. Wagner about this."

"No," I responded, shaking my head. "I can't trust Dr. Wagner. I think they've already gotten to him."

"Who are we talking about here?"

I hesitated, not knowing what to say. "I don't know for sure," I told him, which was close enough to the truth. "But they're powerful enough to make someone disappear. I don't want that to happen to Jason."

Paul studied me cautiously, and I waited for him to laugh or tell me I was crazy. I sat there and watched hope dangle from a fishing line over a river, waited for something to leap from the current and snatch it away from me in the turn of a thin second. In the hall outside, I could hear the muffled conversation of two nurses as they passed, their voices hushed and secretive.

"What do you want me to do?" Paul asked. His voice sounded small and unprotected, reminding me that he too had something to lose—that *he too* could become a target if he got in the way. If anything happened to him, I would bear the weight of that responsibility for the rest of my life.

"I want you to keep your eyes open, to watch out for Jason and to make sure he remains safe here. I don't know if anyone will come for him, but if they do . . ."

He sat across from me, as still as the furniture. I reached into my pocket, removed a slip of paper, and handed it to him. On it was written the contact numbers for Linder and Remy.

"If anyone comes for him, if anything happens," I told him, "I want you to call one of these numbers right away. You make that call, and help will come running."

"And until they get here?" he asked.

It was what worried me the most as well.

"Do what you can," I said. "Don't let them take him."

"Because if they do?" he asked, although I think he already knew the answer.

I exhaled slowly, the tension in my muscles refusing to loosen. "If they do," I replied, "then we may never see him again."

Chapter 28

I t's time for us to speak frankly," I said, closing the door behind me. Jason and I had entered Menaker's modest library, a room whose brown plaster walls were lined on three sides with cheap metal shelves hosting an assortment of used books, many of them tattered and missing large swaths of pages since they'd first been introduced to this place two decades ago. Most of the hospital's literature was donated by local libraries and a few semigenerous individuals wanting to rid their bookcases of titles they hadn't looked at since college. And the bindings—worn and nearing the end of their life spans when they'd first arrived—had reached a state of decrepitude surpassed only by the buildings themselves. They sagged on the shelves, leaning against one another for support, and were seldom held in human hands. One of two small tables in the room supported a computer monitor, mouse, and keyboard, their black wires descending like necrotic umbilical cords to the processor that rested on the carpeted floor beneath the right side of the table. Like everything else here it needed replacing, yet no one bothered to do so—perhaps because a pulse of electricity still flowed within its withered circuits, and like an old mongrel who can do little more than lie curled near the hearth, gathering for comfort what heat it could in its final days, there was a tendency to simply let it be, knowing that sooner or later the life inside would wink out forever.

There was no one there but the two of us. Jason plopped himself down into the only chair comfortable enough for long spells of reading, and its cushions let out a soft, miserable wheeze that reminded me of the way my grandfather's labored breathing had sounded as he lay in a hospital bed he'd been trudging toward through sixty years of heavy smoking.

I pulled a plastic chair from beneath the second table, its rigid form pressing into my spine as I sat.

"I know what happened to you," I said, "and I know why you're here."

He looked at me, only half interested in what I had to say.

"I know that your sister works for the CIA, that she suspected Amir of plotting to bomb a D.C. Metro station. I know that she warned you and eventually confronted him in May of 2010, and that during that confrontation there was a struggle and Amir was killed in the process. I know you volunteered to take the blame, and that a short stay in a state psychiatric hospital was part of that deal."

My words seemed to barely register with him, as if what I was saying held little relevance to his current situation.

"But," I went on, "recent events have made the outside world more dangerous for you and your sister, and you were transferred here for your own protection."

He said nothing.

"When's the last time you spoke with her?" I asked.

He remained quiet, his gaze turned in the direction of the bookshelf on his right.

"*Dammit, Jason!* You need to *talk* to me." My words ricocheted off the walls of the library. I stood, walked across the room, turned to look at him once again.

"Look," I said, forcing my voice into a calmer tone. "I know you're trying to protect her. I get that. But I want you to know that you can confide in me. You can trust me. I will help you in any way I can."

"You don't know *how* to help me," he said, his words barely more than a whisper. "You can't even help yourself."

I stood there, not knowing how to respond.

"Am I in danger?" I asked him at last. "Is there anything else I should know?" I walked over to him, touched his shoulder. "Jason," I said, and he looked up at me from where he sat. "Tell me what you think is going to happen. Will they come for us?"

He nodded, and the expression on his face was not fear or anxiety so much as resignation. "They always do."

"They've come for you before?" I asked. "When you were at Eastern State Hospital?" I could feel the tiny hairs on my forearms rise.

He sighed, buried his face in his hands. I studied him, tried to imagine the things he'd been through.

"During one of our first conversations," I reminded him, "when I asked about your sister, you told me, 'She's been gone for five years now, and alive or dead, I don't think she's ever coming back.' What did you mean by that? Didn't she ever visit you during your time at Eastern State Hospital? Didn't you ever hear from her?"

He lifted his face toward mine, his eyes red and a little glassy. He looked muddled. Lost. The muscles of his shoulders and back bunched awkwardly, like an ill-fitting coat he'd forgotten to remove. When he spoke, his words were thick and sloppy.

"I can see her," he said, "but she doesn't see me. Not really. Ever since the night Amir was killed . . . she's"—the features of his face drew together, a purse string cinching itself tight—"she's different now . . . like a ghost. I . . . I know she's there, but . . . I can't find her." He turned a beseeching gaze up at me. "Do you understand?"

"I'm sure the incident with Amir affected her deeply," I said, trying to offer something reassuring. "The guilt of taking his life—even if it was an act of self-defense—is not something I'd expect her to recover from easily. Seeing you might cause her to"—I sought for the right word—"disengage. Emotionally. It's a defense mechanism, you see? It doesn't mean she's abandoning you."

He shook his head. "You don't know her the way I do."

"No," I agreed. "I don't."

"I can't force you to see it through my eyes."

I nodded. He was right, of course. I was trying to convince him of something I couldn't be certain of myself. She'd gone missing, after all. She could be anywhere. She could be dead.

"Well, *I'm* not going anywhere," I told him. "I won't leave you." It was the type of promise a parent makes to a child, the words well-meaning but naive, as if the world is theirs to control. As if they have every expectation of living forever.

Chapter 29

November 15, 2009

S he stood in the kitchen doorway, watching him fumble with the dial that controlled the heating element for the range. He was wearing a hoodie with a sweatshirt underneath, his body hunched slightly at the waist, the arms held close to his chest when they weren't busy with other tasks.

"You shouldn't be here," Jason told her. He turned, and she could see that he was sweating—*a good sign*, she thought—his body's attempt to counteract the fever.

"I'm your sister. It's my responsibility to look out for you."

"You're going to get sick, too."

"I've had my flu shot."

"But you don't know that it'll work," he replied, and she had to admit to herself that this was true. The swine flu pandemic had begun in Mexico, then quickly spread to the United States. Initial outbreaks had been particularly severe in Texas, New York, and California, but by now there'd been confirmed deaths in all fifty states. Three days ago, the CDC reported an estimated twenty-two million Americans infected—close to 15 percent of the entire population—with a death toll of around four thousand. It was terrifying, and when both Jason and Amir had fallen ill within the same two-week period there was nothing to do but come and watch over them.

"When's the last time you took something for the fever?" she asked.

"An hour ago."

The fact that he was obviously still burning up filled her with dread, turned her mind to images of the thousands of new tombstones that had been set into the earth over the past eight months.

In the next room, Amir was in even worse condition. When Jason had called to tell her that Amir hadn't been out of bed in four days, that this morning he'd been delirious—mumbling about bombs and subway trains, conversing with his dead mother—she'd gotten into her car and driven the forty-six miles to their apartment in thirty-five minutes flat. Now that she was here, watching her brother—his body shaking with chills, his gaunt face the color of limestone—she realized that Jason hadn't been completely honest with her. He hadn't told her that he was sick as well—that he *had been* for days—and that it was the fear that he, too, might slip into delirium, leaving no one to care for Amir, that had made him call.

"Whatever you took an hour ago isn't working," she told him. "You need to take something else—Tylenol or Motrin."

"I took them both. And we've been taking Tamiflu for three days now." He crossed the kitchen, opened a cabinet to retrieve a box of tea bags, and on his way back to the range stumbled and nearly fell. She stepped forward to steady him. *"I'm contagious. Don't touch me,"* he said, but she paid him no mind.

"Forget the goddamn tea. If it's so important to you, I'll make it."

"It's what he asked for—this morning," he told her, "before he became confused. I was thinking it might bring him around."

"He should be in the hospital."

Jason shook his head. "I took him to the ER three days ago. So many sick people, far worse than us. The doctors and nurses seemed overwhelmed. They gave us a prescription and sent us home."

"But he's worse now, and so are you. If he's delirious, he should be—" She stopped, not wanting to argue. She would assess him. If Amir was as bad as Jason said, she'd call the ambulance herself—*insist* that he be hospitalized. She turned off the stove's burner, took Jason by the arm, and led him to the couch in the other room. "Sit. If you fall down, I'm going to have a hard time picking you up off the floor."

He complied, lowered himself onto the sofa. She removed his shoes, hoodie, and sweatshirt, then pivoted his body into a horizontal position, placed a small pillow beneath his head.

"I need a blanket. I'm freezing," he protested.

"You're running a fever. All the clothes don't help."

He mumbled in response, then closed his eyes and lay still as the sound of his breathing grew long and regular. She watched for a moment, then went down the hall to the bedroom.

The room's lights were controlled by a dimmer that had been turned low but not off, and she could see Amir lying on the bed in the semidarkness. The apartment was heated by central air, and it should've been no warmer here than in the rest of the place. But she could feel the temperature shift as she entered the room and—as ridiculous as it was—she was certain the extra heat was coming from the human body in front of her. She walked to the side of the bed, the temperature seeming to click up a degree or two as she neared him.

Impossible, she thought, then went ahead and believed it anyway.

He was lying on his left side, his eyelids only three-quarters closed, his mouth gaping slightly. Either he or Jason had removed his shirt and rid the bed of heavy blankets so only a thin sheet remained. *Good*, she thought, as she slid the sheet down to get a better look at him. Whereas Jason had been sweating, Amir's skin was desert dry, and the heat—*Jesus*, the heat coming off him did not seem compatible with human life.

There was a thermometer lying on the nightstand to her right. It was an old-school version, a thin glass tube of mercury. She picked it up, shook it out, and lifted his right arm just enough to place it into the armpit. While she waited for the mercury to rise, she went to the adjoining bathroom and turned on the cold water in the tub. If the fever was a hundred and five or greater, she decided, she would figure out a way to get him in there. She stood for a moment, listened to the sound of running water. *Don't let him die*, she told herself. *Call an ambulance if you have to, but don't let him die.*

There was a half-full bottle of Tylenol capsules in one of the drawers, but she didn't think she'd be able to get him to swallow the medication in his current condition. Liquid or even suppositories would've been better, but the capsules were all she had. She set the bottle on the counter anyway—just in case—then returned to the bedroom.

Amir's body was in the exact position it had been in five minutes before. There was something ominous about that, as if rigor mortis had set in even though the heart continued to pound away. She plucked the thermometer from under his armpit, the skin so dry it clung briefly to the tube before letting go with a soft pop. There were black numbers etched in the glass. She turned it to see where the mercury had settled, and her first thought was that the damn thing wasn't reading properly because the red on the inside of the tube stretched from one end to the other. The highest number was one hundred and seven degrees Fahrenheit. The mercury was well past that.

"*Shit*," she whispered, grabbed him by the arms, and pulled the upper half of his body over the edge of the bed. He was a lean man, not more than six feet tall, but his inert body was heavier than she'd anticipated. The fever rolled off him in slow undulating waves. As she wrapped her arms around his chest to drag him from the bed, he moaned something unintelligible in her ear.

"Come on," she said, hoping he might stand, and backed away from the bed with his upper body in her grasp. His legs and feet cleared the edge of the mattress, then fell to the floor with a loud *thwack*. The jolt yanked her forward. Her body reflexively countered the movement, but she overcompensated, fell backward onto the hardwood floor. Her ass took most of the impact, hitting the floor with a cracking sound that could've come from the wood beneath or her own pelvis and tailbone, she wasn't sure. She felt the pain, though, blossoming from her sacrum, spreading across her lower back, and a quarter second later her head struck the boards, everything going white and quiet.

She lay on her back—teeth clenched, breath quick and shallow—until the worst of the pain subsided. All the while, Amir's limp body, clad only in boxers and a suffocating shroud of sickness, lay on top of her without moving. She realized he might already be dead, or close to it. The body can go on even when the brain ceases to function, and more than anything else it was the dead weight of him that frightened her. She rolled him off, managed to stand, then bent down, grabbed him by the wrists, and dragged him across the floor toward the bathroom. The muscles of her lower back screamed in protest, but she could hear the cold water running into the tub behind her, the sound of it giving her something to focus on besides her own agony and the heat from the body she was hauling. When she made it to the tub she sat him up against the side, then sat on the lip herself, one foot in and one foot out of the water, and hoisted him up and over. His waist and torso entered the tub with a splash, and a wave of water sloshed over the side onto the tiled floor, lessening her traction. She'd thought his eyelids might fly open at the cold shock of the water, but he barely stirred. Kneeling down beside the tub in jeans that were now soaked and clinging, she placed one hand on Amir's chest to keep his head from sliding down below the surface. She shut off the faucet, looked back through the open doorway into the bedroom, her eyes searching the night table for a phone. *Should have called 911 from the start*, she admonished herself, but for now she was stuck, keeping his head above the water so he wouldn't drown.

" . . . we will be . . ."

Her eyes returned to his face. His lids were partially open.

" . . . the judgment hand . . ." he croaked, his voice the sound of tires on gravel.

"Hey," she said, putting a wet hand on his forehead. "Glad to see you're with me."

He wasn't with her entirely. His gaze slipped past her, as if focusing on someone behind her, a face he could see just over her right shoulder. It was unsettling, him talking to someone else in the room when it was only the two of them. She felt the urge to follow his gaze, but knew that there was only the mirror behind her, that it would be nothing more than her own reflection staring back.

She leaned forward slightly, her thighs pressed against the side of the tub, and something in the right front pocket of her jeans pressed back. She fished it out, surprised for a moment to be staring at her own cell phone. *It got wet in the tub. It won't work*, she thought, but when she dialed 911 and hit SEND she could hear ringing from the small speaker.

" . . . of God," Amir whispered, and closed his eyes once more. She wasn't paying attention to his ramblings now, only to the female voice on the other end who was asking for the nature of her emergency.

"Medical," she said. "I need an ambulance." And she gave her the address.

"I'm dispatching an ambulance to your location now, ma'am," the operator assured her. "They should be there in a few minutes."

"Thank you," she said, and after answering a few more questions hung up and placed the phone on the toilet beside her. Her hand returned to his face. She spoke his name, tried to rouse him, but his eyes remained shut this time and she decided to let him rest. The water seemed to have quelled his fever a bit, but he was still delirious. *He's been talking about bombs and subway trains and conversations with his dead mother*, Jason had told her earlier over the phone. And just a moment ago:

. . . we will be . . . the judgment hand . . . of God.

She took in a breath, let it out, studied the soft placid lines of his face. "You are not checking out on us today, Amir Massoud," she told him. "You will *not* be the judgment hand of God, but will remain with the living awhile longer."

He uttered a snore in response. She shook her head, placed her forearm on the side of the tub, rested her head upon it. She could hear the approaching siren of the ambulance now, and the relief washed over her, a conviction that Amir would survive this illness that had already taken so many.

Six months later he would be dead—not from influenza, but at the hands of a different fate altogether—and there was no way of knowing that her very presence that evening had set the chain of events in motion, that it would have been better had she never come at all.

Chapter 30

After speaking with Jason, I'd gone to my office—a private place to sit and think—but was surprised to find the door partially open when I arrived.

I paused, looked left and right but saw no one else in the hall. I put out a hand and pushed. The door swung another forty degrees on its hinges before bumping into something lying on the floor just inside. *A body; it will be a body*, I told myself, but when I reached inside and flicked on the light it wasn't a person but an overturned chair. I considered calling security, but whoever had gained access—forcibly, from the look of the doorknob—was clearly gone, leaving my ravaged desk and file cabinets in his wake. Anyone who's had their home burglarized would understand how I felt: frightened, dismayed, yes—but also angry. There are few spaces in this world that are ours alone, and when one of those spaces is broken into—violated—the emotional response it elicits is something primal.

I stood there with my hands shaking, looking around at the wreckage. Papers lay everywhere. Two of the desk drawers had been yanked from their recesses and were lying facedown on the floor. My framed diploma, medical license, a few pictures I'd hung on the wall to make the place feel more like home, were all smashed and either lying on the thin gray carpet or hanging at precarious angles from their remaining hooks. My progress notes from my meetings with Jason were gone, I had no doubt. But there was more to it than that. Whoever had done this could have easily taken what he'd come for and left. There was no need to trash the place. This wasn't a mere break-in. It was an assault, an act of malice, and it was aimed directly at me.

So here it is, I thought, *a message that cannot be misconstrued.* But when I went to Wagner to report it, his demeanor was dismissive.

"I agree," he said, barely looking up from his papers. "It's unfortunate that the room was vandalized. We'll of course have security investigate the matter."

"We should report it to the police," I said.

"There's not much the police can do about it," he responded, putting his pen down and lifting his eyes to meet mine. "Whoever did this was probably a patient. We can't really charge them with a crime. And besides, hospital security is our responsibility. It's an internal matter."

If I'd been harboring any lingering doubts about Wagner's involvement, those doubts all but dissipated. I could feel tears of frustration trying to surface, and I pushed them down, not wanting him to misinterpret them as a sign of weakness. *Keep a low profile. Don't do anything to attract attention*, Remy had instructed me, so I nodded, told Wagner I'd appreciate it if security could look into the matter.

"Of course," he said, bringing the tips of his fingers together in front of him on the desk. "I'll take care of it right away."

"Thank you, Charles," I said, then excused myself to go attend to my patients.

Chapter 31

Things have been set into motion. Jason is certain they will come for him, and as much as I want to protect him, I don't know if I can. A week has passed since our conversation in the library. When I see him—when we speak—he seems resigned but restless, a soldier awaiting deployment to a battlefield from which he is unlikely to return. A quiet has descended upon the grounds and buildings of Menaker. It makes me nervous. I move through my days with mechanical stiffness, completing tasks and activities I've performed thousands of times before. Linder and Remy receive a call from me twice a day. It helps to hear their voices, to know they're still out there, ready to respond at a moment's notice if I need them. I've lost track of who I can trust, and I'm frightened—for myself, but mostly for Jason. Something is coming. I can feel it.

In all this, I am alone. And this, I think, is among the worst kinds of loneliness: being alone with your fear. It eats at my middle like a cancer. Someday it may consume me completely. If I try to ignore it, if I try to look away, its face mutates into something even more horrible than itself. And there is nothing to do but watch as it slides across the floor, wraps twice around my body, and sets its teeth to work.

I lie now awake in my bed, looking up at the ceiling. An hour and a half ago, I glanced out the window to find the man in the overcoat staring up at me from across the street. I'd panicked, called Remy, but by the time he and Linder arrived the man was gone.

"We'll keep an eye on the place tonight," Remy had assured me. "We'll be parked in the car just outside. I'll leave the engine running so you can hear us."

"Don't waste the gas," I told him, somehow knowing the man wouldn't return that evening.

"One of us can stay," Linder offered. "I can sit here in the living room and just—"

"No," I replied. "I'm okay."

So they left, advising me to call them if I changed my mind. In the time it took for them to ride the elevator down and emerge from the building onto the sidewalk, I considered calling them back a half-dozen times.

In the apartment at the far end of the hall, I can hear the screamer start up again. Over the past few weeks, I've become accustomed to being jarred awake in the middle of the night by his outbursts. As a psychiatrist, I know there are many possible explanations for such behavior, but the one I imagine is that he is an autistic man still living with his parents. *What must it be like for them*, I wonder, *not only caring for him, but enduring that constant state of worry, being responsible for his actions?*

I struggle with the urge to go to the window, to look down at the sidewalk below. To see if the overcoat man has returned.

But what good would it do me? Would I call them back—Linder and Remy—or simply draw away, pace the room, spend the rest of the night stealing glances through the thin pane of glass?

No, I decide. I do not want to know. There is a certain protection in not knowing—for the mind, if not the body.

Sometimes, it's all we've got left.

Chapter 32

April 2, 2010

She sat back, closed her eyes, pressed her thumb and index finger to the bridge of her nose. Images from the photographs on the desk in front of her flipped through her mind, one after the other. They had been taken from different angles, some using a wide-angle lens to capture much of the sidewalk and surrounding shops, others focusing on the group itself, close-ups of three of the men sitting at the street-side bistro table off Connecticut Avenue in Dupont Circle. All of them appeared to be of Middle Eastern descent—not unusual given the ethnic diversity in that area of the city. She knew the names of all four men but had only spoken to two. One of them was the undercover agent who'd intentionally positioned himself with his back to the camera, allowing the photographer a facial view of the others. The second man she knew well—her brother's partner, Amir. Four and a half months ago, she rode in the back of an ambulance with him while he was delirious with the flu. And now she'd just listened to surveillance tapes of Amir's conversation with men from Al-Termir. If not for the mic embedded in the undercover agent's necklace pendant, very little of the conversation would have been available for her to review. As Amir's role in the domestic terrorism scheme became clear to the CIA, she'd been cut out of the investigation—amputated with the cold precision she'd witnessed from the agency many times before. In a way, she wished the recording didn't exist, that there had been an equipment failure or interference with the signal. She wished that Amir's words—"I am ready to act. Tell me what to do."—had been garbled or inaudible, leaving more open to conjecture. She did not want this proof of his intentions, longed for the small comfort of doubt once again.

"Will you tell him?" the man sitting next to her—a friend and low-level technician with the agency—asked. He was referring to Jason, not Amir. He had clearly done both the right and wrong thing in coming to her.

"I don't know," she answered. But in her mind, the decision had already been made.

Chapter 33

I stood at the counter of Allison's Bakery, one hand wrapped around my morning coffee, the other cradling the obligatory cup of sweets that Amber insisted on making a part of our morning ritual.

"Thanks," I said, offering her a smile but keeping our interaction brief. I was running late.

"No problem," she replied. "Making people's mornings better is what I do."

"And you do it well," I responded over my shoulder as I headed for the door, slipping the cup of chocolate morsels into the trash as I walked past.

Ten minutes later, I entered Menaker's grounds through the front gate as I do at least five days a week, but today there was no security officer in the watchman's booth to greet me. It was possible, I thought, that an incident somewhere on campus had called him away from his station. But that wasn't protocol. There was always supposed to be someone manning the front gate. If a patient became so out of control that the clinical staff and the six security officers who roamed the premises were unable to safely subdue him, then the next course of action would be to call in the police to assist us—not for the security officer at the front gate to abandon his post. And yet here was the watchman's booth, silent and empty. It wasn't just that, I realized as I scanned the grounds. There was no movement. The place was utterly still, as if the hospital had purged itself of its inhabitants and closed its doors permanently ten years before, the weeds growing high against the brick walls of the buildings and the sound of the voices that had once filled this place nothing more than the scarce whispers of ghosts on the tail end of a gusting breeze.

In my pocket was the phone Linder and Remy had given me. *I should call them*, I thought. *Something is not right here.* I pulled it out, found Remy's number, my thumb hesitating for a moment above the screen before I tapped it, sending the call. The image of a small green phone wobbled back and forth as I waited for him to pick up. "Connecting . . ." the screen advised me, and I waited. "Connecting . . ." it flashed again, the green icon of the phone doing its frantic little dance, my heart going *thunk, thunk, thunk* in my throat. And then . . . "Unable to connect."

I stood there, dumbfounded, staring at the phone. The message "Unable to connect" regarded me coolly from its digital realm. Sweat broke out along the back of my neck. My heart continued to wallop in my throat, whispering, *I told you so, I told you so, I told-you-told-you-told-you so.* I hit Linder's number and held my breath. The icon did its gleeful jig and "Connecting . . ." remained on the screen long enough for me to feel hope peek its feeble head out of its shell. But four seconds later the message "Unable to connect" confirmed what I'd already anticipated.

"*Shit*," I whispered, and began to slide the phone back into my pocket—then paused, pulled it out again, and hit 911 on the keypad.

"Unable to connect," it responded after a few seconds. I read the words aloud, not quite believing what was plainly displayed before my eyes. The signal was good, showing all four bars. Which meant . . . *what*, exactly? *Since when was 911 unavailable?*

I told you so, I told you so, my heart went on and on. I advised it to shut the hell up and let me think.

I considered turning around right there and running away; I'll admit that. But I had to believe that Jason was still in one of those buildings, that he'd seen them coming and was hiding in some janitor's closet or under a desk in an office somewhere as they went from room to room searching. *If I could find him before they did . . . If I could get him out of here . . .*

The grounds remained empty, the buildings regarding me with the cold indifference of reptiles. All I could hear was my own shallow breathing and the frantic thrum of my heart. I forced myself to take a deep breath, to hold it for four seconds before letting it out, then repeated the process until I could feel my joints loosen, my body settling into a state of readiness.

Nothing moved in the yard as I made my way up the concrete path to the front of the main building. It was quiet, the atmosphere surreal. The thought occurred to me about halfway up the path that I might be dreaming. But there was too much detail in the building in front of me, in the walkway beneath my feet, in the warmth of the coffee cup in my left hand. *If this was a dream*, I told myself, *the coffee cup would be gone*. I had forgotten about it when I'd entered the front gate and found the security booth empty. I'd absently switched it from my right hand to my left so

I could use my dominant hand to work the phone, and because it was no longer relevant to what was happening I hadn't thought about it again since. Until now. And yet, here it was, still clutched in the curve of my fingers.

Too many details, I thought. *This is real.* I dropped the cup into a trash can at the entrance to the building, then grasped the metal door handle, thumbed the lever, and swung it open. Its hinges protested the disturbance, emitting a shrill shriek that filled the entryway and scampered up the old wooden staircase to my right.

Like the grounds, the lobby was devoid of people. There were voices coming from the far end of the hall to my left, and I headed quickly in that direction, my footsteps a loud, hollow echo on the tile floor.

Along the right-hand wall ahead, two doors gave way to a large multiuse area. Many decades ago the room had been an auditorium, but a psychiatric hospital whose patients stay for years instead of days needs activities to fill that time. The space had been converted into a series of rooms separated by retractable partitions that could be opened or closed to suit various needs. Today the partitions were retracted, accordion style, so that the full space—roughly the size of a basketball court—was able to accommodate what appeared to be the entire patient population. Astonished, I looked through an interior window at the scene where patients milled about restlessly. Several nurses and orderlies moved through the crowd, attempting to maintain order. A few of the patients—the more stable ones—were keeping their calm for now, but many were becoming agitated, their vocalizations like the moans of the walking dead through the muffling effect of the glass.

At the far end of the hall, I spotted Nurse Haskins instruct-

ing a young red-haired orderly. He looked hesitant, a bit skeptical, as if the instructions he received involved actions he was
not comfortable carrying out. She gave him a soft swat on the
shoulder as I approached. "Go," she said, her voice strained and
urgent, and he went, shooting me a brief look as he hustled
down the hall.

"What's going on?" I asked. Nurse Haskins half turned to go.
I reached out and caught her by the arm. She did not look happy
to see me.

"Lise." She opened her mouth to say more, then shut it without another word.

"Why are all the patients in there?" I inquired, gesturing
toward the multiuse room. "Who authorized that?"

"Dr. Wagner."

"Wagner," I echoed, feeling my stomach lurch at the sound of
his name. "Why? What's happening?"

She looked around. "Where have you been? You should . . .
you should be with the others."

"I've been at home," I told her. "I was running late this morning. *Jesus, never mind that.* The front gate is unmanned. The
grounds are empty. The entire patient population is stuffed into
the multipurpose room. *What the hell is going on?*"

She glanced around again. It was just the two of us in the hall.
For some reason she seemed nervous about that, and what she
said next gave me a pretty good idea as to why.

"There's been an attack," she advised, her voice low and
guarded. She gestured toward the room. "They're in there for
their own protection. You should probably join them. We haven't
caught the assailant yet. Security is searching the premises for
him now. An ambulance and police are on the way."

As she said this, I could hear the sirens approaching, and once more my stomach did a slow uneasy roll in the shallow pit it had dug for itself.

"Someone was injured?" I asked.

"Paul Drevel," she said, and the shudder that slipped through her body made me wonder if Paul was still alive.

I put one hand on her shoulder. "Where is he?"

She shook her head. "You should go into the room until we know it's safe. Dr. Wagner said that everyone should be—"

"Where *is* he?" I repeated, stooping a bit to make eye contact. I could hear the emergency vehicles pulling up outside.

"He was attacked on the grounds in front of Morgan Hall. Dr. Wagner is tending to him until the ambulance arrives. I . . ." She looked around, then reached out and took my hand. "Don't go out there, okay? Not until we're sure security and the police have apprehended him. He's dangerous, Lise—much more than the others here. I've felt that for some time now."

"Who are you talking about? Who attacked Paul?"

She looked at me almost apologetically. "Jason Edwards."

"You saw this happen?"

"No," she said. "Dr. Wagner found Paul lying on the grass. Before he lost consciousness, Paul was able to tell him what happened. That's when we were advised to round up the patients and get them to a secure area. Security has been looking for Edwards for the past fifteen minutes."

I took a step backward, pulling my hand free from her grasp. "I'm sorry, Lise," she continued, but I wasn't listening anymore. There was something wrong with the information she'd provided. If all this happened the way she'd said, why wasn't there anyone on the grounds in front of Morgan Hall when I arrived?

Why had they left the front gate unmanned? More important, why would Jason attack Paul? It didn't add up.

I turned and headed for the nearest door, one that would return me to Menaker's front grounds. "Where are you going? You're supposed to stay here," Haskins called after me, but I didn't respond. The door's push bar yielded as I hit it with the outstretched palms of my hands, exiting onto an exterior walkway adjoining the building I'd just departed with several other structures, one of them the administrative complex of Morgan Hall. As I stepped into the sunlight, I heard the *chunk* of a door slamming shut. Turning in that direction, I watched as one of two ambulances flipped on its lights and tore out of the parking lot, its tires screeching on the asphalt.

So I'd missed him already—had missed seeing Paul as he was loaded into the rig. I looked toward Morgan Hall, could see the steps flanked by broad white support columns on either side as they ascended toward the building's front entrance. The door was partially ajar, and as I watched, an arm appeared through the lowest section of the opening, followed by a head and torso as a figure pulled itself onto the front landing, rolled onto its side, and then lay still.

Jason, I thought, and ran along the concrete walkway toward the building. Behind me, I could hear the sound of men's voices as they climbed from their vehicles. Someone was barking orders, and I could hear Wagner's voice as well, telling them, "This way. He's over here."

I took the steps two at a time. When I reached the top, I stopped. Lying on the platform—his face battered, the bright red blood flowing freely from a long gash in his scalp—was Paul.

I dropped to my knees beside him, uttered his name. His eyes rolled up at me, and at first there was no look of recognition on his face. The skin under his right eye was purple and swollen, his lips cracked, caked with specks of blood. His throat made a clicking sound as he swallowed. He coughed twice, wincing and bringing a hand to the left side of his rib cage as he did so.

"Paul, it's Lise," I told him. My eyes kept returning to the gash in his scalp, which continued to bleed profusely. I removed my jacket, pressed it against the wound, applying pressure.

"Who did this to you?" I asked.

He closed his eyes, and for a second I thought he was losing consciousness, but when he opened them a moment later, he appeared clearer, more present.

"Lise," he said. "They got Jason. I'm sorry. I tried to stop them."

"Who?" I looked around frantically. Four men were making their way toward us across the grass. Wagner was in the lead. "Where?" I asked, but Paul's eyes were slipping shut once again, and I gave him a gentle shake. "*Where, Paul? Where did they take him?*"

"Don't know." He coughed, and a few fresh specks of blood appeared on his lips. "They put him in the ambulance, I think."

My mind turned back to the sound of the ambulance door closing, the vehicle's driver flipping on the emergency lights as he pulled out of the parking lot. *Dammit.* The first ambulance had been for Jason, not Paul. And the men who'd loaded him into that rig had no intention of taking him to a hospital, although where they *would* take him I had no idea.

"Hang on," I told Paul. "The other ambulance is here." I felt something clamp itself around my wrist, and when I looked down it was Paul's hand, the knuckles white with effort.

"No, Lise," he said. His voice sounded distant and distorted, as if he were speaking to me from behind a thick pane of glass. I saw his chest hitch—his lungs needing to cough up more blood, I imagined—but he fought against the urge and this time won. "That ambulance is not for me."

I could hear Wagner calling out to me now—"Lise . . . Dr. Shields. Wait right there for us, please."—as he and the men covered the last hundred yards to the building.

"None of these people are who you think they are," Paul whispered. "That second ambulance . . ." A round of coughs tore through him, and once again he winced from the havoc it was playing with his broken ribs. "That second ambulance," he managed, "is for you."

I looked back at Wagner and the men. They'd reached the foot of the steps, were starting the thirty tiered strides it would take them to reach us. If what Paul was saying was true, I was trapped. There was no going back down the way I'd come up.

"Don't let them take you," Paul whispered. "Here—use these," and he placed a large key ring—his personal collection—in my hand.

"Paul, I . . ."

He shook his head, pushed me away with his hand. "No time, Lise. They've been looking for you, searching the grounds. I overheard the orders." He shot a look toward the top of the stairs, then back at me. "There's a small padlocked gate at the rear of the hospital property. You know the one?" he asked, and I nodded. "You can get out there. It's the one on the far right. Find Jason later if you can. But right now, you've got to go. *Now, run!*"

I stood up, the keys in my hand, just as the men reached the edge of the platform. I gave Paul one last look, then stepped over him and disappeared through the front entrance. The sound of a commotion erupted behind me, the clatter of men's feet as they broke into a run across the landing. As I pulled the door shut, a hand stuck itself through the remaining space, grasped the edge of the door, and began to pry it open once again. An additional two inches of daylight poured through the widening crack. I yanked back hard, putting one foot against the wall for added force and throwing my head and shoulders backward. The sudden move took the man on the other side by surprise, the door smashing his fingers against the frame. He let out a howl and a flurry of curses, the fingers disappeared, and the door swung shut. I flipped the lock on its handle and set the deadbolt. Wagner was yelling for them to get out of the way, that he had a key, but I didn't stop to listen as I moved through the lobby. Along the far left wall was a door to a stairwell. I flung it open, raced down the steps to the ground floor.

Most of this level was used for storage: rooms lined with metal file cabinets, the faint smell of mildew, the overhead lights meager at best. I'd never been down here, but on my walks around the property I'd noticed that the building had a rear door at ground level. I went searching for it now. The hall I was in passed several rooms on either side, then intersected with a short corridor that led to the rear of the building. Footsteps pounded on the floor above me as the men gained access.

Reaching the rear door, I glanced through one of its glass panes to ensure the coast was clear, then put a hand on the doorknob and turned the lock. Something moved in my peripheral vision. My hand froze. I glanced out at the yard once again. There was no one I could see. But a lanky shadow fell across the grass on the other side of the door—a human shadow, I realized. Someone was pressed against the back of the building, waiting for the door to open, waiting for me to run out, his arms poised to grab me the moment my body appeared.

"*Shit*," I whispered, standing there, not knowing what to do next. The door to the stairwell banged open on the floor above. It would be five seconds—maybe less—before they stumbled into the hallway perpendicular to the one I was in. If I was still standing here when that happened, there would be nowhere to go.

My next move was instinctual. I bolted down the corridor, turned left at the main hall, sprinted to the end of it, and smashed through the door to the men's restroom on the right. My fingers spun the deadbolt, and I stood there breathing hard. A moment later I could hear them moving from room to room, searching for me, calling out my name.

There wasn't much to the bathroom: one stall with a toilet, a sink and a small mirror above it, a single urinal against the far wall. A slant of natural light filtered through the translucent glass of a modest rectangular window situated high on the wall above the urinal. Planting a foot on the porcelain lip of the urinal, using it as a high step, I was able to reach the window, sliding it open as far as it would go. There was a moment of despair when it slid only a quarter of the way—not wide enough for me to squirm through. The thing hadn't been fully opened in a long time, and several layers of paint bonded the wooden frame to its track. *Screw this*, I thought, and slammed the side of my fist against the wood, giving it another sideways yank. It slid open another quarter of the way.

"This one's locked!" I heard someone call out to the others, and the door to the bathroom shook on its hinges. It was unlikely Wagner had a key to *this* room, but I winced anyway. They'd soon discern my intentions and go searching for the room's exterior window. The man at the building's rear door wouldn't see me coming out a front window, but if they alerted him before I was through, I'd be boxed in and out of options.

I stepped onto the upper shelf of the urinal, palms on the windowsill. There was no screen, but I'd have to go headfirst through the opening, the hole too small and my balance too unstable to maneuver otherwise. The window was high—about two feet below the ceiling—and I could see that the ground outside was another few feet below the floor level of this room. The fall I'd take would be roughly eight feet, headfirst. I'd have to get my hands out in front of me. *But still, I could break my neck.* If there was another way, I couldn't think of it, and when someone banged loudly on the door behind me I decided that the time to do this—if I was going to do it at all—was now.

I poked my head out through the window and could see there was no one standing on the ground below, no one at all on this side of the building. The thought occurred to me that someone might be waiting in ambush around the corner, but there was nothing I could do about that. My arms were extended straight out in front of me, like I'd done as a child diving into the neighborhood pool. I was worried my shoulders might not make it through, but they did, and now I was hanging halfway out of the opening, my waist and upper thighs resting against the metal track at the bottom. With my palms on the exterior wall, I inched myself forward and downward, attempting to control my descent, my hips snug against the wood of the window frame. *What if I get stuck here, my body half out of the building? They could stand right next to me and beat me senseless as I hung here, unable to defend myself, waiting to lose consciousness.*

I turned my pelvis diagonally and was able to get the widest part of my body through. Then, bending my knees to about ninety degrees, I braced myself with my feet against the bathroom wall. *If I could hang by my feet from the lip of the opening, that would put me close enough to the ground to—*

That was as far as *that* plan got. As soon as my knees cleared the opening, I fell. My hands were splayed out in front of me, the wall of the building inches from my face. I hit the ground, rolled to the right. Something broke as I landed—I could hear the crisp snap—and because there was no immediate pain my first thought was that it had been my neck.

Everything will go numb, I thought, but a moment later the pain in my right wrist rose to the surface, the intensity washing over me, suffocating. I knew better than to cry out—only lay in the grass, allowing the scream to fill my head instead of the air. My eyes dropped to my right arm where I'd developed an extra angle about six inches above my wrist. The area was already beginning to swell, and when I touched the site with the index finger of my left hand, I could feel a jut of broken bone just beneath the skin.

Never mind that, an inner voice instructed. *Get up and get going. Or a broken arm will be the* least *of your problems.*

I rolled to one side, pushed myself to my knees with my good arm. The world went white and distant as I stood, the grass tilting away. *I'm about to pass out,* I realized—something I could not afford to do—so I leaned over at the waist, grabbed my broken forearm, and squeezed.

Words cannot describe the severity of pain associated with *that* action—the scream once again filling my head—but it brought me back to where I needed to be, the color slowly returning to the world around me. I gritted my teeth, took a tentative step forward. My left leg supported my weight. That was good. *But could I run if I needed to?*

Get going, get going, get going! the voice hammered inside my head. I did as I was told, lurched across the grass as fast as my legs would take me. It was only a matter of time until the men noticed the open window, either by gaining entrance to the bathroom or returning outside. When they did, they would come for me full tilt across the open yard. They would either spot me heading toward the front gate or assume I had done so. From that moment on, it would be a footrace—one I did not think I could win with my arm in its current condition, the pain crashing against my skull with the impact of each step.

There's a small padlocked gate at the rear of the hospital property, Paul had told me. *You know the one?* Yes, I knew the one. Since it was always locked, I'd never considered it functional, assumed the key was long since lost, the padlock rusted shut. A door to a room that is never opened is no better than a wall, or in this case a fence. But here I was with a key and instructions to use it, Paul's advice clanging in my head. Beyond the rear fence was a dense thatch of woods that descended into a ravine. It would provide cover, a place to hide. Right now, that was all that mattered.

I ran toward the Hinsdale Building, expecting with every step to hear someone yell for me to stop right where I was, the sound of hurried footsteps on the grass behind me. My mind turned to the image of Jason being chased through the woods when he was younger, of Billy Myers waiting in ambush, a switchblade coiled like a serpent in one pocket—and I thought, *Where is the stealthy one, the only one with murder in his eyes?*

I rounded the corner of the Hinsdale Building, breathing a sigh of relief, knowing the brick structure would help shield me from sight. A dash along the southeast wall took me to the rear of the building. Across the open grass, I could see the locked gate some fifty yards ahead.

Warm brick pressed against my back as I closed my eyes, readied myself for the next part. *Hurry, but don't rush,* I told myself. *You will move faster if you stay calm.* Opening my eyes, I listened for the sound of approaching feet. There were voices in the parking lot now. One of them sounded like Wagner arguing with another man. I pushed them from my mind, instead focusing on the small gate in front of me. *Ready?* I asked myself. *Ready enough,* my mind answered. I stepped away from the building and crossed the grass to the rear gate.

There was a nasty moment when I reached into my pocket with my left hand and came up with nothing. No key ring, no way to get through. It had fallen out of my pocket while I was hanging upside down from the bathroom window. *Why hadn't I noticed?* The answer, I realized, was my broken arm. I'd been in too much pain to notice anything else.

"*Now* what?" I hissed.

I took a breath, told myself to slow down, to not panic. *Easier said than done,* but at the same time my mind argued that I was right-handed, that I'd probably been holding the keys in my right hand before shoving them into my pocket.

My right arm and hand were essentially useless at this point, so I reached across my body with my left to fish around for Paul's keys in the opposite pocket. The angle of entry was unnatural, and for a few seconds I couldn't find them there either. The panic started to rise up again, but I plunged my hand deeper, and suddenly my fingers brushed against metal. "*Thank God,*" I whispered, closing my hand around the ring and pulling it out.

At least thirty keys stared back at me.

I glanced over my shoulder. *Still alone, but for how long?* And how the hell was I going to find the right key with limited time, a rusted lock, and only one good hand to sort it all out? The keys were color coded, but I didn't understand the color scheme. The lock, I could see, was a Master Lock, but none of the keys were similarly marked. A few had numbers or letters inscribed into the metal, but none of these made any sense to me either.

Climbing over the fence with its ten-foot spear pickets curving inward at the top was not an option, even if my arm wasn't broken. *Should've gone for the front gate*, I told myself, shoving one key after the other into the lock, hoping one of them would turn. It was slow going with one hand, and as I pulled the fourth failed key from the cylinder the entire ring slipped from my hand and fell to the ground, landing on the soft, slick grass at the foot of the fence where the land sloped downward toward the ravine.

I watched in horror as the keys slid away from me between the pickets.

They came to rest on the opposite side of the fence against a rock jutting up from the earth some four feet away. I kneeled and reached through the fence with my left arm, my shoulder butting up against the pickets. Even when I stretched my arm as far as I could, the ring was still a good twelve inches from the tips of my fingers. *Gone*, I thought, and panic scurried over me like a sewer rat. There was no way out now, nothing to do but hide until they eventually found me. They would drag me into the ambulance—alive or dead—and wherever they took me, there would be no coming back.

Find a stick, the inner voice—the voice of self-preservation—

instructed. *Snag the key ring, pull it back under the fence. And don't . . . drop it . . . again.*

"Right," I agreed, looking up and down the length of fence for something I could use. The stick closest to me appeared long enough, but also flimsy. I couldn't chance nudging the keys off the rock only to watch them break free and slide the rest of the way down the hill. I kept searching.

This is taking too long. I'm going to get caught.

Don't think about that. Keep looking.

My right forearm ached incessantly. Beads of sweat clung to my face, then cast themselves into the grass as I moved—hunched over, eyes sweeping back and forth—along the fence. Finally, I found a stouter branch on the ground some sixty feet away. *This has got to work*, I told myself, returning to the spot closest to the keys. Getting back down on my knees, I reached with the stick through the space between the pickets. Distance was not an issue now, but the ground's surface was irregular. As I hooked the ring and began to move the keys away from the rock, I had to concentrate on maintaining contact between the stick and the earth. Halfway to the fence, the tip of the stick briefly lost contact with the ground and the ring started to slide away once again. I jabbed for it, striking the ring itself, pushing it farther away, then lunged again, catching not the ring this time but a single trailing key. I froze in place. My heart walloped inside my chest.

Careful. Don't lose it.

My index finger pushed down hard on the top of the stick, pressing the key into the ground at the other end. This, I hoped, would be enough to stop its slide during the fraction of a second it would take me to lift the tip of the stick off the key and reposition it within the ring. The word *please* formed silently on my lips, then the far tip of the stick flicked up, down, and into the circle where it was meant to go.

"*Now slowly*," I whispered, and pulled the ring toward me. It reached the fence. I placed a knee on the thing to hold it until I could let go of the stick and grab the ring with my good hand.

I exhaled the breath I'd been holding, scooted back from the fence and the sloped ground beyond, the keys clutched to my chest. "*Okay, now which key?*" I mumbled, thumbing through them, unsure about which ones I'd already tried.

There's a small padlocked gate at the rear of the hospital property. You know the one? Paul had asked as he hovered close to unconsciousness. *You can get out there. It's the one on the far right.*

The one on the far right, I thought, looking up at the rear gate from where I sat in the grass. But there was only one gate back here. For Paul to stipulate that it was the one on the far right made no sense. Unless . . .

The men's voices were closer now, approaching from the other side of the building behind me. They didn't know I was back here—*not yet*—but they were methodical, searching every corner of the grounds.

"Unless he wasn't referring to the gate, but the keys," I said, and looked down at the collection again. The keys were strung along the ring in a circular fashion. There would have been no reference point for right versus left if not for a flat rectangular piece of metal—engraved with the hospital's name—attached to the ring. If I positioned it at the top of the ring with the keys hanging below, then the far right key would be . . .

"This one," I said, grasping the key's silver handle between my thumb and index finger. I stood, moved to the gate, inserted the key in the lock, and tried to turn it.

It wouldn't budge.

"*Shit*," I hissed. In another few seconds the men would be rounding the corner—would see me, shout for the others, break into a run. I started to pull the key from the lock. Paused. *No, no, this must be the right one. It* has *to be.* With my thumb, I nudged it deeper into the cylinder, felt a small click as it settled home, and this time when I turned it the key rotated begrudgingly and the padlock sprang open.

"*Thank God*," I whispered for the second time, removing the lock and swinging the gate open. The hinges had endured many seasons of rain and snow over the years and moaned loudly. I winced, looked back at the building behind me, then stepped through the opening, closed the gate, looped the Master Lock through the latching mechanism, and snapped it shut.

The earth sloped away quickly, and I made for the woods, knowing that, in all likelihood, I would never set foot in Menaker State Hospital again.

Part Three

Beyond the Fence

Chapter 34

The woods were thicker than I'd expected, the brush thorny and difficult to push through as I descended the slope, listening for sounds of approaching footsteps or voices—and certain that at any moment the men who'd taken Jason would realize where I'd gone and enter the forest in search of me. There was no escaping the persistent throbbing of my shattered forearm, the image of Paul lying on the concrete platform of the administrative building, his eyes rolling up at me, the skin of his right cheek purple and swollen, the gash in his scalp flowing freely.

They got Jason. I'm sorry. I tried to stop them, he'd told me, and this realization I wanted to escape most of all: that I'd been charged with the responsibility of protecting him, and despite all the warnings I'd been given, failed to do so.

I will find him, I told myself, but it was an empty promise, devoid of any real hope or conviction. *You will* not *find him*, said a small voice inside my head, and I suspected that it was right. *He's gone. You will never see him again. And that is something you will have to live with for the rest of your life.*

There was nothing to say to that, so I snaked through the trees, my body bent slightly at the waist, shoulders hunched low, trying not to jostle my right arm too much as I stepped over fallen limbs and focused instead on the sound of moving water coming from somewhere down the hill and to my right. It was hard to tell how long I continued that way. It couldn't have been more than a few hundred yards, but it was slow going and there is something slippery and unreliable about gauging distance in the woods. The sharp tines of bramble and holly leaves snatched greedily at my arms and legs, snagged my clothes, biting through the fabric like they had a score to settle. Halfway down the embankment, I walked face-first into a spiderweb. My body twisted and danced in revulsion, my left hand flying to my face to yank loose the sticky strands of silk. The pain in my right forearm had settled into a dull ache, but the sudden movement caused the agony to rise up, an angry white geyser. I got down on one knee, shut my eyes, and forced my way through the pain until it was something manageable.

My plan was to follow a straight path through the woods—down into the ravine and up the other side—until I made it to Old County Road to the east. From there I could flag down a car, and then try to get in touch with Linder and Remy. It was early enough in the day that the sun was still positioned in the east, and I used that as a rough compass, reminding myself to keep my bearings, to not get turned around.

The murmur of the stream grew louder, becoming a chuckle as the water pitched and tumbled across its bed of uneven stones. There was something nasty in that sound, almost berating, accusatory. Twice I stopped to listen, wondering if there were voices coming from the ravine's lip high above me. I didn't think so, although it was impossible to say for sure. My line of sight was blocked by the foliage, and the stream did its best to muddle the sounds of the forest.

Before long I came to the stream, its tortuous course stretching through the woods like a vein, the water casting sporadic glints of sunlight from its restless, rolling surface. I got down on my knees along the bank, dipping my cupped left hand into the steady flow, then splashed my face to wash away the dirt, sweat, and grime. The water was shockingly cold against my skin, making me shiver as tiny rivulets twisted their way down my neck and disappeared beneath the collar of my shirt.

I looked down at my right forearm, studying it more fully. Beneath the swelling, I could tell there was an angle to the break of about twenty degrees. It would need to be straightened if I wanted the bones to heal correctly, if I wanted to regain full function of my arm. I still had good sensation to my fingers, could move them all right, and the color and warmth of my hand was normal—a sign that the nerves and blood supply were intact.

I sat there considering. *Should I try to straighten out the angle of the fracture myself?* I didn't think I could do it, not only because of the incapacitating pain I'd endure in the process, but also because it would be difficult to get the bones straight with only one hand to use for the manipulation. And then the arm would need to be splinted. *What would I use for that? Some sticks with vines for lacing?* That might work in a movie, but in real life the bones would shift and heal at an angle. The arm would never be the same. No, I needed medical attention—an emergency department—and the longer I waited, the more difficult the repair would be.

Again, I listened for the sound of voices, for the rustling tramp of feet through the woods. There was nothing, only the indignant shriek of a blue jay from its perch on a branch above. The relative silence made me nervous. I rose to my feet, moved downstream to the point where the water grew shallow and a series of stones protruded through its surface. The bird screeched once more, a flutter of wings behind me as it moved from one branch to the next. I picked my way across the stones. When I'd reached the other side, I started upward along the far side of the ravine. Getting myself to a hospital, keeping a low profile, making contact with Linder and Remy—these were my goals.

The ache in my arm was blossoming once again, the skin stretched tight from the swelling beneath. *You can do this,* I told myself. *You can find him. Just take one step at a time.* And I did, concentrating on each step as I made my way up the hill. Before long, I was thinking of Uncle Jim—which was no surprise. The woods were our special place that summer. And even now it was hard to be here without searching for him in the shadows.

"Whatcha listenin' to, honey dew?" Uncle Jim asked as he walked into my room and plopped down on the bed next to me. I was sitting on the mattress, legs crossed Indian style, my back against the wall.

"'Step by Step,'" I told him, surprised he didn't recognize it. It had been at the *Billboard* #1 spot for the past three weeks, and was playing on the radio, like, all the time. The cassette had come from the record store a week ago, bought with money I'd earned helping Mom around the house.

"Who sings it?" Uncle Jim asked, nudging me lightly with his elbow, then settling back against the wall.

"New Kids on the Block," I said. My fingers fiddled with the scrunchie I'd pulled from my hair, twisting it this way and that, my body moving in time with the music. I offered him the case and he studied the picture on the front.

"Oh yeah, I've heard of these guys," he said, although his tone wasn't convincing.

"Donnie Wahlberg is pretty cute." I pointed him out on the cover.

"I'll take your word for it."

"He has a younger brother, Mark, who was part of the band for a little while, but then quit."

"Why?"

I shrugged. "Guess he didn't wanna be famous like his brother."

He nodded.

We sat together for a while as the song finished and the next one began. Outside, I could hear the plastic tires of my brother's Big Wheel rolling down the driveway, the machine-gun spray of the sprinkler firing away in the front yard.

"What kind of music do *you* listen to?" I asked—not that I had a wide selection to choose from: Madonna, Bon Jovi, Duran Duran, some Cyndi Lauper . . .

"Oh, I don't know," he said. "I grew up in the sixties and seventies, listening to stuff from The Beatles, The Doors, Jimi Hendrix, Bob Dylan . . ." He motioned to the small collection of cassettes I had in the tape rack next to my bed. "I don't suppose you've got any Dylan in there."

"I don't even know who that is," I admitted. "What kind of stuff does he sing?"

Uncle Jim ran a hand along the stubble on the side of his face. He didn't shave every day like my father did. Some of the whiskers were gray.

"Well, he's not a new kid on the block, I'll tell you that," he said. "Kind of an old kid, I guess. Like me. Been around for a while."

I opened my mouth to tell him that he wasn't *that* old—not ancient, anyway, like Grandpa—but my eyes fell once again to the gray in his beard and all at once it occurred to me that there are different kinds of old, that sometimes it's not the years but the stuff you've been through that makes you old. I had the feeling that Uncle Jim had been through a lot.

"He's sort of a poet, Bob Dylan," he continued. "Uses his songs to talk about human nature, about the way we live—the way people treat one another—things that aren't right and ought to be changed. He . . . he sings about a lot of things."

"I don't understand most poems." I'd gone across the room to turn down the volume on my stereo, and now I climbed back onto the bed and sat beside him, our feet dangling off the side.

"Yeah, I know what you mean," he agreed. "But sometimes it's not important to understand *everything* about a poem. Sometimes a good poem is like a fun-house mirror: it shows you the same world but in a different way. It offers you a different perspective."

"And you get to see how you look."

"To other people, maybe. Or you get to see how *their* world looks to them. You can learn a lot by seeing things through other people's eyes."

A car pulled up outside at the end of our street. For a moment I thought it was my father, returning home from wherever he'd been this morning, and I could feel my body tense, draw in on itself as it often did when he was around. I hopped off the bed again, went to the window, and looked out in time to see the neighbors' car pulling into their driveway across the street.

"Sometimes I wish people weren't so different," I said, turning from the window. "In school, the kids tease you if you don't act like everyone else, if you're interested in different things. And I think: maybe it would be easier if we were all the same."

"Wouldn't be any fun that way."

"I know, but . . ." I went to my dresser, took the loose knob on the top right drawer in my fingers and gave it a spin. "I mean, *you're* different, right? You know what that's like."

"Yeah. I guess I do." He turned his eyes from me and looked across the room and through the window at the oak parked in the front yard just outside. "Your parents told you about me, I guess, how I'm a little off my rocker."

I shrugged.

"Well, it's true." He sighed, the fingertips of his right hand drumming lightly on his blue jeans. "The doctors call it schizo-phrenia."

"What's it like?" I asked, my ears turning red like I was asking him something that maybe I shouldn't. His face looked tired now, the eyes cast downward at the rug between us.

For a long time neither of us spoke, and I thought that maybe I'd gone too far, that it was something he didn't want to talk about. Through the thin walls of my bedroom I could hear the springs on the front screen door squeal as it opened and slapped shut again, the sound of my brother's footsteps making their way down the hall into the living room.

"The first time I was admitted to a psych hospital the doctor asked me if my mind sometimes played tricks on me. And I remember thinking, *Yes, that's it exactly. Sometimes my mind plays tricks on me.*" His eyes flicked up toward my face, then down again at the floor. "I hear things, mostly. People talking to me who aren't there. They say . . ." His face contorted a bit, grimacing. "They say horrible things."

"Do you hear them now?"

He shook his head. "They're not always there. They come and go—like headaches, Lise. Or sometimes I get so used to them that I can tune them out, ignore them for a while. But there are other things, too. I'll get an idea in my head that I can't shake, something that isn't right but *seems* right at the time. That's the hell of it, you know: separating out what's real from what's not real. Trying to keep things straight. Knowing when your mind is playing tricks on you."

"Can they fix it? The doctors?" I asked.

"No," he responded. "I mean . . . they can't take it away. Some of the medicines make things better for a while, but . . . it will always be there. I'll always be fighting it."

"Are you scared?"

"No, not scared," he answered. "I've been living with it a long time. It's just . . . part of who I am now."

"It sounds lonely."

He nodded. "It can be."

The last song on the cassette had ended. From the living room, the television was playing the opening song for *Teenage Mutant Ninja Turtles*, a show my father had proclaimed *idiotic*.

"*Hey, Lise,*" Uncle Jim said, brightening. "How about you and I take a walk down to the record store. We'll see if they have any Bob Dylan albums. Or The Doors—I think you'd like them. If they do, I'll buy something for you, let you take a listen and see what you think."

"Okay," I said, stooping to gather my shoes. "We should tell Mom we're going."

"Maybe she'd like to come with us."

"She's lying down in her room," I told him. "I don't think she feels well."

I followed him into the hallway, waited while he rapped lightly on the bedroom door, then poked his head in to check on her and tell her where we were heading. She wouldn't come with us, said she had a headache and needed to rest with the lights off and the shades closed for a while longer, but to have a good time, and we *did* end up finding that Bob Dylan album on sale. Also *Strange Days* by The Doors—"You're going to love this," Uncle Jim told me—and Madonna's new single, "Vogue." When we got home Mom was up and out of her room—feeling a little better, she said—and that made me happy because tomorrow was her birthday, and everyone should feel good on their birthday.

Chapter 35

I stood near the edge of the woods, still concealed within the protective cloak of the trees, peering out at the empty stretch of roadway in front of me. Now that I'd gotten here, I was hesitant to leave the safety of the forest, afraid to step out onto the shoulder and allow myself to be seen by the next passing motorist. *Would the men who'd come for Jason be driving the streets looking for me?* I didn't know—*couldn't* know—but I could imagine flagging down a car that would roll smoothly to a stop, the front passenger door opening and a man in a dark suit stepping out. *There you are, Dr. Shields,* he would say. *We've been looking for you.*

I could hear the heavy drone of tires now. Instead of stepping away from the woods I stepped deeper into them. A semi rounded the corner, the vertical slats of its front grille glistening like narrow rows of teeth, its driver only a hulking shadow behind the glinting glass of the windshield. Crouching low, I made myself even less visible from the roadway, holding my breath as the tractor trailer blasted by me, its brake lights winking for just a moment before it disappeared around the next bend.

I can't do this, I thought, but there were no other reasonable options. I'd already tried the phone—still no reception and the battery getting low—and decided to shut it off for the time being. The closest hospital was Anne Arundel Medical Center in Annapolis, about six miles away. It was within walking distance, but there was no shoulder or pedestrian walkway across the heavily traveled Severn River Bridge into Annapolis, and I'd have to catch a ride anyway if I wanted to head in that direction. But going to the closest hospital seemed unwise for another reason: it was too obvious. Instead, I decided to head toward Baltimore Washington Medical Center at the north end of the county. I wasn't certain of the distance. The phone Linder and Remy had given me was a basic model and didn't have access to the Internet or a GPS mapping program. I estimated the hospital to be about ten to twelve miles from here. I *could* walk the distance if I had to, following Route 2—a major thoroughfare—for most of the way, but I'd be conspicuously visible to hundreds of passing motorists, and this seemed even more risky than flagging down a random car.

So it came down to this, waiting here, concealed by trees, until something nonthreatening came along—something benevolent and nurturing. A Prius, maybe. Then I'd step out toward the roadway where I could be seen, wave a hand for them to stop, and hope for the best.

I mustered my nerve, readied myself, focusing my attention to the left, on the far stretch of asphalt that disappeared around the curve. A deep breath slid out of my body through pursed lips. The front sole of my right shoe dug into the earth: a sprinter settling into the blocks. The deformed, swollen mess of my forearm pounded with the quickening wallop of my pulse, and the forest itself grew quiet, as if sensing the intensity of the moment and pausing in its persistent subtle murmurings to watch.

We spend so much time in the midst of others, navigating our way through the seven billion people with whom we share this planet, that it is often a shock—an outrage—to find ourselves alone and in need of help, and for no help to come. For ten minutes I stood and waited, my heart gradually slowing, the adrenaline spent and tapering into nothing. Even the forest began to chirp and twitter again with the call of birds, the tree limbs awakening to a soft breeze and swaying impatiently, irritated with the time they had wasted in pausing to watch. I wasn't even looking at the road anymore—was, in fact, studying the faint blush of reddish purple beneath the taut skin of my forearm—when I heard the sound of tires approaching from the left. I looked up, and for a moment was too surprised to move. "*Son of a gun,*" I whispered, as a sky-blue Prius materialized from around the bend in the road. It covered half the distance to where I stood before I realized it was going to shoot right by me if I didn't get a move on. I lurched forward, the front of my left shoe snagging on something—a root, maybe—that held me midstride for a second, then broke loose and almost sent me sprawling out into the roadway. Instead of stepping out calmly to where the driver could see me, I stumbled onto the shoulder, my upper body bent forward at the waist and too far out in front of my feet. The grass was high here, the terrain uneven, and I stepped on the edge of what might have been a gopher hole, twisting my right ankle in the process. For a panic-stricken moment, I thought I was going to fall directly into the path of the Prius with no time for the driver to react or even slow. I had a clear vision of the car slamming into me at the knees, my body rolling up onto the hood, my head smashing into the windshield, starring it, leaving behind a small wet patch of blood and hair on the safety glass—and then the brief, curious span of weightlessness as the driver slammed on the brakes and I was flung twenty feet through the air, my body rotating a quarter turn before landing in a bone-splintering heap on the asphalt and sliding another six feet before it finally came to rest. The image was so clear, my conviction that it was going to happen so certain, that the blast of the horn and the whoosh of the car speeding past me—the passenger-side mirror snapping the fabric of my pants but missing my right hip beneath by less than a centimeter—seemed incongruous with the moment. I had difficulty merging the two—what I *thought* was going to happen and what had actually happened—but then the car was beyond me and I was somehow still alive. I stood there, shaking uncontrollably, with one foot on the roadway and the other in the overgrown grass of the shoulder.

She will stop, I thought. *She nearly hit me, and she'll want to make sure I'm not hurt. I will show her my arm, tell her I fell and injured it in the woods, and ask her to take me to the hospital.* Given what had just happened, I couldn't imagine her refusing such a request. She'd feel compelled to help me.

I was still thinking these things when the car vanished around the next curve and drove out of my life forever.

One of my faults, I will admit, is that I cling to the premise that human beings are endowed with a tendency toward basic goodness and decency. History is, of course, replete with irrefutable evidence to the contrary, and yet time and again I am shocked when people do not behave as I expect. This may sound odd coming from a person who narrowly escaped being kidnapped and possibly murdered less than two hours before, but I stood there flabbergasted, puzzling over how the woman in the

Prius could possibly have driven away without stopping. I stood there with my mouth hanging partially open, everything else temporarily forgotten, and listened for the sound of her returning vehicle. It would come around the bend any second now. She would flip on her hazards and bring the car to a gradual stop along the side of the road, check her mirrors for other cars before stepping out of the driver's door and approaching me with a distressed look of concern on her face. *Are you okay?* she would ask. *Are you hurt? Should I call an ambulance?*

That was going to happen, and I stood there waiting for it—believing in it—until at last I registered the growling, gutteral idle of a diesel engine behind me. Turning, I saw a mammoth red pickup truck had stopped on my side of the road five yards from where I stood. It was a ridiculous, obnoxious, fossil-fuel-gulping contraption straight out of a country music song. The front wheels cut to the left and the driver began to ease the truck around me, but then he stopped as the cab of the pickup pulled even with where I stood. Looking through the open window at the man sitting behind the wheel, I could see the tanned flesh of his heavily muscled right arm resting on the steering wheel. He wore a sweat-stained olive baseball cap with a John Deere logo planted on the front, and there was at least two days of thick black stubble on his face and neck. But his eyes—his eyes were a deep cobalt that reminded me of the blueberry patch on my grandfather's farm in Vermont—and there was kindness in his expression. He asked me if I needed a ride. I reached out with my good hand and opened the door without hesitating, grasped an interior handhold, and hoisted myself into the cab. He glanced at my swollen right arm held protectively against my stomach, then back at my face.

"Can you take me to the hospital north of here," I asked, "to the one in Glen Burnie off Route 100?"

"Sure," he said, and dropped the truck into gear and accelerated smoothly. We drove on in silence for a while. I looked out the window mostly, watched the world—one I barely recognized anymore—slipping by around us. He didn't ask any questions, and although part of me wanted to confide in him, to tell him what happened and to maybe ask for his help, in the end I decided it wouldn't be fair. He'd shown me kindness, after all, and I didn't want to reward an act of altruism by placing him in danger. I'd placed enough people in danger as it was.

The trip was not a long one, and when it became clear that I wasn't up for conversation, he flipped on the radio, and sure enough, the music was country—something sweet and earnest and a little lonesome. It made me think of Jason—and, of course, Uncle Jim. And for the next eight miles I sat with my face turned toward the window and tended to the ache in my heart without ever making a sound.

"Whatcha lookin' at, Uncle Jim?" I asked, standing behind him as he sat looking out through our living room window at the street below.

I'd been getting a snack from the kitchen refrigerator— standing on my tiptoes to reach the corn bread on the upper shelf—when I'd heard him talking to someone in the other room. His voice had been low and hushed, as if sharing a secret, and I'd closed the refrigerator and left the kitchen to see what was going on.

But standing in the passage between the two rooms I could

see it was only him, leaning forward in my father's recliner, his face turned toward the window. He was muttering to himself, his head cocked to one side as if listening to the faint call of birds from far away. "No, no, that's not true," I thought he said, although the words were muttered, difficult to make out.

"What is it?" I placed a hand on his shoulder, thinking maybe it was a game he was playing, that it might be something fun. He startled a bit at my touch, his muscles twitching, but when he saw it was me, smiled and nodded to himself, seemed happy I was there.

"What's new, Lindsey Lou?" he asked, using one of those made-up names he sometimes called me.

"What're you looking at?" I asked, but he didn't answer—just left the question hanging there between us, and for some reason I was scared to ask him again. I removed my hand from his shoulder, thinking maybe he was sick or something, that I might get it too if I wasn't careful.

"What d'ya think of that kid out there, Lindsey Lou?" he asked me.

I looked out the window to see who he was talking about. "The one on the bike?" I asked, but he shook his head.

"Nah, the other one." His head did a little twitch and I thought I heard him whisper, "*Leave me alone,*" but I couldn't be sure and, at any rate, it didn't seem like he was talking to me. "The one sitting on the curb," he said, pointing to the neighbors' boy, Ronald McBee, who was three years younger than me but almost as tall. He had a plastic truck in his hand, his blond head tilted down to study it as he spun its wheels.

"That's Ronald," I told my uncle. "He lives next door."

"Ronald," he echoed. "Yeah," he said, tapping the fingertips of his right hand on the chair's leather armrest. "Yeah, I can see that now."

"Uncle Jim," I asked, "are you feeling okay?"

"What d'ya mean?" He didn't even turn his head to look at me.

"You're not . . ." I started. "You're not sick or anything, are you?"

"Sick," he said, but there was no inflection in his voice and I couldn't tell whether it was a question or an answer.

I turned to go, feeling like I shouldn't be here, like maybe I should go tell my mom that something wasn't right with him. *Would they take him away,* I wondered, *if he got sick again?* But on the cusp of that thought I could hear my mother telling my father, *He's got no place else to go.*

I was heading toward my room, the plastic-wrapped corn bread a forgotten thing in my hand, when I heard him call my name.

"Lise. Hey, Lise," he said, his voice just above a whisper.

I turned around. His eyes moved back and forth before coming to rest on my face.

"Why does he keep looking over here?" he asked. "The Ronald kid. What d'ya think he wants with me?"

I went back to the window, looked out at the boy sitting on the curb. His attention was focused on the toy truck, not our house, and although I watched him for a while, that never changed.

I turned to look at Uncle Jim. "I don't think he's—"

"*See? See there?!*" he said, and I spun my head back around but nothing was different.

"He just looked up again," Uncle Jim told me, his body rigid, his eyes never leaving the window. "Why does he *do* that?"

"I don't kn—"

"He knows we're in here. That's what *I* think," he said, nodding to himself.

"So what if he does?" I responded, but Uncle Jim had gone back to ignoring me.

I walked away, left him sitting there. I should've gone straight to my mother and told her what was going on. Uncle Jim could be weird sometimes in a way that felt more like a game, like the acting I'd done in my school play the year before. This didn't feel like one of those times—but I wanted it to. I wanted this to be something we would laugh about later.

They come and go—like headaches, he'd told me two weeks before when I'd asked him about the voices in his head, and I clung to that idea, telling myself that tomorrow he would feel better.

If it gets worse, I'll tell Mom, I promised myself, and that seemed like a good enough plan.

Only I never would.

Chapter 36

Anyone wanting to get a firsthand look at the vulnerable, unpredictable nature of the human condition need only travel as far as their local hospital emergency room. During medical school, I spent two months working in the ER at Johns Hopkins, where I was afforded a front-row seat to the ebb and flow of the many lives that passed through those daunting translucent sliding glass doors. The waiting room itself is a kind of purgatory, not only for the patients who have come to be treated, but also for their families, who sit among a sea of slack-faced strangers and wrestle with the horror of the unknown outcomes in front of them. A young mother holds her crying four-month-old child in her arms and wonders why the fever will not abate. A middle-aged couple alternate their stares between blank registration forms and the silent automated doors to the resuscitation rooms beyond as their seventeen-year-old daughter is rushed to the operating room to remove a shattered spleen and left kidney resulting from a hit-and-run accident with a drunk driver. An old man looks down at his brown, sensible old man's shoes and tries to remember what his wife was like before the Alzheimer's.

He agonizes over the guilt of bringing her here, of realizing—finally—that he can no longer take care of her.

At the registration desk, I gave a fake name and address, advising the clerk that I'd left my ID and credit cards at home in my rush to get to the hospital. She'd been doing her job long enough to know I was lying, but she also understood that I couldn't be turned away. She dutifully entered my fabricated information into the computer, fastened a patient ID to my left wrist, and added my chart to a rack of fifteen others behind her. "Have a seat, the nurse will call you shortly," she said in one practiced monotone breath, and her eyes moved to the gentleman waiting behind me.

I got up and moved to the waiting area. Every chair was occupied, so I stood against a wall and tried to busy myself with other thoughts while I waited for my name to be called. In a seat in front of me, an old lady clutched a blood-soaked towel in her lap, kneading its edges with her fingers. She caught me looking at it, and we locked eyes. "My husband . . ." she started to explain, and then trailed off, her gaze shifting down and to the right. On the other side of the room, a man erupted in a ratcheting series of coughs. His lungs sounded heavy and wet, as if they'd been left out in the rain overnight. He brought a handkerchief to his mouth, spat in it, then grimaced at what he'd expectorated.

I stood in that room for an hour and a half before I was called into the treatment area. The nurse led me past a row of three gurneys, all of them occupied by disheveled, malodorous gentlemen who appeared to be recovering from various stages of drunkenness. There was a pungent, eye-watering scent of urine emanating from that section of the hallway, and I wondered if the nurse—for all her years of service in such an environment—even noticed it as we passed. If she did, she didn't comment, but instead drew back a curtain and tossed a gown onto the bed.

"Please undress and put on the gown," she told me, "opening in the back."

"It's just my arm that's injured."

"The doctor can't properly examine you if you're not undressed," she said, and her voice had the same flat intonation as that of the registration clerk, the explanation something she was forced to utter over and over every working day of her life. I felt sorry for her, so I drew the curtain closed, removed my shirt—gingerly easing the sleeve over my right forearm—and put on the gown. The rest of my clothes stayed on, however. There is just something too unsettling about unnecessarily forsaking one's pants in public.

I waited only a short time for the ER physician to appear. He swept aside the curtain and offered me a smile as he stepped up to the bed. "I'm Dr. Mathers. Sorry to keep you waiting."

I told him it was okay, that they seemed busy today.

"We're busy every day. You should see this place during cold and flu season."

"I'd rather not," I said, and he smiled.

"Me, either, but they make me come in anyway." His eyes glanced down at the chart in his hands, then back up at me. "What happened to your arm?"

I shook my head. "I'm embarrassed to tell you, but I managed to do this gardening. I'd just come back from the nursery with a bunch of potted plants that I'd lined up along the edge of the yard. I got distracted and forgot they were there for a second, took a step backward and tripped over them—managed to get my arm out enough to break the fall, but . . . well . . . this was the result."

It amazed me how easily the lie slid out, how I didn't stammer or blush or avoid eye contact when I said it. It was like I'd practiced delivering the story in front of a mirror several times until I'd gotten it just right. I was so impressed with myself that when he asked what I'd been planting, I didn't stop to consider my answer before responding. "Tulips," I replied, and then winced, realizing that was the wrong answer for this time of year.

"Does that hurt?" he asked, his fingers paused on my upper arm.

"I was just anticipating how it's going to feel when you get to my forearm."

"I'll be gentle," he promised as he began to examine the lower part of my arm, probing delicately over the deformity and feeling for my pulse. He asked me to move my fingers, and I did, although the action caused the pain to intensify. His right thumb pressed against the nail of my index finger, blanching it, and he watched as the pink returned to the nail bed.

"Okay. We'll get some X-rays of your arm and go from there."

"Thank you."

He nodded and started to leave, then paused with one hand on the curtain. "I don't know if you usually garden in your work clothes, but I think you'll have better luck planting tulips in the fall. And they usually start out as bulbs, not potted plants." We were both quiet for the next few seconds. I could hear a baby crying in a room somewhere off to the right.

"I'll have the nurse bring you that pain medication," he said, and was gone as quickly as he'd appeared.

Chapter 37

The X-ray technician couldn't have been more than twenty-two, but he'd been careful with my arm. He chattered on about the Orioles' chances of making the playoffs this season, about Manny Machado's incredible play at third base the night before. None of this exuberant monologue required much comment from me, and I leaned back on the stretcher and let the words wash over me, the pain in my forearm ebbing to a vague presence as the Vicodin started to take effect.

"Well, it's as I suspected," Dr. Mathers said as he entered the room. "The radius and ulna are broken and angulated enough that we should straighten them out before putting you in a splint. I can reduce the fracture here, but you're going to need some sedation. When's the last time you ate?"

"Breakfast," I replied, thinking back to earlier that morning. The time since then seemed like weeks instead of hours. "It was no more than a few sips of coffee."

He nodded, had me sign a consent for the procedure, and a few minutes later a nurse came in and started an IV.

I was worried the visit was taking too long, that the longer I stayed, the greater my chance of getting caught. It was important to keep moving.

"You ready?" Dr. Mathers asked, returning to the room.

"Ready as I'll ever be."

They redosed my pain medication, then I watched as Dr. Mathers drew something white and milky into a large syringe. He screwed the tip of it into one of my IV ports and slowly depressed the plunger. "Here goes," he said as the milky fluid snaked its way through the plastic channel and into the vein in my left hand. I could feel it sliding its way up my arm toward my heart, where it would be pumped to the rest of my body. It tingled a bit, not quite burning but—

"You tell me when you start to feel sleepy," Mathers said, but his voice sounded far away and I was already drifting.

I could feel myself being reclined in the bed. Cool oxygen flowed into my nostrils, reminding me of how the first few breaths of night air felt after emerging from the stale confines of my childhood house on Cedar Street.

"DON'T STAY OUT too long," my mother called, the screen door clapping shut behind me. I walked down the three steps to the front yard, ignoring my brother as he shot past me down the driveway on his Big Wheel, the hard plastic tires rumbling on the asphalt. I could hear the pulsing drone of insects, could see the sporadic glow of fireflies against the dim backdrop of dusk. The oak tree in our front yard held its limbs out to either side just as it had always done. *It looks tired,* I thought, *weary of the day.* To punctuate this point, it let go of a few leaves, allowing them to flutter to the grass, a hint that summer was almost over and the season of surrendering would soon be upon us.

Uncle Jim sat on the far side of the oak with his back against the coarse skin of its trunk. I couldn't see his face or upper body from where I stood—just the partially bent stretch of one blue-jean-clad leg in the grass. His left hand rested on his knee. The other, I knew, would be holding a cigarette because this was where he came to smoke. My mother had put her foot down about him not smoking in the house.

I kicked off my flip-flops and walked across the yard in my bare feet, the soft, cool tickle of grass on my skin. I moved slow and quiet, thinking that maybe I'd sneak up on him, would yell *"Boo!"* when I got to the tree. When I got there, though, he looked so lost in thought that it didn't feel right to break the silence. I sat down next to him, folded my legs Indian style, and picked at the grass in front of me.

He didn't say anything for a long time, just sat there smoking, looking out across the street. I didn't mind the silence. We had a connection, Uncle Jim and I. We could spend an hour working on a jigsaw puzzle in my parents' garage, the whole time neither of us saying anything, just concentrating on connecting the pieces. It was different from my mother's silence because I knew that Uncle Jim was right there with me, not lost in a world that I couldn't reach. Over the past few weeks we'd started to lose some of that. I could feel him withdrawing a bit—not from me, but from the world in general. He was getting sick again. I didn't blame him—didn't hold it against him. During those times I just . . . missed him. But then his eyes would clear and he'd look over, see me and give me a smile, and I'd grin right back because the warmth of that smile felt good, the minutes or hours that he'd been gone just washing away like dirt in the rain.

He held the cigarette out, offering me a drag. The first time he'd offered, I brought it to my lips and sucked in the smoke, gagged, coughed, and almost threw up. But I held on to it with my fingers because it had come from Uncle Jim, and the second time I brought it to my mouth I only coughed a little bit. Two drags was about all I could take. He'd nodded and smoked the rest of it down to a stub, his arm wrapped loosely around my shoulders. Now it was something else we shared, something we did together as we sat beneath the tree in the evenings and watched the world go by. And neither my mother nor father ever seemed to notice. Because, like I said, they were distractible people who looked past the family in front of them. As if anything else in the world could be more important.

"There," he said, making me jump. I'd started to reach out for the cigarette, but his hand had moved, and now he was pointing with the two fingers that held it. "You see that, Lise?" he asked, his voice low but clear in the stillness of the yard.

I looked across the street to where he was pointing, in the direction of our neighbors' house, but there was no one on their lawn or standing in the driveway. The garage door was closed. The only interior light I could see was coming from a lamp in their living room, the flicker of their television.

"What?" I asked, but he dropped his hand to the grass, stubbed out the cigarette, and was quiet for a long time.

I sat there studying the house as the last of the daylight ebbed from the sky. I could hear the sound of my brother's Big Wheel up the street, the sound of running water through the screen door behind me as my mother washed dishes in the kitchen. But I wasn't concentrating on that. My focus was on the house across the street. My eyes moved over the modest patch of shrubs, the brown rectangle of the front door with its single glass pane at the top, the slope of the roof tilting toward us, the darkened square of the side window that I could just make out in the shadows because the house wasn't facing us directly.

"You see it now?" he asked. I shook my head no. "At the window," he said. "The one on the side of the house. You see him looking out at us?"

"Who?" I asked, straining to see what he was talking about, but suddenly I knew the answer to my own question. "Is it Ronald?"

He smiled. I didn't look at him—kept my eyes focused on the house—but I could *hear* him smile in the darkness. The slide of dry lips pulling back against his face. I could picture it in my mind: the humorless, doomed smile of a man who suddenly realizes he is cornered and has no choice but to fight his way out. I could sense the fear settling on him, moving across his skin like a reptile.

"He sneaks over to our house at night," he told me. "I can hear him running around on the lawn just outside my window. Sometimes he scratches to come in."

What could I say to that? Tell him it wasn't true? Have him turn that suspicious eye toward me?

"He'll come for you first, I think, or maybe your brother. Because he's smaller and won't fight as much." He sat there in silence, considering this. The night things continued their clamoring all around us—calling out to one another, searching for each other in the dark. Hunting.

"You think your parents will protect you?" he asked. "You think they'll put a stop to it?"

I tried to answer him; I really did. Because he listened to me, and maybe I was the only one who could get through to him. I felt that responsibility pulling me down—the grass sprouting vines as thick as my fingers that wrapped around me as I sat there next to him. *Are you getting sick again, Uncle Jim? Should I go to Mom and Dad for help? Should I tell them something's wrong?* Those were the questions I should've asked. A braver, more responsible person would've asked. But I was afraid he would close himself off, become as distant and inaccessible as my mother. I didn't want to lose him, couldn't bear the emptiness that would be waiting for me in his wake. So I sat there like a statue and let the vines do their work. I could feel them winding their way up the back of my shirt, encircling my ankles, my waist, my neck. The one around my right forearm tightened, biting into my flesh. At first the pain was a distant thing—something happening to someone else, in another time or another town far away from here. "We've got to do whatever it takes to protect one another," he was saying, but in the light of a half-moon I could see it was Jason sitting next to me now. The small scar on his left temple— the place where he'd been struck so many years ago—was bleeding. He reached up and touched it with the fingertips of his left hand, turning the trickle to a smear. I started to speak, to tell him I was sorry I hadn't been able to stop them, but he shushed me, pressed his finger to my lips. The blood he left behind was salty against my tongue.

The vine around my forearm tightened further, pressing into the bone itself—the pain more intense, no longer distant. I moaned, and when I looked down I could see that the bone was beginning to twist and splinter in its grasp. "Try not to fight it," Jason told me, "or it'll never let you go." But I reached for it anyway, tried to free myself.

"Watch that arm," someone said. "She's coming around." And there were hands on me then, holding me down, and the warmth of a second bolus of sedative worming its way into my bloodstream. I could feel myself sliding back down, but there was no one there to meet me—only darkness this time, and maybe somewhere far away, the sound of a child's feet scurrying across the lawn beneath my bedroom window, the tiny hands scratching to be let inside.

Chapter 38

The second time I regained consciousness I resurfaced gradually to the sound of a soothing voice, a light touch of skin on my cheek. The room was darker than when I'd left it. An overhead surgical light that hung from the ceiling above had been switched on to its lowest intensity, but its beam was directed toward the far corner of the room, providing a soft, ghostly illumination to this otherwise unlit section of the ER. The curtain was closed, but I could see light coming from the hallway beyond. A nurse stood at my bedside, stroking the side of my face and repeating an unfamiliar name over and over. Something was tickling the inside of my nose, but when I tried to raise a hand to scratch at it my arm only went up a few inches and then stopped.

The nurse leaned over me a bit more, studying my eyes as they moved about the room. "It's okay, Candice," she said. "You're just waking up, that's all."

My thoughts were muddled. I was uncertain of where I was or how I'd gotten there. I'd been sitting outside talking with someone, I seemed to recall, although I couldn't remember who.

It had been getting dark—I remembered that much—the last of the day disappearing from the sky, the shadows spilling out across the grass.

"Time to wake up, Candice," the nurse said again, adjusting the thin plastic loops of tubing running behind my ears and coming together to form two short prongs that rested in my nostrils.

I looked up at her, feeling more present in the room now. "Who's Candice?" I asked.

The nurse smiled. "Supposedly, you are. At least that's the name you gave the registration clerk."

Of course, I realized, more awake now. *I'm in the emergency room. Because*—I concentrated, reaching for it—*because I broke my arm.* Yes, *that's* what happened. But how had I broken it? I worked it over in my mind, willed it to come back to me. Snatches of conversation resurfaced.

You don't know how to help me. You can't even help yourself.

Am I in danger? I could hear myself asking.

You call one of the two numbers on that phone, and we'll come running.

Will they come for us?

They always do.

And then suddenly I remembered everything: Jason and Linder and Remy; Dr. Wagner and the men pursuing me through the administrative building; the fall I'd taken from the bathroom window, my right arm sustaining the brunt of the impact, the bones snapping like kindling.

"What time is it?" I asked.

The nurse glanced at the digital display on the wall behind me. "About eight o'clock."

"*At night?*" I exclaimed, shocked it was so late. I tried to jerk myself into a sitting position, but I was still woozy and my left wrist was anchored to the side of the stretcher.

"Hold on," the nurse told me. "The restraint's just there for your safety until you're fully awake. We usually don't need to do that, but you got pretty wild there for a while and we had to give you extra medication. The doctor thought it would be best to let you sleep it off."

She removed the restraint from around my left wrist. My right arm, I could see, was wrapped in a hard splint that ran along the underside from just below the elbow to the tips of my fingers and was held in place by an ACE wrap. The ache in my forearm was better now—not gone completely, but manageable. I'd done the right thing in coming here.

"There's someone who's been waiting to see you," the nurse said, and that sent my pulse going, triggering the alarm on the monitor behind me.

"Whoa, take it easy. You don't have to see him if you don't want to."

"Who is it?" I asked, wondering how in the hell they'd tracked me down so quickly. On one hand, I'd half expected it. But the reality of them showing up to claim me was—

"I think he said his name was Haden."

I looked at her blankly. "I don't know any Haden."

"Okay," she said, sighing a bit. "I'll send him away."

She'd turned and made it as far as the curtain before I called out to her.

"Wait. What does he look like?"

She turned back to me. "Tall. Dark hair. Blue eyes." She paused, considering. "He could use a shave, I suppose, but if a guy like that showed up in the ER to check on me, I sure as hell wouldn't send him away."

I frowned. "John Deere baseball cap?" I asked, but she shook her head.

"No. He says he drove you here earlier and wanted to check on how you were doing. 'Course, if you don't know him . . .'"

"No, no. I . . . I know who you mean now. I'll see him."

"Okay," she responded, an amused smile on her lips. "I'll go get him."

She drew back the curtain and disappeared down the hall. A minute or two later she ushered the man in.

"This is Haden," she said. "You know him?"

I nodded.

She stood there, looking back and forth between the two of us. "So we're okay here?"

"I think so," he told her, a touch of southern drawl to his voice. "Thank you."

She didn't reply, just stood there for a few seconds longer. "We'll get you going shortly," she advised me, then left the two of us alone and walked off to attend to her other patients.

"I don't think she likes me," I told him.

He smiled. "The waiting room looks like a third-world refugee camp. I can't imagine having to work in this type of environment every day."

"I think she knows I've been lying to her ever since I showed up here."

I expected him to frown, to ask me what I'd lied about and why, but he only nodded, taking it all in stride. "When she was younger, I used to tell my daughter that it's always best to tell the truth."

"And now?"

"And now she's old enough to know better." He stood there awkwardly for a moment before adding, "And so am I."

I started to extend my right hand to him, then realized that shaking hands was a social ritual I wouldn't be able to partake in for a while. "I'm Lise."

"Haden," he replied. "It's nice to meet you, Lise."

"Thanks for driving me here, and for checking up on me. It was really nice of you."

He gave me another smile. He'd gone home and showered, changed clothes, and run a comb through his hair. The stubble was still there, but it suited him. The jeans he wore now were clean, his shirt a soft plaid button-down with an actual collar. His hair was dark and wavy, combed straight back from his forehead. I could see brown cowboy boots—of course—jutting out from beneath the cuff of his pants.

"You looked like you needed help," he told me, "and probably a ride afterward." He looked toward the corner of the room, then back at me on the stretcher. "I wasn't sure if coming back here was the right thing to do. But I got home and cleaned up after working in the yard, and I just kept thinking, *A person with no one to drive her to the hospital when she's hurt is a person who could probably use a little help afterward.* I hope that doesn't seem too . . ."

"Presumptuous?" I offered, and he nodded.

From where I lay on the gurney, I considered him carefully. The possibility occurred to me that he might not be as nice as he seemed. He could be a womanizer, a rapist, a psycho who would chop me up into little pieces and then bury my remains in the woods if I was foolish enough to get back into that giant truck of his. To be honest, it shamed me that I was thinking that way.

It really did. But it's important to remember where I worked, the kinds of things I'd seen in people's files during my years at Menaker.

Then again, I thought, *he'd had an opportunity to do those things the first time I got into his truck, and instead he brought me to the ER like I asked.* And now, many hours later, he'd come back.

"It *was* presumptuous of you—coming back here like this," I told him. "But it was also kind. Right now, I could use a little kindness."

"Well," he said, "how can I help?"

"I could use another ride. And, quite frankly, a place to stay tonight."

"Okay," he replied with no more than a second's hesitation. "You can stay with me."

"Just like that?" I asked. "You don't want to hear my situation first?"

"If you want to tell me, I'm happy to listen. But, no," he said, "it's not a requirement."

I eyed him suspiciously. "I'm not sleeping with you. We should get that on the table right now."

He laughed, blushed a bit. "What makes you think I'd wanna sleep with *you*?"

I should've bantered with him, used the opportunity to break the ice, but my mind was back on Jason. The thought of him locked away in a concrete room somewhere—or facing something far worse—made my stomach knot. He must've sensed this, Haden. His good-natured grin evaporated as he looked at me, his lips holding back the questions he'd promised not to ask.

"I'll bring the truck around, give you a chance to get dressed and to finish up in here."

"Okay."

"I'll be parked and waiting right outside."

"Thanks," I said, and watched him sweep past the curtain as he stepped into the hallway.

I looked around for the call button, but couldn't find it. Nor could I figure out how to lower the side rail. I removed the tubing from my nose, detached myself from the monitoring equipment, slid to the foot of the bed, and climbed off. The plastic bag with my clothes and other belongings was under the gurney. I removed the hospital gown and dressed. The splint, I found, was too bulky to fit through the sleeve of my shirt, but I'd worn a silk cami underneath, which gave me something besides my bra to wear on top.

Eager to get out of there, I stepped out of my room to look for my nurse, to ask her if there was anything else that needed to be done before I left. The ER remained a study in controlled chaos. The drunks lined up on gurneys in the hallway were still there, although a few of the faces—but not the smell— had changed. As I passed some of the rooms, I caught brief glimpses of activity in my peripheral vision. In a room to my left a child screamed bloody murder as several people held him down and the doctor bent over him, fishing for something with a long-nose pair of forceps. "This is why you don't stick toys in your ears," his mother was saying, but I don't believe the child was listening. A different patient looked up from his iPhone. "Can I get some pain medication over here or do I have to get it myself?" he yelled to no one in particular, then scowled at me when I glanced his way.

The computer stations were in the middle of the ER, an island of doctors and nurses hunched over charts and keyboards. Dr.

Mathers was on the phone, standing with his back to me as I approached the station.

"Yes, we have her here," he was saying. "Came in a few hours ago and should be waking up shortly."

I stopped, listened.

"You'll need to send someone to come pick her up," Mathers continued. "We can only keep her here for so long."

Against the far wall to my right was a security guard, sitting in a chair with his body turned obliquely to where I stood. He was looking toward triage, not in my direction, but the triage doors were the way I'd come in and the only exit I'd seen so far. Taking that route out could mean trouble. But standing near the station and heading back to my room both seemed like bad ideas as well. I turned left, my back to the security guard, and walked past a curtain and into an adjacent treatment room.

It would have been nice if the room was empty, but instead there was an elderly woman lying almost flat on a gurney. A younger man—her son, I guessed—sat in a chair next to the bed. He looked up at me expectantly. I smiled, tried to think of what to say.

"I'm . . . Candice," I told them, sticking with the alias I'd used thus far. "One of the hospital volunteers."

"Oh," the man said. "I'm Henry and this is my mother, Dorothy. Are you here to take her to X-ray?"

If I paused, it was only for a second.

"Yes," I told him, warming up to my role. "They'd like me to bring Dorothy over to X-ray now."

"Looks like you've had some X-rays yourself recently," the man said, gesturing to the splint on my arm.

I looked down at it. "Slipped and fell a week ago right here at the hospital," I lied. "Broke my wrist. But at least I didn't have to go too far for treatment."

He nodded, smiled sympathetically.

In the larger room just beyond the blue curtain, I could hear my nurse calling out to Dr. Mathers: "She's gone. Left the gown on the bed and took off."

"We can't just let her leave like that," Mathers advised her, his tone sharp and irritated. "I just told them we had her."

"Well, we don't have her anymore."

"—some time off," Henry was saying, but I wasn't listening.

"Activate a Code Gray," Mathers ordered. "Let's see if we can find her."

"I'm sorry, what was that?" I asked, turning my attention back to the man.

"I said, 'You should take some time off,'" he repeated.

"No," I said, dismissing the suggestion. "I enjoy volunteering here."

"CODE GRAY TO THE EMERGENCY DEPART-MENT. CODE GRAY TO THE EMERGENCY DEPART-MENT," the overhead paging system blurted a few seconds later.

"Sorry about the commotion," I told the patient and her son as I moved to an isolation cart and donned a cap, booties, and a blue plastic gown. I considered the gurney for a moment, imagined it would be difficult to maneuver. There was no wheelchair in the room, but I'd seen one parked against the wall near one of the bathrooms. "What are we X-raying today?" I asked.

"My shoulder," the woman told me.

Perfect, I thought, and was about to retrieve the wheelchair when Henry spoke up.

"Um, Mom has dementia," he confided. "She fell out of bed this morning. I'm worried her right hip might be broken."

My hopes sank. So much for the wheelchair.

Outside of the room, the uproar raised by my disappearance had subsided a bit. Peeking out past the curtain, I saw neither Dr. Mathers nor my nurse at the computer station, and the security guard was gone as well—*looking for me*, I thought. If I could figure out how to control the gurney, I'd have a pretty straight shot down the hall and around the corner, hopefully to another exit.

"Well, let's get you over to X-ray," I said, giving the gurney a light push and finding that its wheels were locked. A brief inspection revealed a black lever—tilted toward LOCK—at the foot of the bed. I stepped down on it, flipped it to the neutral position, and found that the bed moved freely on all wheels. Stepping down again and tilting the lever toward STEER reduced the side-to-side play, making it easier to control the forward direction.

"You sure you know how to drive this thing?" Henry asked.

I gave him a reassuring grin. "You'd think they'd stock the same type of bed throughout the hospital. But no"—I shook my head—"they're all a little different."

I grabbed a mask and strapped it across my mouth and nose, the elastic bands looping behind my ears to hold it in place. "Shall we?" I asked, positioning myself at the head of the gurney. Henry stood up and pulled back the curtain.

Even with the lever in the STEER position, the bed was more difficult to maneuver than I'd expected, particularly with only one good arm to do the work. The wheels at the foot—the leading edge—were locked straight, so that any steering was done by moving the rear of the bed in the opposite direction of where I wanted to go. I hit a chair, almost toppling it, and sideswiped the bed where one of the drunks was sleeping. He awoke with a snort. "Hey, watchit," he mumbled, reaching down with one hand and pulling the sheet over his head. "Sorry," I told him, and pushed on.

The ER continued to buzz around me. From a curtained room to my left came a gagging sound, then retching, a nurse telling a patient, "Bear with me. You'll feel better once we get this tube in place." As I was nearing the hall's next intersection, I could hear Dr. Mathers's voice as he approached us from around the corner. I eased the gurney toward the wall to my right, then bent over, pretended to fiddle with the oxygen tank attached to the under-carriage. Mathers rounded the corner, a portable phone held to his ear. "I don't care if she has no risk factors, she's got new ST depressions across the anterior leads," he was telling someone on the other end, but he was walking fast—shot past me without slowing—and his voice trailed off as he continued down the hall toward the front of the ER. I stood up and gave the gurney a nudge, swung wide into the turn and bumped the far wall with the bed's left front corner.

"Ooh," my patient remarked.

"Sorry, sweetheart," I apologized in a low voice, forcing myself to take it slower.

This hall, I found, was more narrow and cluttered than the first, but my driving skills were improving, and I was able to ne-gotiate the remaining obstacles without incident.

We turned another corner. There were double doors at the

end of the hall, and a push plate that I assumed would open them. Standing next to the door was a security guard.

I paused for a moment, not knowing what to do. Reversing course—trying to back up the bed in the crowded hallway—would draw even more attention to myself. Leaving the bed, turning around, and walking off in the opposite direction would be equally conspicuous. But the security guard was there for a reason, and suddenly my spur-of-the-moment disguise seemed meager at best.

In the space of time that I was considering these things, the double doors swung wide and two paramedics entered—one leading and one trailing—an empty stretcher between them. I saw my opportunity and went for it, gave the gurney a shove and moved through the doorway while the medics were between us and the security guard, partially obstructing his view. I didn't cringe, wasn't tentative, but walked quickly and confidently through the opening, knowing this was the secret to passing unchallenged through most limited-access venues. Still, I expected to hear him say, "Hold on a second. I need to check your ID," and readied myself to run if I had to. But the doors clapped shut behind us and it was quiet in the hallway, the bustle of the ER inaudible in this section of the hospital.

"Here we are," Henry said from beside me, and I realized he was right, that the placard hanging from the ceiling read X-RAY, marking the entrance to the department.

I made a right through the doorway, then brought the gurney to a stop at the counter in front of us.

"Who do you have?" the clerk asked me from behind the desk.

"Patient from the ER here for a hip X-ray," I told her.

"Name?" she asked.

"Dorothy Jacobs," the man volunteered.

The clerk typed the name into her computer, waited, then frowned. "It says here they ordered a portable. We could've done that in the ER."

I shrugged. "They told me to bring her over."

"Let me call Dr. Mathers and see what he wants," the woman said.

I figured this was my cue to say good-bye.

"Good luck to you both," I told the woman and her son. "Someone else will take you back when they're finished taking pictures."

The man smiled. "You've been very kind. Good luck with everything."

"Thank you," I replied. I started to go, then turned back, taking the old woman by the hand. "Get well soon, Mrs. Jacobs," I told her.

"Oh . . . well . . ." She laughed, a look of confusion passing over her face. "I don't . . ."

"It's okay," I said. "You're in good hands now."

"That's my daughter," she told the clerk.

Henry stepped forward, put a hand on her shoulder. "No, Mom," he said, exchanging a glance with me. "You don't have a daughter."

Chapter 39

I found a side exit to the hospital, walked out pushing a laundry cart, a loose towel draped over the splint on my right arm. The key to being inconspicuous is not only looking like you belong someplace, but also acting the part. A busy, hardworking individual is not someone people usually pay attention to, and for the thirty minutes that had passed since I'd overheard Dr. Mathers talking about me on the phone, I was the hardest-working non-employee at Baltimore Washington Medical Center.

I didn't want to risk meeting Haden in front of the ER, but I could see the truck parked there, Haden waiting for me, leaning up against the tailgate. It took five minutes of staring at him from where I stood behind the laundry cart, but he eventually noticed me, got back in the truck, and drove over.

"What's with the gown and mask?" he asked as I climbed in, a look of amusement on his face.

I stayed low in the cab, most of my body in the passenger foot well, head below the dashboard. "Tell you later," I said. "Let's go."

He pulled out of the parking lot onto Hospital Drive, turned left onto Oakwood Road, then right, accelerating onto the entrance ramp for Route 100. I sat up, buckled my seat belt, looked over at him.

"Thank you," I said, and then because those words didn't seem like enough, I added, "You may have just saved my life."

He nodded, as if it were no big deal—as if he were in the business of saving women's lives all the time—and drove on without saying a word. Beyond the windshield, the open road lay ahead of us, empty except for the distant red glow of a few taillights. I thought about rolling down the window to let in the night breeze, but when I lifted my arm to reach for the button I felt the weight of the splint and realized I'd have to do it with the other hand. *It's funny,* I thought, *how the brain tries to protect us sometimes. It works so hard at blocking out the bad things in life: a broken arm or a broken promise, the things we've done to ourselves and others that can never be put right. Our worst moments and deepest regrets. The things we are most ashamed of.*

We got to the end of Route 100 and merged onto Mountain Road heading east. I'd removed the cap, gown, mask, and booties, placed them on the floor of the cab near my feet.

"This used to be just one lane in either direction," he said. "During my grandfather's time it was a dirt road."

I squinted into the headlights of oncoming traffic. We passed a few shops, most of them dark. On either side of the road, I could make out the entrances to sporadic driveways disappearing into the woods. We drove for a while, then turned right at a sign that said NORTH SHORE ON THE MAGOTHY. A representation of a sailboat rode along the sign's imaginary waters. Community athletic fields stood silent in the darkness, patiently waiting for the scores of young athletes to return for another day of practice. A quarter mile farther and it was all forest now, the blacktop winding through the trees, the reflective eyes of a possum watching us from the woods as we swept by. The truck slowed, the trees closed in even more, and I could feel the rough jounce of the suspension negotiating the potholes and uneven terrain of the gravel road we'd turned onto. There was nothing now, just the sound of pebbles beneath the tires, the pulsating symphony of crickets all around. We traveled for less than a quarter mile before the road ended, coming to a stop at a red barn. Haden put the truck in park and killed the ignition, the only sounds from the insects and the ticking metal of the engine as it cooled.

"This is it," he said, looking over at me before opening his door and stepping out.

I stepped out myself, slid down from the height of the cab onto the dirt driveway. A motion-sensing exterior light blinked on as we approached the house, a modest one-level structure with white siding. He stuck a key in the lock, turned it, and walked in, flicking on the kitchen light.

"You want anything to eat or drink?" he asked, but I told him no, that I was feeling a little nauseated from the sedative they'd given me. Despite everything that had happened that day—or maybe because of it—all I wanted to do was sleep.

"Well, the bedroom's back there," he told me, pointing toward a short hall and an open doorway beyond. "There's a bathroom right next to it. I'll sleep on the couch in the sunroom."

"Thanks," I said, suddenly feeling awkward about taking his room, about leaving him standing here in his own kitchen.

"Good night," he replied, then he disappeared into another part of the house. I turned out the light and made my way to the bedroom, easing the door shut behind me until I heard the latch click—loud in the stillness of the house. Kicking off my shoes,

I sat on the bed, then lowered my head to the pillow. My sleep, I knew, would be fitful—my dreams plagued with nightmarish images of Menaker, the ambulance doors closing as they made off with Jason, Paul looking up at me with his swollen, beaten face, the blood flowing freely from the wound on his scalp. Regardless of my exhaustion, the night would be a long one. And with those thoughts running through my head, I fell asleep and dreamed of nothing that I could recall the following day—only the sensation of falling, of not knowing when or if I would ever land.

Chapter 40

I awoke the next morning in an unfamiliar house to the muffled clatter of pots and pans in the kitchen. The bedroom, I noticed as my eyes adjusted to the brightness of the sunlight passing through the window, was the room of a single man. The oak dresser was decorated with a few wood carvings, but that was all. Hanging on the wall to my right next to a large mirror was a single framed picture of Haden smiling into the camera, his arm wrapped affectionately around the shoulders of a teenage girl, presumably his daughter. In one corner of the room was a nail that he'd tapped into a wooden support beam, and several belts hung from it by their buckles like a collection of skinned snakes. There was nothing feminine here to soften the decor, and I suspected the rest of the house would be just like it.

I rose and gathered my shoes, sitting back down on the side of the bed as I slipped them on. My own face stared back at me from the lower portion of the mirror. I looked like hell and felt even worse. My back ached, and my legs and upper arms felt stiff, heavy. There were scratches on my cheeks from my harried trek through the woods. My hair was a matted, tangled mess—my eyes weary, still reflecting the fatigue and horror from the day before. The bandaging around my right forearm had already begun to unravel.

Making my way across the room, I paused to take a closer look at the photograph of Haden and his daughter. She looked to be about seventeen here, her long brown hair pulled back from her face into a ponytail that fell across her left shoulder. It was an outdoor picture, the two of them standing on the rocks beside a river. You could make out a rowboat in the background, a few fishing poles stretching their long thin spines above the gunwale. They looked happy, the two of them, like they'd just finished laughing over some inside joke. It was something personal, this picture, something he loved. As far as I could tell, it was the only personal thing in the room.

The doorknob felt cool in my hand as I swung open the door and stepped into the hallway. Like in the bedroom, the floor here was wood, the sound of my footsteps loud and hollow in the morning stillness. The hall opened into a dining room, and here at least was the presence of a woman's touch: a thick oriental rug on which the ornate legs of the dining table rested; a glass display cabinet with an assortment of china; a decorative serving table in front of a plaque on the wall that read, *Home is slippers, laughter, and a warm cup of tea.*

"Good morning," he said, causing me to jump. He winced, offered up a weak smile. "Sorry. I didn't mean to scare you. I . . . I've gotten used to living on my own here."

"It's okay," I replied, feeling a little guilty. I could see that he'd showered already, his hair combed back like before but still wet. He wore a light gray T-shirt and a different pair of jeans, his feet clad in the brown cowboy boots I'd seen yesterday. A cup of coffee was clasped in his left hand. He looked like a farmer, like he might be heading out to till the land.

"Would you like some coffee?" he offered.

"Please," I said.

He turned and left the room, and I followed him into the kitchen. It was a well-lit space, the way kitchens are supposed to be. Sunlight filtered through a series of windows over the sink and counter. A small table stood near the wall, a folded newspaper resting on its surface. I took in the usual amenities: stove, range, a refrigerator strikingly devoid of pictures—just a single magnet with the caricature of a stern-looking turtle posing above the word *Terrapins*.

He poured me a cup of coffee, turned, and handed it to me. "There's sugar in the bowl on the counter," he said, "some milk in the fridge."

"Thanks."

He gestured toward a large skillet on the range. "I was going to make some eggs and toast if you're interested."

My stomach growled at the mention, and I suddenly realized I was ravenous. "That would be great," I said, going to the fridge to retrieve the milk, then taking a seat at the table. I sipped my coffee and opened the newspaper, wondering if there would be anything in it about the incident at Menaker, but the paper was from yesterday and the news was the same as always: political posturing over a stalemate in Congress, more religious and ethnic violence in the Middle East, a humanitarian crisis in eastern Africa. Bad news, all of it, so I folded the paper and sat back in my chair, enjoying the smell of frying eggs and waiting for the caffeine to kick in.

He came to the table with plates and silverware, then headed back for the toast, butter, and jam. A few minutes later, he slid two eggs onto my plate with a spatula. He was quiet through all this, and we ate in comfortable silence, listening to the distant sound of a neighbor's lawn mower.

"Thanks again for everything you did for me yesterday," I told him, dotting my mouth with a napkin. "I realize it's probably more than you bargained for."

"Happy to help you out," he said, taking another sip of his coffee and looking at me over his mug.

I could tell he was prepared to leave it at that, that maybe he didn't feel it was his place to grill me with questions, but I felt the need to explain—hell, the *absolute necessity* to talk to *someone* about this. I opened my mouth to tell him only the basics, and before I knew it I was telling him *everything*, the grief and terror spilling out of me in a torrent. I spoke for a long time, unable to hold it back any longer, and he sat there listening, barely moving, until at last the pressure inside diminished enough for me to fall silent, my voice tapering away into nothing.

This is when he calls the police, I thought, *or the hospital. This is when he washes his hands of the whole thing and tells me he'd rather not get involved.*

"These FBI agents," he said. "Linder and . . . I'm sorry, what were their names?"

"Special Agents Daryl Linder and Aaron Remy," I told him.

"Right." He nodded, fiddling with his fork for a second before looking up at me. "It seems to me that they're your greatest asset here. I mean . . . the FBI, you know. They have resources. They can help you."

"Why didn't they answer their phones when I tried to call them?"

"I don't know," he admitted.

"You know what I'm afraid of?"

He shook his head, watching me.

"I'm afraid that someone might have already gotten to them, that the men who kidnapped Jason from Menaker also knew about Linder and Remy's involvement—that they did something to take them out of the picture before coming for Jason and me. That's why I couldn't reach them. I'm afraid they're already dead."

"You couldn't reach an operator at 911, either," he reminded me. "Maybe it was just a problem with your phone. If you can pull up the numbers, we can try calling from my phone here at the house."

I thought about this. "If the men who took Jason also got to Linder and Remy, then *they* have the agents' cell phones. If I try to call them, they could trace the call. I'd be giving away my location."

A subtle chime sounded in the dining room, the blink of a single solitary note. Haden cocked his head at it. He stood up and went to the sink, peered out through the bay window.

"What is it?" I asked.

He was still for a few seconds before answering. "I live on a private road. Just me and one neighbor farther up. We don't get many visitors, but when we *are* expecting someone it's nice to know they've arrived before they actually pull up out front." He shifted his position, leaning over the sink with his head closer to the window.

"You're a bit of a recluse, aren't you?" I asked, but he ignored the question.

"We have a line stretched across the dirt road at the point

where it merges with the public street. When a car rolls over it, it sends a chime to both our houses."

"The mailman," I suggested.

"Too early for that, and the mailboxes are out at the main road. Like I said, we really don't get many visitors. Tell me, does that phone of yours have GPS tracking?"

I thought about it for a moment. Linder had made a point of telling me that it did.

"Yes, I believe it—"

"Wait," he said, holding up a hand. "You hear that?"

"What?" I asked, getting out of my chair and joining him at the window.

"The lawn mower. It stopped. But now it's starting back up again."

"So?"

"So someone's coming," he said, "and my neighbor's house is not their destination. He wouldn't still be mowing if it was."

Despite what I'd been through the day before, I was having a hard time convincing myself there was reason for concern. Maybe I was just tired of running. "They could've just stopped by his house to drop something off," I told him, "and now they're leaving."

He shook his head. "No second chime. It would've sounded by now. They're coming here." He looked at me with genuine concern on his face. *At least he believes me,* I thought. *Thank God for that.* "We should go," he said. "Right now."

He moved quickly then, and I did my best to keep up. He went to his bedroom, opened a large cabinet, and brought out a hunting rifle and a box of ammunition. "Oh," I said, realizing that I'd been sleeping next to it the whole night.

"No need to lock this up," he said, referring to the gun. We were heading through the house, entering another hall and then a sunroom that faced the water. "It's just me who lives here now," he finished. He pushed his way through a side door and hurried down the exterior steps to a small walkway. I expected him to round the house and head for the truck, but he took the steps at the back of his property that descended toward the water, and a few seconds later we were out on a wooden pier. There was a rowboat with a small outboard motor tied up to the dock. I recognized it from the photo I'd seen in his bedroom.

"Get in," he said, dropping to one knee and untying the rope that tethered the boat to the pier.

I looked back up at the house, thought I could hear the sound of tires pulling into the driveway.

"Get in," he said again, sitting down on the pier and lowering himself into the boat, then steadying it as I climbed aboard. He'd placed the rifle and ammunition on the walkway and retrieved them before pushing off. I expected him to start the motor, but he handed me the rifle and box of bullets and went for the oars instead, rotating them in the oarlocks and easing the wooden blades into the water. The metal locks squeaked a bit as he did this, but it was much quieter than the motor would have been. Still, I could hear the sound of men's voices from the vicinity of Haden's house on the hillside above us.

Haden pulled on the oars, propelled us through the water, distancing us from the shoreline. We'd made it about a hundred yards—enough for me to relax slightly—before I heard shouting and then a loud crack that echoed off the creek's opposite embankment. Something splashed in the water to my right.

"Get down," Haden instructed, pulling the oars back in and

stepping past me toward the stern. He put one hand on my shoulder and pushed me off the wooden seat and onto the bottom boards of the boat. "Do you know how to load that thing?" he asked, not bothering to look back at me as he tilted the motor's propeller into the water. The air filled with another loud crack and this time the bullet went high, smashing into the water a good hundred feet behind us. Haden flipped a switch, then jerked back on the pullcord. The motor sputtered, but didn't catch. I could hear the reports of two more gunshots from the hillside. At least one of the bullets came close, passing by my head with a *ssssszeew* that made me flinch, press my body even tighter against the floorboards. I stared at the rifle in my hands, at the box of cartridges. I'd never loaded a gun before and wasn't sure if trying to do it now with only one good hand would put us in more or less jeopardy of getting shot.

Haden jerked the pullcord again, and this time the engine caught. He eased back on the throttle, put it in Forward, then gunned it. The boat lurched ahead through the water. The men kept firing and I heard Haden grunt once. Alarmed, I looked back at him, but he shook his head, indicating that it was nothing as we angled toward the bend in the creek. There were a few more shots from the hillside behind us, but we were rounding the bend, putting earth and trees between us and the men, and for the next few minutes it was just the drone of the motor, the soft slap of water on the underside of the boat.

Haden slowed, and I came up off the floorboards and sat on the seat opposite him, the fear still pulling at me, not wanting to let go.

"Jesus! They were actually firing at us!"

"Yes, I . . . I know," Haden answered. He was looking back at the shoreline behind us.

I was shaking, the adrenaline so thick in my system I could taste its bitter, metallic tang. We were entering the mouth of a larger body of water now, the surface choppy in the wind. The community sign I'd seen the night before had said NORTH SHORE ON THE MAGOTHY, and I assumed that *this* was the Magothy River. Just beyond it would be the massive Chesapeake Bay, and from there—eventually—the vast expanse of the Atlantic Ocean. We wouldn't make it that far, I knew, but sitting in the small craft with the shores spread wide around us and the waves lapping at the thin sides of the wooden vessel, it almost felt like we could. I opened my mouth to speak, then stopped. There was blood on the sleeve of Haden's T-shirt, a line of bright red fluid coursing down the length of his arm and spilling onto the floorboards.

"*You're shot!*" I stood up and moved toward him, forgetting to keep my weight balanced. The boat tipped precariously.

"*Sit down!*" he ordered. "*It wouldn't take much to tip us over out here.*"

I did as he directed, centering myself on the seat, but continued to stare at him in horror.

"It's not that bad. It just grazed me."

"I'm a physician. I want to take a look."

"Not now," he said. "I'm going to take us downriver a ways. Then we'll find a suitable shoreline to get off the water for a minute. You can look at it then. For now, sit still. The water's getting rough."

He was right. The wind had picked up, pushing my hair back

from my brow. The boat rocked heavily on the waves, and I had to hold on to the side to keep from being tossed about. The sky was gray and overcast, the air cool in my lungs—the heat and humidity of the day not yet upon us. Haden pointed the bow into the waves and opened the throttle, propelling us downriver in the direction of the Chesapeake. I forced myself to turn and face forward—away from the wound—narrowing my eyes to protect them from the wind buffeting my face, and for the next forty minutes I concentrated only on the good fortune that we were both still alive.

Chapter 41

We eased into an inlet at the mouth of the Magothy River, adjacent to Sandy Point State Park. It was a protected harbor, and the water here was smooth, the only sound coming from the rumble of our motor and some activity along the docks to our right. Haden guided us onward until the banks narrowed, forming a thin creek that we followed for a short distance until it dead-ended in a patch of reeds. He hoisted the motor's propeller out of the water and used the oars to nudge the boat through the reeds until the underside found purchase on the sandy bottom. We were within a foot of the shore now, and I was able to step out over the lip of the bow onto dry land. Haden did the same, handing me the rifle and box of ammunition before climbing out himself. I held them cautiously, as if the rifle was already loaded and might go off at any moment.

Haden gave me a brief appraising look as he disembarked. "You hurt?"

I shook my head, my eyes going once more to the darkly matted sleeve of his T-shirt, the blood there already drying. He studied me for a second, then went about the short task of tethering the boat to the closest tree. His hands moved quickly, despite his injury, and when he was finished he turned, took the rifle and ammunition, and motioned for me to follow him up the slight grade. We found the fallen trunk of a large tree and sat down, the rifle across Haden's lap.

"I should look at that wound now," I told him. He started to pull up his sleeve, but I made him remove his shirt so I could get a full look at the area. I'm no trauma surgeon, but I know enough to not get tunnel vision on the most obvious wound and run the risk of missing any less obvious ones. I inspected his back, chest, and neck—eased his arm upward to get a good view of the left chest wall and underside of his arm. There were no other injuries and no exit wound, so I returned to his shoulder, which was caked with blood but not particularly swollen and seemed to have good range of motion. I used his shirt to wipe away some of the blood. He was right. The bullet had only grazed him, leaving behind a long but relatively superficial gash. The bleeding had stopped, and there did not appear to be any significant damage. The wound would need to be cleaned—*but not here*, I thought, glancing down at the brackish water below us. I handed him back his shirt and he slipped it on, careful with his injured arm. We were quite a sight: me with my splinted right forearm and him with dried blood on his sleeve.

"We should get that cleaned as soon as possible. Some stitches and antibiotics would be ideal. When was your last tetanus shot?"

"I left the army five years ago," he said, and I felt a piece of his background snap into place. "They kept us updated on those things."

I looked up at his face. "Did you see combat?"

"Iraq," he said, but the way he refused to look at me told me not to press further. "I got out after my second tour of duty."

I allowed the silence to spool out between us, wondering if he would say anything else about his experience. He didn't. I looked out across the creek. Near the shoreline to our right a blue heron waded through the water, its eyes searching for fish, the beak opened slightly in anticipation of the downward lunge.

"What do you do now?" I asked finally, glancing at his faded jeans and cowboy boots, my mind turning back to his massive pickup truck, the John Deere hat he'd worn the day before.

"I write children's books."

His response took me by surprise. I gave him a thin smile, assumed he was joking. He looked back at me blandly, and a good five seconds elapsed before it occurred to me that he might be serious. "What—" I said. "You're kidding, right? I mean . . ."

"I don't look the part?" he asked, one eyebrow cocked slightly.

"Well . . ." I said, trailing off once more, checking his expression to be certain he wasn't having me on. "You seriously write children's books?"

"I do."

"Have you sold any?"

"Does it matter?"

I thought about it. "Only if you're trying to make a living at it, I guess."

He looked down at the boat, then back at me. "I've written about ten stories over the past couple of years. Published my first one about a year ago."

"And the others?"

"In time," he said. "My illustrator's busy with college right now."

I thought of the Terrapin magnet clinging to the refrigerator in his kitchen. "Your daughter?" I asked, hazarding a guess.

He nodded. "She's really talented," he said, studying the back of his hands. "You should see some of the work she's done."

I heard a splash and the soft flap of wings, looked up in time to see the heron take to the air, a small fish grasped in its beak.

"So what makes you go from serving as a soldier in combat to writing children's books?"

He shifted his weight on the tree trunk. "We all have to atone for something," he said, lifting the rifle and pulling back on the lever.

I started to apologize, but he waved it away.

"Listen, if people are going to be firing weapons at you, then you should at least know how to load this thing." He looked at me. "You've never used a bolt-action rifle before?"

I shook my head.

"Fine. This is a Remington 798. It's a hunting rifle. You see this?" he asked, pointing to the far end of the weapon. "That's the muzzle. You keep it pointed in a safe direction at all times. And this"—he grabbed the metal lever on the side, sliding it forward and flipping it down—"is the bolt handle. Watch what happens when I flip this up and pull back."

"The top part opens."

"Right. You load rounds in there." He opened the box of ammunition and removed one for me to see. It was longer than I'd expected. And heavier. There was a quiet lethality to it.

"This is how you load it," he said, taking the bullet back from me. "There's a receiver just in front of the bolt. You place the round in here and press it down with your thumb until it snaps into place. Here"—he handed me the rifle—"you try loading a few."

I laid the gun across my lap, muzzle pointed toward the trees, then took a round from the box and placed it in the receiver, pushing down until it clicked into place.

"Keep going. The magazine will hold five rounds, but you can put one more directly in the chamber, like this." He placed his hand over mine, guiding the bullet. I felt my skin break out in goose bumps. "Now, since your right hand's in a splint, you'll have to use your left hand to slide the bolt handle forward and down."

I practiced loading and unloading the gun until I could do so with reasonable proficiency. Once I got the hang of it, I found that I enjoyed it—the sound of the bolt sliding back and forth, the rounds snapping into place, the smooth grain of the wood pressed against the flesh of my palm. Haden watched me for a while, then walked down to the boat and covered it with fallen branches, allowing the camouflaging shelter of the reeds to do the rest. When he was satisfied, he returned to where I sat on the log, the Remington resting on my lap. "When do I get to fire it?" I asked.

"It's going to be hard to do with your hand in the splint. Whether you use your right hand to hold the forestock or pull the trigger, you'll need some working fingers on that hand. Can the splint be shortened?"

"Yes. The fracture is in the lower part of my forearm, not my hand."

"Okay. Even so, the recoil might hurt. You'll have to see." He looked out over the water, then back at me. "A friend of mine lives close to here. It'll be a good place to clean my wound and shorten your splint."

He turned and started to make his way up the embankment. I followed, the leaves crunching under our feet.

"Do you cover that in any of your children's books?" I asked. "How to load and unload a Remington 798 bolt-action rifle?"

I was walking behind him and his back was to me, so I couldn't see if he was smiling.

"Most of the story lines so far have been about fully automatic machine guns," he replied. "But I've been considering branching out."

Chapter 42

The trek through the woods was longer than I expected as we moved through the northern section of Sandy Point State Park. A smattering of residential houses were backed up against the park's heavily foliaged perimeter, and one of them belonged to Haden's friend—a veterinarian who owned a small animal practice not far from here. The two of them were apparently fishing buddies, which was how Haden was familiar with the creek and surrounding waterways, why he seemed so confident that we were heading in the right direction. The Remington was still in my hands, my left palm on the grip with the fore end cradled in the crook of my right elbow the way Haden had demonstrated. I looked down at it, struck by how comfortable and natural the firearm felt in my grasp. We'd been lucky to escape with our lives, and that got me thinking about Jason—of where he might be, if indeed he was still alive at all.

I stopped short, nearly bumping into Haden. We'd emerged from the woods and were standing on the outskirts of someone's back lawn. There was a wooden shed to our right, the sides painted barn-door red with white trim. Affixed to the side facing us was a life-size image of a black cat, the fur on its arched back standing on end, the mouth drawn back into a silent hiss, the pointed teeth like an irregular row of tiny daggers. The grass here was not completely unkempt, but it was clearly overdue for mowing, and the gray siding on the back of the house looked tired, a little dirty, holding up the best it could under what appeared to be years of neglect.

"Your friend," I said. "He lives alone?"

"Since his wife died," Haden replied. "He's been . . ."

"Depressed?" I ventured, reminded once again how often our inner world bleeds out onto our external one, how the crosses we bear in silence are reflected all around us.

"I try to visit at least once a week," he said, moving toward the back door. "He looks forward to our outings together." Haden got down on one knee, fished behind the shrubbery, and brought out a key that he inserted into the lock on the doorknob. "We both do," he said, turning the key and knob together and swinging the door open for us to step inside.

"I guess security's not a big concern for him," I commented, following Haden in and standing just inside the doorway as my eyes adjusted to the dimness of the house's interior. There was a sudden scurry of movement near the floor as an orange cat shot past me and out into the yard.

"His cat just—"

"It's okay," Haden said, walking across the room and flipping on a light to make up for the paucity of sunlight coming through the open doorway, the one solitary window looking out onto the backyard. "That's Tabitha. She's allowed."

I remained near the open back door, hesitant to follow him much farther into the house. "Your friend . . ."

"Richard."

"Your friend Richard," I said. "He doesn't mind you rummaging around inside of his house while he's not here?"

Haden had disappeared into an adjacent room. I had to step inside a bit deeper to hear his response.

"I take care of the house and Tabitha when he's out of town. I wouldn't normally just walk into the place when he's not home," he said, reappearing once again, "but I think it's safe to say that this is sort of an extenuating circumstance."

I nodded, feeling uncomfortable just the same.

"Listen," Haden said, one hand resting against the door frame. "I'm going to clean this wound, and after I'm done maybe you could sew it up for me. I know Richard's got a medical kit around here someplace. In the meantime, why don't you see if you can shorten up that splint of yours so you can at least use your right hand if you have to. There's a heavy-duty pair of scissors in the kitchen upstairs. If that doesn't do it, he's got some shears in the shed."

He retreated into the bathroom and shut the door before I could object. A moment later I could hear water running in the shower. I stood there a moment, then placed the Remington on a table behind me and went in search of the stairs leading to the second story.

The house was a split-foyer. The upstairs kitchen and living room were considerably better lit than the rooms below. The furniture throughout looked like it had once been nice but, similar to the exterior siding, was now weighted down with a weary, worn-out appearance, as if this whole place—and its owner— were merely marking time until the inevitable end. There were a few framed pictures on the living room's bookshelf, but I tried not to look at them. They would be of Richard and his wife, I figured—maybe a few children if they had them—but it was evident that this place maintained none of the vitality that had once thrived here. I was surprised at how that knowledge weighed on me. Maybe it reminded me of my own childhood home, of the years of emptiness I'd lived through and the person I'd become because of it. I looked in the direction of a chair perched near the front window, could see him sitting there, peering through the glass at the street below. *I can hear him running around on the lawn just outside my window,* Uncle Jim whispered to me, and for the span of a few seconds I was eight years old again, confused and terrified, not knowing what to do about this man I loved who was deteriorating in front of me.

Sometimes he scratches to come in.

I shook my head, blinked, and he was gone, leaving me standing alone in the living room, the knot in my throat so tight I struggled for breath. I sat down right there on the floor, lowered my head, and squeezed my eyes shut. And though I could no longer see him I could still hear the sound of his voice—almost imperceptible—calling to me from far away. It was hard to make out what he was saying, although I tried, I really did. Because suddenly it seemed important, maybe the *most* important thing he would ever tell me. But then it, too, was gone, and the voice that took its place was Haden's as he knelt down beside me.

"Lise."

I opened my eyes and there he was, in his jeans although he'd left his blood-encrusted shirt behind in search of something clean to borrow from Richard's collection. He was well muscled, but a little too thin, the lower ribs clearly visible along the sides of his body. A midline scar ran the length of his abdomen, reminding me of the trauma patients I'd encountered during my medical training.

"What happened up here?" he asked, but I didn't feel it was something I could explain, and I turned the subject to him instead.

"Why aren't you living with your wife, Haden? Did she pass away, too? Like Richard's?" I knew it was none of my business, that I had no right to ask if he wasn't ready to tell me. And yet it was something that was hanging out there between us.

"No," he said, looking away from me toward the window. "She didn't die."

I waited for him to continue, but he was quiet for a long time. I could hear a clock softly ticking away the seconds through the open entryway to the kitchen. It seemed to give voice to everything I hated about this house.

"When I returned from the war," he said at last, "I was a different person from the one she'd fallen in love with—the one she'd known through most of our marriage." He ran his gaze along the hardwood floor beneath us, his eyes restless. "I tried to be the same. I *wanted* to be the same. But some things in life, they just . . ."

"Change you," I said, and he nodded, looking back at me.

"That's right. They change you, Lise. And you can never go back to being the person you once were."

My thoughts returned briefly to Uncle Jim. It was not his face I pictured this time, but for some reason his hands—the strong fingers dangling loosely at his sides. And on the heels of that was the image of Jason kneeling beside his lover's dead body in the stillness of the hallway as the sound of approaching sirens grew near.

"People who've survived military combat talk about how hard

it is to return to civilian and family life afterward. It's not just that it's different. That's to be expected. The problem is: *you're* different. And the people who love you, that tears them up inside. They've been waiting so long for you to come home, you know? But when you finally do . . . you're a stranger to them, no longer the person they've been waiting for. You can see the confusion and disappointment in their faces."

"I'm sorry," I said.

"Yeah. Me too. Deborah—that's my wife—she rode it out for almost a year. I was drinking back then, and that didn't help matters. There was just so much . . . guilt and rage inside of me, and I turned some of that on her. Eventually, she couldn't take it anymore. Got in her car and left one evening after an argument and never came back. That was rock bottom for me. I've been working my way up ever since."

"Maybe it's not too late to—"

"She's remarried now. And six months pregnant." He smiled, shaking his head. "You believe that? We had our daughter, Rebecca, when we were so young. I always assumed there would be more, but . . . as it turned out that was it for us."

"Haden, I . . . I'm really sorry."

"It's all right," he said, helping me to my feet. "Probably better this way. For both of us." He opened his mouth to say something else, but then stopped and turned his attention toward the front door.

"What is it?" I asked, but a moment later I heard it too. The sound of a car on the driveway.

Chapter 43

Richard Davenport did not look like a depressed man, which is only to say that he put up a good front. Besides, the workings of people's inner worlds are seldom revealed to others. He had a short, reedy build and a gaunt, clean-shaven face that conjured images of a bird of prey. His nose was long and thin, a little too sharp at the end, and the wire-rimmed glasses he wore had a tendency to inch along its bridge until a quick dart of his index finger sporadically pushed them back up again. He did not seem displeased or even particularly surprised to find Haden and me inside his house, but he did watch me with a touch of distrust that made me uncomfortable and eager to leave. Haden, as well, seemed impatient for the two of us to move on, but he took advantage of the resources available by locating a pair of shears and shortening my splint so that I would have use of my right hand. Richard did indeed have supplies in the house to repair Haden's laceration, but he elected to suture the wound himself rather that turn the task over to me.

Instead of remaining in the house and enduring Richard's suspicious glances, I found my way back outside and waited for Haden there. Kneeling down in the soft grass, I practiced loading and unloading the Remington, but before long I heard arguing from inside the house. A few minutes later, Haden emerged through the back door.

"We should go," he said, walking past me at a hurried clip without breaking his stride.

"What is it?" I asked, falling in step behind him as we crossed the yard and entered the woods.

"He's called the police on us. Or rather, on you," he advised me over his shoulder, quickening his gait so that he was almost jogging now. I did my best to follow him, the smaller branches yielding or snapping as I shouldered past.

"What the hell for?" I asked. "Breaking into his house?"

"You're wanted. By the police. The incident at Menaker, it made the paper. They say you attacked an orderly there. Nearly killed him."

Paul, I thought. *Jesus*. I couldn't believe Wagner was trying to pin that on me.

Sirens could be heard in the distance, rapidly getting louder, and Haden doubled his pace. A police patrol car must have been close by when Richard called. I had to run to keep up with Haden.

"The orderly . . . they're talking about . . . is a friend of mine." I was breathing hard now as we tore through the woods. Somewhere behind us I could hear the sound of a dog barking. "Paul was attacked . . . because he was trying to protect Jason. I told you all this . . . this morning."

"I know," he said. "But that's not what the paper says." We had reached the embankment, and Haden was near an all-out run now. I had fallen behind, but I saw him reach the boat, and he began flinging away the branches he'd used to camouflage the craft. "*Hurry up!*" he urged without bothering to look up in my direction, his fingers working furiously to untie the rope. The sound of barking had stopped, but I could hear something coming through the woods, moving much faster than any human being was capable. The rifle was still in my arms. *Was it loaded or unloaded?* Didn't matter, I decided. If that was a police dog, there was no way I could shoot it.

"*Get in!*" Haden ordered, already pushing the boat away from the shoreline. I could hear the animal panting behind me—so close now—and as I splashed through the shallow water and dove into the boat I didn't turn to look back, knowing that seeing it closing those final few yards wouldn't make one bit of difference.

There was a final thrust as the boat was pushed one last time, the vessel tipping a bit as Haden vaulted into it from the water, the thud of his boots landing on the floorboards. He was behind me, rotating the oars into the water, trying to distance us from the shore. I turned in time to see the German shepherd launch its body at the rowboat. Its fur bristled as it arced through the air, the snout pulled back into a snarl. It was angled *right at me*, and without thinking I swung with my right arm, crossing my body hard and fast. The splint connected with the side of the dog's head just as its paws touched the front of my shirt.

The shepherd's momentum carried it forward, its body rotating so that it struck me with its left flank. The impact sent me stumbling backward, tripping over the seat behind me as I fell to the floor of the boat. The dog's body ricocheted to the right, struck the gunwale, and a second later was in the water. Haden pulled at the oars, backing us away, the dog's front nails scratching for purchase on the side of the boat.

"Sorry," I called to the animal as we reached a safe distance in the middle of the creek. It was back on the shore now, barking once again.

"*Sorry?*" Haden asked, rotating the oar blades back into the boat, then lowering the propeller into the water and firing up the motor.

I looked back at him. "I didn't mean to hurt him."

Haden shook his head. "I think he's fine."

"I hope so," I responded, the agony in my shattered forearm awakening in a fury now that the adrenaline was spent.

Haden turned the boat around so the bow was facing outward, then gunned the motor as we headed for the mouth of the Magothy River and the open waters of the Chesapeake Bay beyond.

Chapter 44

The Chesapeake Bay is roughly two hundred miles long and separates Maryland's Eastern Shore from the remainder of the state. Whereas the Baltimore-Washington corridor is among the busiest thoroughfares on the Eastern Seaboard, residents of the Eastern Shore have been blessed with the opportunity to enjoy a quieter, more tranquil existence. The numerous inlets and waterways give refuge to an abundance of waterfowl, and the grasses of the low-lying marshes stretch on for mile upon mile with only the breeze and the occasional local fisherman to disturb them. In Maryland, two parallel bridges span the width of the Chesapeake, connecting Anne Arundel County to the west and Kent Island to the east. In this section of the Bay, it is just over four and a quarter miles from one side to the other. Still, the water can be choppy, the swells dangerous for small vessels on days when the wind is really up. As Haden pointed us toward the Eastern Shore and the immense structure of the Chesapeake Bay Bridge loomed high above us, I was grateful that today was not one of those days.

It's an odd thing to hear the drone of traffic so high above you, the waves lapping spiritedly at the sides of your boat while the gulls cruise low along the waterline, eyeing you as if there were parts of your body they'd prefer to simply pluck off with their beaks. The light wind, the motor, the traffic overhead all made it too noisy for conversation, but I stole a look back at Haden a few times during that crossing, and he refused to meet my gaze. I'd read James A. Michener's *Chesapeake* many years ago, and the opening line—*For some time now they had been suspicious of him*—came to me as I looked out across the Bay. I shivered at the recollection, although the day was getting warm, and I wondered why it was that we as human beings can never truly trust one another. *It is the fatal flaw in our species,* I thought, *that silent ever-present potential for lethality we all carry inside of us, and the reason we do not trust one another is because we do not trust ourselves. We know all too well what we are capable of.*

I assumed Haden planned to dock at the harbor on Kent Island, but he seemed to change his mind as we drew closer, pointing our bow to the island's northern peninsula and leaving the bridge behind us. The water grew rough as we approached, and I began contemplating how long it would take us to swim to shore if it came to that, but then we were around the point and into a more protected area and the waves settled. We were still heading east, toward a smaller island that appeared to be a wetland marsh. We'd covered about half the remaining distance when the boat's motor sputtered, our forward progress slowing to intermittent lurches and then stopping altogether as it went dead.

"No more gas," Haden said, and motioned for me to switch seats with him so he could work the oars.

After the persistent whine of the motor, the thrum of traffic crossing the Chesapeake, a day populated by gunfire and barking, it was suddenly very quiet now—as if we'd passed through a thin white veil into a small, gardened courtyard about which the world had long since forgotten. I could hear birds calling from the island's trees ahead of us, but they were still far away. We'd moved from the Bay into the mouth of the Chester River, and things were calm, the surface disturbed only by the passage of our boat and the rhythmic glide of the oars through the water.

As we neared the island I could see there were no houses, only the sounds of shore birds and the soughing of the wind through the tall grasses. Haden craned his neck upward as a large winged animal passed overhead.

"Turkey vulture," he said, bringing us into the shore and hopping out of the boat.

The bird settled onto a branch some fifty feet away, watched us disembark. I looked back over my shoulder at it, unsettled by its persistent, patient glare.

"Would they eat humans?" I asked.

"They're scavengers. They'd eat just about anything dead."

Maybe he was tired, or frightened like I was, but his tone sounded irritable and I couldn't help but assume it was directed at me.

"I'm sorry I got you into this," I told him. "I didn't mean for things to turn out this way."

"No," he said, scanning the open grassland. He held his hand out for the rifle, and I gave it to him, watched him pull back the bolt handle and check the chamber. "I need a few more rounds," he said, and I reached into my pocket and handed them to him one at a time while he loaded the magazine.

"You work there?" he asked. "At the state hospital?"

"For five years now," I told him.

"And these special agents who contacted you, they showed you their badges and everything, right?"

"Yeah. Why?"

"Richard," he said, running a hand across his face. "He didn't believe that story you told me. The newspapers, you see, they've got it all turned around. They say you attacked that man—the orderly."

"I told you I didn't."

"I know, I know," he said. "And I believe you, Lise. I do. It's just that . . ."

"It's just what?"

"It's just that there are some things that don't add up."

"Such as?"

"Such as those FBI agents who contacted you—Linder and Remy."

"I know," I said. "I don't know why I couldn't reach them. All I can think is that maybe they were captured—"

"Lise," he said, cutting me off. "Richard called the FBI—the Baltimore field office where they said they worked. He did it right before he called the police."

"And?" Something was approaching in the distance, a soft mechanical whir that became choppier as it neared. The turkey vulture spread its wings and lifted off, heading for the far end of the island.

"And they don't have any agents with the last name of Linder or Remy, either in the Baltimore office or elsewhere."

"But I saw their IDs," I insisted, although it was beginning to dawn on me how foolish I'd been to trust them, how foolish I'd been to trust anyone.

"What if they were connected to Al-Termir instead?" he suggested. "What if they were only using you to confirm Jason's location, to keep tabs on him until it was time to take him?"

"Are you saying I may have actually *helped* them capture him? And when it was over, Linder and Remy—or whoever they were—simply disappeared?"

The whirring noise was louder now, and we both looked skyward. A helicopter was approaching from the south.

"Shit," Haden said, his voice sounding as if it were close to the point of resignation. "Stay low and follow me."

He turned and disappeared into the high grass that composed much of the island. I followed, crouching at the waist. "Keep your head down and don't look up," I heard him say from up ahead, but it was hard to tell exactly where the voice was coming from. The blades of the helicopter were loud in my ears. I could feel the rotor wash pressing down on me, the grass being pushed flat. *There's no way they don't see us*, I thought, my chest and stomach no more than a foot above the wet earth. The downward current of air moved on ahead of us, and I experienced a moment of hope that we'd somehow gone undetected, but then the helicopter turned, gained some altitude, and began moving in slow circles above us.

"THIS IS THE POLICE," a voiced bellowed over the chopper's external speaker. "STAND UP, PUT YOUR HANDS IN THE AIR, AND MOVE TOWARD THE ROADWAY."

"It's over, Lise," Haden called back to me, standing so that his head and upper torso appeared above the top of the grass. I hesitated a moment, then stood as well. I could see the road they were referring to, a single finger of blacktop that extended down the center of the island. A black van was pulling to a stop at the edge of the asphalt some fifty yards away. Several men emerged from the vehicle, none of them in uniform. Four of the men lifted assault rifles to the ready position as we approached, the helicopter continuing to circle overhead, and it occurred to me that it too had no identifying markings.

"They'll take us in and we'll explain it to them," Haden was saying, and I could see that his hands were empty, the Remington left behind in the grass. I took a few more steps forward, saw it lying there in his wake. "Leave the weapon," he called back to me, as if reading my mind. "Don't give them any excuse to shoot us."

I looked up at the men, their faces more distinguishable now. They watched us approach through the sights of their guns—a firing squad awaiting orders to shoot. A fifth man climbed out of the vehicle and joined them. He was dressed differently from the others—in a tan overcoat despite the heat of the day, his face obscured by the low-riding brim of his fedora.

"Haden, wait!" I exclaimed. "That's the man I saw—"

But it was too late. By then they were already firing. A few steps ahead of me, I saw Haden's body jump as the first round took him high in the chest. He let out a soft grunt of surprise, the hands of murderous men finally catching up to him five years after the war. The next shot caught him in the throat, and he fell backward at my feet, his body cradled in the soft grasses of the marsh.

"No!" I screamed, dropping to my knees and pressing my hands against the wounds, trying to hold back the rush of blood pumping out through the newly formed circle in his neck. "No, no, no . . ." was all I could manage as the life drained out of him with sickening speed. I could hear the sound of footsteps pushing through the high grass, the sound of someone yelling orders, but it barely registered in my mind.

Haden reached up and touched the side of my face. His hand had gone to his chest as he fell and it was covered with blood. I could feel the wet mark it left behind on my cheek.

"It's okay, Lise," he told me. "You're going to be okay now."

But *he* was the one who'd been shot, and I shook my head violently back and forth. "Don't die on me, Haden," I said, the tears spilling down my face. "Please don't die on me."

He brought a finger to my lips, shushing me. *His flesh is cold*, I thought, *much too cold*, but before I could say anything further he locked eyes with me and whispered, "No, Lise. I was never what you needed."

A moment later his gaze slid away. He looked up at the sky and it had begun to rain, the drops washing away much of the blood from his chest and neck, and he looked clean—cleaner, perhaps, than he'd ever hoped to be again. "Oh," he said, as if God himself had extended a hand down to lift him away from this Earth, and in the next instant he was dead. I laid my head against his chest and wept until I could hear the boot steps of the men as they gathered around me, then a loud crack and a shooting pain in my head as everything went dark.

Part Four

Captivity

Chapter 45

Movement: the brief sense of weightlessness as my body was lifted into the air for a fraction of a second before coming down again with a thud.

"*Hey, watch the bumps,*" a voice spoke up beside me.

"Sorry." A more muted response.

I swayed to my left, felt the cold touch of metal against my forearm, but when I tried to lift that hand to my face, I couldn't. Something was holding me down at the wrist, a thick band of rubber maybe two inches in width. There was something similar attached to my legs at the ankles. Only my right arm, with its thickly wrapped splint, was free to move.

I kept my eyes shut, feigning unconsciousness. My body was resting on a thin, narrow mattress, short spans of railing on either side. To my right, just beyond the rail, there was a flat pane of plastic that I could slide back and forth a few centimeters with my fingers. Working my way to its edge, I found that I could reach past it into a compartment of some sort. Inside were individually wrapped sections of tubing.

An ambulance, I thought. *I'm in an ambulance.*

There was no reassurance in this. We drove onward—no

sirens to call attention to ourselves, no hospital waiting for us at the end of *this* line.

"She's starting to stir," the man sitting beside me called up to the driver.

"So give her more of the juice. I don't want her waking up back there."

"Right," the man snarled in agreement, his voice rough and callous in the small compartment we shared.

No, I thought. *I don't want to be—*

The sting of a needle as it buried itself in my upper arm.

I tried to fight it, wanting to know where they were taking me. I didn't want to wake up lying on a dirt floor and chained to a concrete wall—no way of knowing where I was or how many halls and doorways stood between me and the light of day.

But I could feel myself rolling away now, the jostle of the road beneath our tires becoming a distant thing. There was a moment or two—before I slid down the steep and muddy slope into unconsciousness—when it seemed as if I were high above the ambulance looking down on its rooftop. The road stretched out long and straight below me, and I could see all the places I had been along the way—the Eastern Shore wetlands where Haden had died, the Bay Bridge looming high over the Chesapeake, the river and the dog, the hospital Emergency Department . . . and near the edge of the horizon: the foreboding grounds of Menaker itself. I could see its scattered buildings, the sporadic oaks that stood like sentries in the grass, the watchman's booth near the front gate, a few patients moving along the concrete sidewalks. But it was the wrought-iron fence that my eyes kept returning to. The ten-foot speared pickets curving inward at the top.

I turned and looked in the opposite direction, trying to make out where the ambulance was heading. But the path ahead was a mirror image of what lay behind us, and with it came a sense of disorientation, a carnival ride that spins and spins and will never stop. *Everything we've done, we will do again,* I thought, but the sun had fallen from the sky and darkness was almost upon us. I could feel myself slipping now, the world becoming dim and full of shadows.

Chapter 46

Dark. Headstone quiet. Before I even opened my eyes, I could tell that I was alone.

The floor was soft and a little spongy against my face. I sat up, tried to look around. There wasn't much to see, only a small rectangle of light at face level along one wall—enough for me to note that the rest of the room was empty. Feeling along the walls, I found they were covered in the same material as the floor. *Soundproofing.* Whatever happened in here would never leave the confines of this cell. They could rape or torture me—or simply leave me in here and never come back—and no one would ever know. No one would hear the screaming, the eventual tapering into silence.

I went to the small Plexiglas window, looked out at the narrow hallway beyond. There was someone—another prisoner perhaps—shuffling away from me toward the far end of the hall. I couldn't make out his features, only his hunched form and the way his clothing—as lackluster and hopeless as the human frame inside—hung from the sharp angles of his body. With a closed hand I banged on the window, the sound filling the room with its hollow, desperate reverberations. If he'd heard me, he made no indication, only turned the corner at the end of the hall and disappeared without looking back.

I stopped banging.

It was quiet again. Just the sound of my own breathing. I tried to slow my respirations, tried to focus and remain calm.

So there are others, I thought, *others like me who are being kept here against their will.* The man I'd seen must be one of them. He'd looked beaten—not physically necessarily, but certainly in spirit. He had more freedom than I did at the moment, but he'd moved without any sense of purpose, the boundaries of his world expanded just enough to reveal how isolated he truly was. I wondered how long he'd been here, and whether I would eventually take his place—someone new awakening here and looking out of this very room at me.

I ran my hands along the wall in front of me, my fingers coming to a crease in the lining, following it to the floor, then back up and over the portal, the crease running parallel to the ceiling for about three feet until it once again ran straight down to the floor. *A door*, I thought. *This is a door. The window is only part of it.* But there was no doorknob, no latch or other mechanism. I pushed on it, then wedged my fingers in the crease and tried pulling it toward me, but there was no give. If this was indeed a door, then the only way to open it was from outside the room.

Running my fingers carefully along the padding, inching my way around the cell, I checked for other points of access. There was nothing other than what I'd already found. I was trapped in here—no way out except by the will of others. Panic started to close in, its jagged fingers digging into my flesh.

You're okay, I told myself, pacing back and forth across the room. *They've put you in here for safekeeping, but they haven't hurt you.*

Yet, another part of my mind answered back. *They haven't hurt you yet. Oh, but they will, Lise. They'll hurt you plenty. You can be sure of that.*

I thought of the shallow grave awaiting me, could almost taste the grit of dirt between my teeth.

"Got to get out of here, got to get out of here," I whispered, but there was no way out, nothing to do but wait.

You will die here, the voice spoke up inside my head.

"Shut up, shut up!" I looked down at my naked feet, tried to think. "I haven't done anything," I reasoned. "I don't know who they are—don't have enough information that could hurt them."

They don't know that, Lise. That's why they brought you here. To be certain.

"I'll just tell them," I whispered. "I'll just have to make them believe me."

Silence.

"I could do that," I said. "There's no need for them to—"

That isn't the way this works, and you know it.

I stopped pacing. The voice was right. That isn't the way this works. They will torture me until I have reached a point where lying is no longer possible. I will tell them everything—*anything* to make the pain stop—and only then will they listen to what I have to say. *Even then* they will not stop. Not until they are absolutely certain. And once they are certain, they will have no more use for me. I will have become . . . dispensable. *That is how things play out from here*—and for once the voice inside my head was in complete agreement.

"Okay then," I said, and continued my pacing, unable to remain still. I concentrated on my breathing: head low, eyes cast downward—*like the man in the hall*, I thought. I was almost to the door before I looked up and noticed the face staring in at me.

For a few seconds, I could've sworn it was Uncle Jim, that he'd been out there waiting all this time because . . . well, because we had some unfinished business between us. Despite his illness, in the end he had shown me what needed to be done—had provided an example for me to follow. And yet here I was, still hiding from it. But Uncle Jim, he was here to help, to take me by the hand and make me face this thing—this unfinished business— once and for all.

I ran the last few paces to the door, put my face to the window so he could see me in the darkness and know that I was ready. The face pulled back, a bit startled, and I could see that it was not Uncle Jim after all, but rather the face of the man I had seen in the hallway earlier.

"*Open the door,*" I begged. "*Please, let me out of here.*"

I doubted he could hear me through the soundproof walls, and yet he seemed to understand what I was asking—reached out for the handle.

Yes, I thought. *Yes, that's it. Just turn the knob a little.*

Then he stopped. Over his shoulder I could see that someone had appeared at the far end of the hall. I couldn't hear what the other man said, but the stooped figure gave me one last glance through the window before turning and walking away.

There. You see that, Lise?

Uncle Jim again, whispering in my ear, his voice low but clear in the still of the room.

At the window. You see him looking in on us just then?

"I saw it," I answered, my voice too loud, too harsh in my own ears—something I barely recognized.

But we'll be ready, won't we? We know what to do.

I swallowed, felt it go *click* in my throat.

"Yeah," I said, not wanting to be part of whatever plan he'd come up with. But still, things had been set in motion.

Good then. We'll wait. We'll wait for the right time. You and I . . . I thought we could do this together.

THE SOUND OF the screen door slapping shut. My eyes open in the darkness.

A bedroom. I can hear the rain outside, the steady drum of drops pelting the rooftop. There is no time to listen. I pull back the covers and ease my feet to the cold floor. A pair of shorts is slung over the back of the chair at my desk. I slip them on over gooseflesh skin before going to the window and peering out. The rain is coming down so hard that I can't make out the front yard or the street beyond, but I have a sense that something is not right out there, that something is about to happen and I'm already too late to stop it.

I slip into the hallway, stepping over the spots where the floorboards are prone to squeak the loudest. I know this house. The door to my brother's bedroom is closed, same as my parents' door. The one to the guest bedroom, though, is open. Uncle Jim's room. And I know before looking in that the room will be empty.

I do not know what to do next. There is an urge to cross the hall, to bang on my parents' door until one of them—my father, no doubt—swings the door wide. *What in the hell's the problem?* he will want to know. *And what will I tell him?* That Uncle Jim's missing—only half the truth—or that Uncle Jim has gone in search of our neighbors' five-year-old boy at two in the morning. *He told you this?* my father will ask, and whether I answer yes or no, it will be far from the whole truth of it—that he'd been telling me in his own way that he was going to do this and I'd done nothing to stop it.

Dad will kill him, or come close enough, I think. He resents Uncle Jim's intrusion on our family. But that's not why he will kill him. My father will kill him because there is something about Uncle Jim that scares him. Maybe it's the mental illness—the wild, unpredictable nature of it. It reminds him, maybe, of my mother's own struggle with depression. Maybe he hates him because Uncle Jim requires patience and compassion, and my father has very little of either. Or maybe he just hates him because he's different: strange and weak, defective in a way that makes him an easy target.

I decide to remain quiet, turn from their bedroom door, and continue down the hall and into the kitchen. We keep a flashlight in the upper drawer here, and I pause long enough to take it with me. There is something wrong with the contents of the drawer, I notice, but I don't focus on that now. Because again I am filled with the certainty that there is no time to waste, that I might be too late already.

The flashlight is dim and weak when I test it, the way all flashlights are when you need them the most. If we have any extra batteries, I don't know where they are, and now is not the time to go looking. At the front door, I can see that the heavier one—the door with the deadbolt—is standing wide open, leaving only the mesh of the screen door to hold back the chill of the night. It is the end of summer, but the September rain has brought with it the taste of an early fall, and I wish for more than a T-shirt and shorts as I step outside. The concrete, wet with precipitation, presses against the bare soles of my feet, and I look down, surprised, realizing that I haven't bothered to put on my sneakers.

No matter, I tell myself. *Get moving.*

I am down the steps and across the street at a half run, feeling the rough texture of the asphalt beneath my feet but not slowing until I've reached the McBees' driveway. The house in front of me is dark and silent, the shrubs like hunkered animals watching me from the shadows. The front door is closed, the small porch vacant and undisturbed. I have the feeling that the house does not want me here. It raises itself up a bit, protective of the family within.

The side yard looks up at a window to Ronald's bedroom. I move around to that side of the house because it is where I think Uncle Jim would go—to the window with a partial view of our front yard, to the one he pointed out to me as we sat beneath the oak a week and a half ago in the gathering dusk.

There, he'd said to me, two fingers raised in this direction, the cigarette nestled between them. *You see it now? . . . You see him looking out at us?*

I hadn't argued with him, hadn't tried to talk sense into him, hadn't gone to my parents to warn them that Uncle Jim was getting sicker. Instead, I'd sat with my back against the tree and done nothing.

He'll come for you first, I think, he'd told me, *or maybe your brother. Because he's smaller and won't fight as much.* The cigarette had burned down to almost nothing in his hand, a forgotten thing. *You think your parents will protect you? You think they'll put a stop to it?*

I stand in the grass looking up at the window, my right hand shielding my eyes against the rain. The window is high enough that I can't look directly through it and into the bedroom. If I jumped, I could maybe touch the bottom portion of the glass with my fingers, but that is all. I won't be able to open it. But Uncle Jim is much taller than me. If the window is unlocked, *he* could've gotten it open.

Where is he now? I wonder. *If he went through the window, wouldn't he have come out the same way? Would he have taken the time to close it behind him?*

I walk around toward the rear of the house. There is a back door, of course, but the chances of the McBees not locking it at night are slim. *So . . . maybe he gave up. Maybe the house did its job protecting them after all. Except . . .*

Except where is he now? And would he have left all this up to chance, hoping for an unlocked door or window? No, I think, *he is smarter than that.* He came here tonight *knowing* he would be able to get inside. Because . . . because . . .

The answer strikes me just as I near the rear corner of the house. *Uncle Jim has a key.* He has a key because my family and the McBees are neighbors, and neighbors exchange such things so that there will be someone to water the plants and take care of the animals while they're away. That's what was missing from the kitchen drawer when I'd fetched the flashlight. If I'd taken the time to notice, I might have—

And there it is as I round the corner: the back door standing open.

He's inside. He's in Ronald's room right now.

I run through the doorway and into the house. I've been inside before and know that Ronald's room is halfway down the hall on the left. My naked feet thud softly on the carpet, but it doesn't matter if I wake the whole house. All I care about is getting there in time. In my mind, I can see Uncle Jim standing beside the bed, the pillow held firmly in his hands and pressing downward on the boy's face, the child's small hands beating uselessly at the thick forearms above him, my uncle's head turning to look at me. *Lise*, he will say, *I did it. I took care of that thing we were talking about.*

"*Noooo!*" I scream, trying to stop him as I burst into the bedroom through the open doorway. I am so convinced that he will be there that at first I *do* see him staring back at me from the darkness—his eyes wide, the sides of his mouth pulled back nearly to his ears, the face nothing more than a grinning skull. But then there is the sound of footsteps within the house, another door being flung open, the hallway light flashing on behind me.

"*YOU THERE!*" a man yells. "*GET DOWN ON YOUR KNEES RIGHT NOW!*" The voice sounds like Mr. McBee, but the pitch is off: high and full of terror. It doesn't occur to me that he is talking to me. I am lucky he doesn't have a gun or a bat because, in his panic, he might have killed me. Instead, I feel a hand on my shoulder and he is spinning me around to face him.

"*WHAT IN THE HELL IS GOING ON HERE?*" But I don't have to say anything, don't have to explain why I am standing here in his child's bedroom in the middle of the night. Because in the next instant he looks past me and notices what I have already seen for myself. The bed is empty.

"Where . . . ?" His eyes widen. A strand of saliva trembles on his lower lip. I look away from him, trying to think. If Uncle Jim has already taken Ronald from the house, he could've taken him anywhere. But the place that comes to mind first is my special place: the creek down in the woods where I go to be alone. I've taken Uncle Jim down there a time or two, wanting to share it with him. There is no particular reason he would go there now, and yet I somehow *know* that he will. Because . . . because we have a lot in common, Uncle Jim and I. He said so himself.

"There's still time," I say, more to myself than to Mr. McBee. I push past him and run down the hallway. He does not reach out to stop me.

My sprint through the woods is frantic. *Not too late, not too late*—and yet I fear that it is. The snap of twigs against my body. The feel of wet leaves on my feet. The dim beam of the flashlight plays tricks on my eyes. Every tree looks like a man carrying the weight of an unconscious boy slung across his shoulder. It doesn't matter. I am relying more on instinct than sight, the flashlight serving only as a beacon for the others to follow.

There is a break in the trees on either side of the creek. It is not a full moon tonight, but it is getting close, and although I can't see everything in the glow, I know this place well enough to fill in the shadows. I stand there, breathing hard, looking in both directions along the banks. There is no one.

The hope that I've been clinging to is gone. He isn't here. He's taken the boy somewhere else. And whether Ronald McBee is already dead or will be soon makes no difference now. There will be no finding him tonight, no chance of saving him. I turn, start to make my way up the embankment. That is when Uncle Jim appears from the trees, carrying the boy's limp body across his shoulder, just the way I imagined he would. The rain has tapered off, and I can see that he is smiling at me, happy to find me here. I've beaten him to the creek. With the weight of the boy in his arms, the woods less familiar to him than to me, it had taken him longer. Somewhere along the way, I must have passed him, his path swinging wider than mine, my own race through the woods covering up the sounds of his passage.

"I brought him down here to wash him off first," he tells me, proud of himself for having thought of this. "He should be clean before we bury him."

I look from his placid face to the body he is holding. There is no movement there. I cannot tell if the boy is still breathing.

"Is he dead, Jim?" I ask, leaving off the "Uncle" part this time. Because if Ronald is dead, then things are different between us. I am as much to blame as he is.

I can hear the others—Ronald's parents, maybe mine too—pushing their way through the woods a short distance above us. They are calling Ronald's name, calling out to both of us, but I don't answer. Everything that will guide the rest of my life is right here in front of me.

Uncle Jim glances briefly at the body resting on his shoulder. "Is he dead, Jim?" I ask again, and I expect him to answer, *Yes. He would've come for you. I had to protect you.* But instead he shakes his head slowly, solemnly, as if I should know better—after all we've been through—than to ask a question like that.

"No, Lise," he says, and he reaches a hand out and touches my shoulder. "I thought we could do this together."

Chapter 47

The next time someone came to the door they did more than just look inside. I'd been doing push-ups, the weight of my lower body on my knees instead of the balls of my feet. I had counted out seventeen, my arms beginning to shake, but I was doing them properly—back straight, lowering my upper body slowly until my chest touched the floor, then back up again to a straight-arm position.

One of the problems was that it was hard to keep track of how much time had passed. There were no external windows to mark day and night, no clocks, no objective way of separating one hour from four or fourteen. Shortly after I'd awoken for the first time, they'd turned on the lights in the room and left them on, probably to keep a better eye on me. The ceiling was higher than I'd originally imagined—fifteen feet, perhaps—and there was a video camera perched in one of the corners where the ceiling met the wall. It looked down on me with unblinking, inanimate indifference.

They slipped food and water into the room once while I was sleeping, and I was still kicking myself for not being awake when it happened. Not that there was much chance of me using the opportunity to escape, but I wanted to observe them. If there was a weakness, something I could exploit, then I might be able to use it to my advantage. I hadn't eaten what they'd brought—a small apple and a sandwich that was nothing more than two slices of cheese on bread—but the water I'd gulped down so quickly I almost barfed it back up a moment later. I fought my stomach on that one, managed to hold it down after all. The body can go without food for a long time, but lack of fluids will incapacitate you faster than almost anything else. Any chance I had of breaking out of here was dependent on me staying hydrated.

There was no particular strategic reason I didn't eat. I wasn't worried about poisoning. They could've poisoned my water almost as easily as poisoning my food. And I knew that not eating might weaken me. The water I saw as an absolute necessity. The food—for the space of at least the next few days—was not vital to my survival, so I chose to refuse it as an act of rebellion, although I seriously doubted that they cared.

Still, I kept the apple—tucked it away beneath the waistband of the loose clothing they'd provided. The outfit was something like hospital scrubs, only the material was much flimsier—almost paper thin. The pants had an elastic waistband, which I used to hold the apple in place. Even then, it had a tendency to slip out as I moved about the room, the apple cascading down my pant leg, landing near my bare foot on the soft floor. I'd stoop, retrieve it, return it to my waistband. I'd think about the watchful eye of the camera above me, wonder whether all this was being observed or recorded.

I was just lowering myself into push-up number eighteen when I saw movement in my peripheral vision and the door swung open. I scrambled away, crab-walked backward into the far corner.

Two large men stepped into the room, and I could see a third standing in the doorway behind them. All three were darkly complected and appeared to be of Middle Eastern descent. The largest of them—the one who spoke—had a thick accent and coal-black eyes that burned into me as I sat there with my back pressed against the wall.

"You are feeling better, no?"

I didn't answer, pressed myself tighter against the wall.

"You will take these," he said, and opened the palm of his hand to reveal several small pills.

"I don't think so," I told him.

He seemed to be expecting a response like this and stepped aside so the third man could enter the room. He was carrying a large syringe with a hypodermic needle attached.

"You will take these pills," the one in charge said, "or you will receive an injection. It makes no difference to me."

I looked from the syringe to the capsules resting in his open hand, then back at the syringe again. They watched me with blank faces.

"I would recommend," I advised them with an air of careful consideration, "that you take both the pills *and* the injection"—I took a moment here to make eye contact with all three of them—"and shove them up your—"

They came for me then, all three at once. I kicked out with the heel of my bare foot and caught one of them in the knee. He gave a grunt and I heard something pop. My left hand reached back and yanked the apple loose from beneath my waistband. One of them had grabbed hold of my right arm, was trying to turn me over and force me into a prone position. With the apple cupped in my left hand, I brought it across my body as hard as I could, felt the satisfying crunch as it smashed into the man's right temple. He rolled to one side, holding a hand to the side of his head. The third man had to step over his fallen partners to get to me. He stumbled and fell awkwardly, cursing as he struck the floor. My feet were under me now, and I bolted past them toward the door. *Gonna make it!* I thought before the one whose knee I'd snapped reached out and snagged me by the ankle. I wasn't expecting it, went down hard and landed on my stomach, the air momentarily forced from my lungs. With my free foot, I kicked out at him, caught him in the nose this time. He howled, let go of my ankle, and I crawled the rest of the way to the door, covering the remaining few feet in less than a second. If I could get through the door and slam it behind me, they would be trapped inside. They were scrambling now, having come to the same realization—all four of us focused on gaining control of the door.

I shot through the opening, was outside of the room, swinging the door closed on its hinges. The space between the door and the frame narrowed to a single sliver before at least two of them went slamming into the door from the inside, throwing it wide open again and sending me flying backward into the hallway. I landed on my ass, felt my teeth click shut as the jolt of the impact shot up my spine. They spilled out of the room, all three of them, and I could see that I'd rattled them—the biggest one most of all. He lurched toward me, breathing hard. Before I could get to my feet, he reached down, took hold of an ankle in each hand, and yanked them out from under me. My head swung backward, cracked against the tile.

He was pulling me back into the room, my body sliding along the smooth flooring of the hallway. I tried to kick out again, working my legs like I was pedaling a bicycle, but he was stronger and my movements were useless. The top part of my garment had torn, and it rode up my back as he pulled me along, the tile of the hallway transitioning into the soft rubber flooring of my cell. I fought harder, knowing I'd never get another chance at escape like this one. The man whose temple I'd struck with the apple got down on one knee and grabbed both of my arms. He and the leader held me down while the third man retrieved the syringe. He walked over, uncapped the needle, then leaned forward and plunged it right through my pant leg into my thigh. Liquid warmth spread quickly through the muscle.

They held me there for a while, until the room was spinning so fast that I no longer had the ability to struggle. Then they let go of my limbs, and I rolled over onto my side, clinging to the floor for fear that, if I didn't, I would slide off into the abyss.

"Next time you take the pills," the one who had done all the talking said to me. They were leaving. All I could see of them now was their shoes.

"Next time you bring more men," I managed, and then closed my eyes as the darkness rose to meet me.

AFTER THE INCIDENT with Ronald McBee, they'd come to take away Uncle Jim, as I'd known they would. Mr. McBee left it to my father to call the police, but it was one of those if-you-don't-I-will situations. My father was more than happy to place a call to his colleagues. He'd wanted to do it since Uncle Jim had first come to stay with us. I think he actually relished the opportunity. He had been right and my mother had been wrong—*just one in*

a long line of such occasions, he pointed out as we watched the officers escort Uncle Jim into the back of a squad car and drive away,
the siren silent but the light bar flashing. My parents stood in the
entryway of our house as the cops loaded him in, but I'd refused
to come inside, standing in our front yard beneath the oak where
the two of us used to sit. The rain had tapered to all but nothing. Mr. McBee had watched from his driveway, but the rest of
his family had gone inside and the house was once again dark.
He never glanced over at me, never said a word to me beyond
the brief, panicked exchange we'd had when he'd discovered me
standing in Ronald's room that night. I knew that he blamed me
too for what had happened. And although his son was safe and
I'd played a critical role in saving him, I had no doubt that he
would never trust me again.

I stood there in the last of the dwindling mist and watched
Uncle Jim go, the only one in my life who'd ever taken the time to
understand me. I raised a hand as he paused outside the cruiser.
His own hands were cuffed behind him, and he had no way
of returning the gesture. But he did give me a nod and a thin
smile before lowering himself inside, and I saw him watching me
through the glass as the officers climbed into the front and the car
shift was dropped into gear. The driver turned the front wheels to
the left and the patrol car followed suit, the tires squeaking softly
on the wet pavement. I watched until they rounded the corner,
until even the flashing remnants of the blue-and-red strobe had
disappeared from view. After a time, my right arm began to ache
and I realized that it was still raised in a half wave. I forced myself
to put it down.

"Come inside, honey," my mother called to me from our front
door, so I did. She walked me to my room, helped me out of my

wet clothes and into my pajamas, ran a towel through my hair. She got down on her knees to tuck me in as I slid beneath the sheets, and for once she seemed completely present.

"Where will they take him?" I asked as she planted a kiss on my forehead.

"To a hospital," she said, "someplace where he can be safe." She stood and walked across the room to my door, flipped off the light. I could just make out the shape of her outline in the doorway. "He belongs in a place that can keep him safe. He deserves that, Lise. Don't you think?"

"I miss him, Mom," I whispered, not wanting to be brave or grown-up any longer. "I miss him already."

Chapter 48

The day after Uncle Jim was taken away, I came down with a fever. I'd been sick before—chicken pox, strep throat, an assortment of viral illnesses over the years—but I don't remember ever being quite so ill as I was during the three days following his departure. I ran high fevers, had shaking chills, and was intermittently delirious. Eight hours into it my parents took me to the doctor's office, and from there I was sent straight to the emergency room. Bacterial meningitis was what the doctors thought at first. They'd given me Tylenol, IV fluids, and antibiotics, stripped me down and covered me with cool wet towels in an attempt to break the fever. They'd even done a spinal tap that I'd slept right through without flinching. That worried them most of all, and I was admitted to the hospital for observation.

I have no clear memory of those three days, only a vague recollection of voices and images that marched through my head, accosted me with accusations to which I couldn't respond. I tossed and turned, poured out liters of sweat from my body, and there was no way of separating delirium from reality.

For an unknown duration of time, this was also the type of existence I endured while in captivity, following my fight with the guards and the first of what would be an entire series of injections. The men came and went, but I had no real way of keeping track of what was happening. I had long, angry conversations with them—only to open my eyes and find myself in an empty room. If I drank or ate, it was because they forced me. I tried to sleep, but there was no relief in it. The brief semilucid moments felt like waking up after a night of heavy drinking with no idea where I was or what I was doing there. At one point, I became convinced that everyone in the complex—even my captors— were dead, and that I was completely alone. The horror of those moments was unbearable, and when the guards had finally come through the door—hours later—with another injection, I had broken down in tears of relief, welcoming them.

There were snippets of interaction I could recall—someone yelling, *Where's Jason?! What have you done with him?!*, although I think that person might have been me. I remember apologizing profusely for something I'd done long ago, although I couldn't remember what it was.

It didn't matter. I was past the point of hope, strategy, or resistance. I wanted it to end, wanted to be clear of this so that I could move past death to whatever came next. And if that turned out to be nothing, well . . . it was far better than this.

And then one day it ended. It happened as quickly as it began. Just as I'd been transported to this place an immeasurable time ago, I found myself suddenly being transported away from it, taken somewhere else, and the only emotional response I could conjure was resignation. There was the thrum of the tires beneath us, the sway of the ambulance, and in my mind I could once again picture the shallow grave awaiting me.

Eventually, we pulled to a stop. The driver and passenger

doors opened and shut. *Chunk-chunk*. I waited for them to come around and get me, listened for the sound of shovels.

Nothing.

I opened my eyes and looked around. I was alone in the back of the unit. The restraints around my wrists and ankles had been removed. They'd dressed me in my regular clothes before bringing me here. I sat up on the stretcher, listening.

Still, nothing.

Getting to my feet, I had to bend at the waist to accommodate the low ceiling. I shuffled to the double doors at the rear of the vehicle and tried the handle. *It will be locked. In a few seconds, I will feel the rig rolling forward, then a brief and disorienting plunge to the water below. The ambulance will strike the surface nose first, and I'll be thrown like a wet towel into the cabinets behind me. If I'm lucky, I'll hit my head and lose consciousness. Better that than clawing at the locked doors and windows as the truck sinks below the surface, the water pouring in around the hinges. Better that than being trapped in utter darkness with my mouth and nose pressed to the ceiling as the last few inches of breathable air are slowly extinguished.*

Yes, it will be locked, but when I pulled on the latch the door swung open, and there was sunlight—so much of it that I had to shield my eyes. Above me, the sky was blue and cloudless. I don't think I've ever seen something so beautiful in all my life. I lowered one foot onto the rear step of the ambulance, paused a moment, then lowered the other until it was touching grass. I got down on my hands and knees, ran my open fingers through the green blades as they prickled my skin. Morning dew still clung to them, dampening my pants at the knees. I lowered my face to the ground, breathing in the soft, clean smell of abundant life.

Chunk-chunk. Doors closing.

I froze.

A diesel engine sprung to life behind me, the sound loud and intrusive in the morning stillness. The sound of the transmission dropping into gear, tires rolling forward on the asphalt.

I didn't look back. If they intended to run me over, I didn't want to see it coming. I wanted to focus on the grass, wanted the last thing I saw to be something good.

The engine revved behind me. But instead of growing louder as it bore down on me, the sound receded. Even then I didn't look back, merely remained where I was, listening as the drone of the engine dissipated into nothing, until the whisper of the breeze became the dominant sound once again.

I got to my feet, took in my surroundings. I was standing on grass adjacent to a parking lot. About a hundred yards away, two women were engaged in a discussion as they traversed a concrete walkway that adjoined two brick buildings. I recognized the buildings immediately. In the distant backdrop behind them was the fence, its towering black pickets arching inward at the top. I turned to the left and there was the watchman's booth beside the large front gates. The last time I'd seen it, it had been empty. Now it was manned, Tony Perkins back at his usual station, his body hunched over a clipboard as he jotted something onto a sheet of paper. I started toward him, then stopped, wondering if Tony had been among the men who'd kidnapped Jason, who had assaulted Paul when he'd tried to intervene.

I continued cautiously toward the booth until I was close enough to catch his eye. If he'd been blameless, outraged by what they'd done to us, it would be apparent in the first moment he saw me.

Tony finished writing and looked up from his paper. His eyes narrowed when he realized it was me, his expression caged and measured. If he was surprised to see me—if he was relieved that I'd shown up here alive—he didn't show it. It broke my heart, that guarded expression. I'd always liked Tony, had always felt that he was one of the good guys. But I saw now that they'd gotten to him as well. And if they'd gotten to Tony, then they'd gotten to everyone. There was nothing left for me here.

"Nice to have you back, Doc," he said, but his eyes had returned to the clipboard, and when I turned my back on him to walk away, I don't think he even bothered to look up.

Part Five

Checking Out

Chapter 49

Menaker,

After all that has happened, I know that I shouldn't have stayed. It sounds ridiculous, even in my own ears, to allege that the place meant to do me harm from the beginning. How could it? The events that took place here were caused by the actions of people, not the institution itself. A series of brick buildings and open grounds do not have the capacity to plan, to conspire, to hate. Accusing Menaker of such things is merely an act of displacement. It is easier for me to blame the place than the people whom I once trusted.

And yet . . .

Places have a memory. A house in which people were murdered is never the same again. Evil and violence have a way of settling into the walls like toxic chemicals. Over time, those chemicals will seep from the pores of the drywall. They will poison the people residing there if given the chance.

I suspect the same thing has happened here. I cannot pass the front steps of the administration building without picturing Paul's beaten face staring up at me, without hearing the wet sound of his breathing as a weak cough racks his body and speckles his lips with a fine mist of blood. Walking by the fence at the west end of the property conjures images of Jason—the way he used to look at me with a mixture of tortured hope and resignation, as if he were forever trapped in his own private purgatory.

The buildings and grounds are a constant reminder of such things, but the hatred that I feel pulsing from the brick and iron skin of Menaker doesn't come from those memories, but from the place itself. *Is it possible for a place to be evil, for it to have enough ill will to elicit violence instead of just witnessing it?* Yes, I think that it is. I think there are some places—just as there are some people—that cannot respond in any other way.

Menaker is alive, and like all living things it must feed. It fed on the eye of the groundskeeper, Kendrick Jones, four years ago when a wayward branch punched through the globe and left him blind on that side. It fed on Paul and Jason, and has been feeding on its chief administrator, Dr. Wagner, for decades now. It has fed on me, too—will continue to feed for as long as I remain here.

Two months have passed since Jason's disappearance, since my abduction and subsequent release. The fractured bones of my right forearm have healed and the splint has been removed. The arm aches sometimes—the area where I broke it. Maybe it always will.

I never did call the police, never reported Jason's kidnapping or my own abduction, never notified the FBI that two imposters had been posing as special agents. What good would it have done? No one would've believed me. It was Wagner's word against mine, and the staff here have clearly been intimidated into backing *his* story, not mine. "You've caused enough trouble here," Wagner told me during our first encounter after my return. "What evidence can you cite for any of this? Any remaining credibility you have will be ruined."

Why, then, did he not fire me? After all that has happened, he must know that I can't be trusted, that I remain a liability. But he allows me to continue here, I think, for the same reason that compels me to stay. We are keeping track of each other, circling, gauging each other's weaknesses.

I continue to take care of my patients. If my experience with Jason has taught me anything, it's that I'm responsible for what happens to the people hospitalized here. I'm not the only one who knows how nasty this place can be, but I feel that I'm the only one left with the courage and dignity to fight it. Menaker will feed on the people here for as long as it remains standing, the weakest among them—the patients—most of all. I can't leave them, cannot walk away and allow it to happen in my absence. I have failed my patients in many other ways, but I owe them that much, at least.

Menaker doesn't like it, this interference. It does not want to be watched while it eats. It hates me and I hate it right back, and someday it will figure out a way to get rid of me. A tree will fall, perhaps, crushing my head in one swift motion. A patient will attack, killing me before anyone can intervene. It will be called an accident or a horrible tragedy. But the people who work and live here will know differently.

Until that time comes—and maybe even after—I have assumed the role of the resident ghost. I show up each day, do my job, and return home to my small apartment in the evenings. The hospital staff ignores me as much as possible. I have fallen into the habit of interacting only with my patients. Still, I keep a close eye on what is happening. I have considered burning the place to the ground, to wipe it off the face of the earth. There is even a remote possibility that I might succeed, although Menaker would take with it a good number of the patients—maybe all of them. The doors would not open. People wouldn't be able to get out. Many of them would asphyxiate in the smoke. Some of them would burn alive. I couldn't live with that. So I wait for my chance, consider the options and weigh the risks. My guard is always up.

I am waiting to act.

Chapter 50

It was either Monday or Thursday. I wasn't certain because I no longer kept track of the days. When every day is the same, it doesn't really matter. For the past month, I've been showing up to work seven days a week. I liked weekends the best because Wagner wasn't here and the staffing was minimal. But today was either Monday or Thursday because Kendrick Jones was raking leaves, and he always reserved that activity for those days during the fall. We were into October now, my favorite month, when Maryland is at its most beautiful. The piles of leaves were so thick and plentiful they reminded me of the clover field from *Horton Hears a Who*, the elephant having spent all afternoon inspecting them one by one during his desperate search for his microscopic friends. I raised my hand to Kendrick, who—like the pachyderm—was working diligently among the piles. He smiled and waved back, the milky white opacity of his blind right eye glistening in the early-afternoon sunlight.

Unlike the others, Kendrick remained cordial. Maybe it was because we'd both lost something irreplaceable to Menaker. I didn't know if he hated the place as much as I did, but I suspected the resentment was there. I sensed it in the way he worked so hard at maintaining the property, combating the deterioration and hopelessness it exudes. Perhaps he saw it as a test of wills, his blind eye flashing like a war wound—a testament to his refusal to surrender to the forces at work here.

"Afternoon, Lise," he said, scooping up a pile of leaves and stuffing them into a large black yard bag.

"Hey, Kendrick," I replied, glancing around at the scattered mounds of burgundy and gold. "Looks like you've got your work cut out for you today."

"Ev'ry day," he said, and offered me a crooked smile, lowered his voice, assumed a conspiratorial tone. "Menaker, she got somethin' waitin' for me ev'ry day."

I looked at him, nodded. "It's got something waiting for me, too, I think."

The upper lid of his left eye—the good one—closed and opened. I couldn't tell if he was winking at me or if it was just a slow blink. The lid of the blind eye hadn't moved.

He stooped at the waist and gathered another armful of leaves, his knees making a soft popping sound.

"Gettin' stiff," he admitted. The armful of leaves disappeared into the yawning mouth of a yard bag, and he stood up, stretched his back, one hand on each hip. "Feel myself slowin' down sometimes," he told me, almost apologetically. "Can't help it. Gettin' old. Turned eighty-four today, ya know."

"You did?" I asked, embarrassed that I hadn't known, but also surprised at the man's age. Kendrick's body had a gnarled and broken look about it. But still, eighty-four was much older than I'd pegged him for. "Why are you *working* today? You should be taking the day off."

"Oh, yah? Ta do what?"

"I don't know." I thought it over for a second, was suddenly struck with an idea. "How 'bout I take you out for dinner after work today."

"Dinner," he responded, as if it were some extravagant luxury enjoyed only by the superrich.

"Yeah, dinner," I said, warming up to the notion. "Nothing fancy, just . . ." I considered the options, then landed on a good one, something I thought he might enjoy. "I'll take you to Marj's Kitchen."

"*Where?*"

"Marj's Kitchen," I repeated, surprised he hadn't heard of it.

He sighed, shook his head.

"What?"

"No, Lise." He studied me for a moment. That cool, one-eye gaze made me want to fidget, but I stood still, resisting the urge. "We're not goin' out ta dinner after work. That's never goin' ta happen. You understan' that, don't ya?"

Quite frankly, I didn't. "I'm sorry," I said, not apologizing for the offer exactly but simply sorry I'd gone out on a limb in an attempt to be friendly. *What* was it *about this place that made people want to hurt each other?*

I moved on, continued past him in the direction of the north end of the property. When he called out to me, I almost didn't hear.

"What?" I asked, turning around. The October sun was already sliding down from its pinnacle in the sky. I had to shield my eyes with one hand to look at him.

"He's back, ya know. They won't let ya see him on account of everythin' that happened, but—"

"Who? Who are you talking about?"

He paused for a moment, maybe unsure if he was doing the right thing in telling me. "Jason," he said. "Jason is back."

My stomach rose and fell like a ship on the open water. It was a sickening, disorienting sensation.

"Where?"

Kendrick held up a hand. "Now, listen," he warned me. "He's not supposed ta even be here. Dr. Wagner was very clear about—"

"*Screw Wagner. Where is he?*"

The old man was looking trapped now, but I wasn't about to let him go.

"You can't just go barreling in there and—"

"*Where?*" The front of his shirt was bunched in my hands. "*Where, goddammit!*"

"Stop, Lise. You're hurting me."

I released him, stood there looking down at my hands, breathing hard.

"*You tell me right now.*"

"I . . . I can't," he said, his voice cracking a bit. "I shouldn't have said nothin'. I'm just a stupid ol' man who doesn't know enough ta keep his *damn mouth shut.*"

"*Where?*" I persisted, but I was only half listening now. My eyes had moved up to the ratty brown belt Kendrick used to cinch his pants. There was a leather holster clipped to the right side of that belt, and from it protruded the dual handles of a pair of garden shears.

Dr. Wagner was very clear about—Kendrick had said. *You can't just go barreling in there*—

I realized then: the one place off-limits to the patient population and most of the staff here, a place where Wagner would have easy, unfettered access to him. I'd been inside the building only once myself, and that excursion had been . . . a little rushed.

My actions over the next sixty seconds required no thought, no deliberation. I reached out with my left hand and snatched the shears from their holster. The tips were tapered to a fine point, the blades held together in a closed position by a small metal clasp near the grips. If Kendrick protested or made a move to stop me, I wasn't aware of it because I was running across the yard toward the front steps of the administration building, taking them two at a time. When I reached the upper landing there was a brief flash of Paul's body lying there, the gash in his scalp pumping a steady stream of bright red blood that saturated my jacket as I pressed it against the wound. I tried the front door, found it locked, then turned and headed back down the steps, around the building to the door at the back of the complex. It, too, was locked—*yes, of course it was*—but the rear door had a window that shattered easily with one blow of a palm-size stone I ripped from the ground. I reached through, flipped the deadbolt, swung the door open, and stepped inside.

The lower level of the building was unchanged from the last time I'd been in here. Dust lay thick on the windowsills. There was a damp, mildewed smell to the place, as if the files kept here were already in an advanced state of decay—the records of the past being methodically erased so that the suffering and injustices could be repeated all over again.

I moved quickly down the hall. At the intersection, I glanced left toward the end of the hallway and the bathroom from which I'd narrowly escaped capture, wondered whether my blood—dry and flaking—still lingered on the wooden frame

of the window. Something told me that it did, that Menaker
wanted it that way.

I turned right, walked to the other end of the hall, swung
the door open, and stepped into the stairwell. The door closed
quickly behind me—too quickly—would've slammed if I hadn't
reached out and stopped it with my hand. I eased it shut. The
hinges—previously soundless—let out a tortured shriek that
filled the stairwell, making me wince. Menaker was trying to
stop me, or to at least alert the others to my presence. Ascending
the stairs, I kept toward the side where I could hold on to the
handrail, expecting to slip or feel one of the steps give way beneath me. I reached the top, my heart beating loudly in my chest,
but when I pushed on the door's bar it refused to budge.

Locked.

There was no reason (*trying to stop you*) for the door to the
stairwell to be locked. It didn't make sense. I engaged the push
bar again, readied myself, then threw the weight of my body forward, hitting the door with my right shoulder. It moved slightly,
still trying to resist me. I took a step back, lunged forward, and
hit it again. This time it gave, swung wide, smashing into the wall
behind it, the splintering thud echoing through the open lobby.

*By now they must know that I'm coming for him. Anyone in this
building would've heard that.*

I paused long enough to check the other side of the door.
There was no locking mechanism. A skid of paint marked the
door's edge, matching the paint on the doorway's inner frame.
The door itself had not been recently painted, only the frame.
Although why anyone would—

To stop you. It wants to stop you.

I stood there in the lobby, listening. At first, all I could hear was the sound of my own breathing, loud in my ears. I held my breath, remained perfectly still.

Nothing. The place was empty except for my—

No. No, wait. There were voices now, their volumes low and subtle—behind at least one closed door, coming from this level. Crossing the lobby, I proceeded down a hall to my right. The discussion grew louder—and yes, one of them sounded like Wagner, his tone stern, lecturing.

The administrative building was of modest size, and it didn't take me long to home in on their location. I made a right, then another right—found myself standing in front of a closed door. There were no placards or markings to announce the room's purpose, just the sound of Wagner's scolding words coming from the other side. And then, in response, the softer pitch of a voice I hadn't heard in a long time.

In my left hand were the shears. For a moment they looked like a knife, and I wondered what exactly I intended to do with them. In a quick motion, I transferred the instrument to my right hand.

My senses were heightened. I could hear the distant sound of traffic from the streets beyond Menaker's iron-guarded perimeter. There was a slight chill, a breeze on my back, as if I were standing in the open night air instead of in the closed quarters of this vacant hallway. My muscles twitched and jumped beneath the thin veil of my skin, my breathing slow and even now, my jaw set as I reached forward and turned the knob.

The door opened soundlessly and I entered a short inner hallway. There was a conference room at the far end, its door already opened. The first thing I saw was Jason's once-familiar figure silhouetted against the window. His black hair hung limply over his forehead, covering the small scar that marked his left temple. He looked haggard, defeated, maybe even drugged. His eyes registered nothing. The shoulders of his thin frame slumped forward, reminding me of the man I saw through the small window of my cell that first day of captivity. There was a quiet desperation in the way he struggled to hold himself erect.

Another man entered my line of sight. His back was to me, but I could tell right away that it was Wagner. He was spouting a rebuke, admonishing Jason, and whether this was part of an interrogation I didn't know and didn't care. I took a step forward. The floorboard creaked loudly beneath my left foot as Menaker dutifully alerted them.

Wagner stopped talking, turned around. Over his shoulder, I could see Jason's face studying me as well. I took another step forward.

"*No*," Wagner said. "This is a private meeting and you are not permitted to be here."

"You go straight to hell," I told him.

"Lise." He was at the far end of the hallway now, taking tentative steps in my direction. "It is dangerous for you to be here. It is dangerous for all of us. How did you even—"

"I'm not leaving here without him."

Another step forward. He held up both hands to show me there was nothing in them. "You don't understand what is happening here."

"I understand enough," I said, trying to keep my voice level. "And one way or the other, I'm taking him with me."

"But where would you take him?" he asked. "Have you even thought of—"

"Doesn't matter. Away from here. And if you raise an alarm or try to stop me"—I locked eyes with him, so he would know that I meant every word—"I will kill you."

His eyes dropped to my hands for the first time, and he saw the shears. "Oh," he said, appearing not so much frightened as fascinated by the sharp metal blades nestled there. "This plays into it, doesn't it?"

I didn't take the bait, didn't bother to ask him what he was talking about. Wagner's gaze slid along the walls of the narrow hallway, touched upon the open door behind me. Again, I could hear the distant sounds of traffic, could feel the chill of the night air coming through the open doorway.

Wagner's head cocked to one side, the look of a praying mantis as he studied me. "Do you know where you are right now?" he asked, and I felt a thin sliver of fear at the question.

"Shut up, and get out of my way," I responded, raising the shears in front of me.

"You are at Menaker, you know. I am Dr. Charles Wagner."

"I know who you are."

"This is not a town house in Silver Spring, Maryland. It is daytime, not night."

"Stop it."

"You are here because you are concerned about Jason's safety. You suspect that I am cooperating with a group of Islamic extremists. You have come to confront me in his presence, haven't you?"

I stared back at him.

"But I am not Jason's domestic partner, Amir Massoud. This is not the evening of May 12, 2010."

"I know what year it is."

"Do you? Do you really?"

For the space of a few seconds, neither one of us spoke.

"Because this is exactly what happened on that night, isn't it? You showed up at their town house, argued in the hallway. I don't know if you planned to kill him or if it was more of an accident—the confrontation turning physical and quickly getting out of control. But you did bring a knife, Lise, and that suggests premeditation. And now . . ."

He looked down at my right hand again, the one holding the shears. We both did. I could feel the hallway tilting a bit, like the long circular tube of a fun house.

"I am Dr. Lise Shields, a psychiatrist at this hospital."

Wagner shook his head no, offered me a sad but compassionate smile.

"I am Dr. Lise—" I began again, but he cut me off before I could finish.

"You are not a psychiatrist. You are a patient here."

The tube was spinning faster now. I put a hand on the wall to steady myself.

A trick, I warned myself. *This is one of Wagner's tricks, some form of hypnosis. When he sees the opportunity, he will go for the knife.*

Shears, I corrected myself. *He will go for the shears.* I looked down at them again to be certain.

"You gave us quite a scare, taking off like that." The sound of his voice made me jump.

"What?"

"Your escape from Menaker," he said.

"They kidnapped Jason and attacked Paul—tried to capture me, too. That's why I had to run."

"No one kidnapped Jason. And as for Paul . . . *you* attacked Paul. Stole his keys. It's how you managed to escape."

"That's bullshit," I replied. "Paul gave them to me."

"You broke your arm going through that bathroom window downstairs. You're lucky it wasn't worse."

A thought occurred to me then—proof that what he was telling me was a pack of lies.

"Haden. They killed him right in front of me."

"Who's Haden?" Wagner asked.

"The man who took me in, the one who was helping me."

He looked puzzled. "This is the first time I've heard that name."

"They executed him, Charles. We started to surrender and they shot him in the chest and neck. I watched him bleed out in that field."

"Are you referring to the place where the police eventually picked you up, on that wildlife refuge on the Eastern Shore?"

"It wasn't the police."

He shook his head. "You were found alone in that refuge. You'd stolen a boat and a gun from *who knows* where." He scowled at me with a look of severe disapproval. "The rifle was loaded, you know. When I think about what could've happened, about how badly you could've been injured . . . or even killed . . ."

"Haden died in that field," I said, trying to hold on to at least one irrefutable truth. "He was innocent, blameless, and there was nothing I could do to stop it. He was . . . he was my friend, Charles."

"I'm sorry, Lise," he responded. He was not conceding the point, I realized—only expressing empathy for my pain.

"The FBI," I countered, although it felt like I was grasping at straws now.

"Do you mean Special Agents Daryl Linder and Aaron Remy?"

"How do you—?"

"You've told me about them many times before. Don't you remember?"

I put a hand to my head.

"They're part of the delusion, Lise. Daryl Linder and Aaron Remy do not exist. In fact"—he smiled disarmingly—"their names are most likely based on medications you've come in contact with here at Menaker. Remeron, from which I believe you constructed the name Aaron Remy, is an antidepressant. Inderal, from which you've created Daryl Linder, is a drug used to control medication-induced akathisia." He paused a moment, looking at me. "You *do* know what akathisia is, don't you? If you're indeed a psychiatrist, as you profess to be, I'm sure you're familiar with the term."

I didn't answer. *Couldn't* answer.

"Akathisia is profound restlessness," he told me. "Any third-year medical student would know that."

"I have an apartment," I argued. "If I was a patient here and not a doctor, I couldn't just—"

"You have a room here at the hospital, and I can assure you that except for your recent escape you haven't set foot off this property for the past five years. Although you sometimes try to. Our security officers have become quite adept at making sure you find your way to the right place."

Out for a walk, Lise?—a recollection of Tony Perkins, calling out to me from the watchman's booth at the front gate.

Goin' home, Tony, I replied, but he held up a hand for me to stop a second.

Let me get someone to escort you. Make sure you get there safe.

"Lies," I muttered, backing up a step, my weight against the wall. It was becoming difficult to breathe.

"For five years," Wagner advised me, as if reading my thoughts, "you have been a patient here at Menaker. I've tried so many times to confront you with the truth. But the nature of a delusion is that it remains fixed and unchanged despite all evidence to the contrary. I could see that direct confrontation wasn't working. You simply refused to hear it, or shut me out altogether."

He ran a hand across his face. Sighed.

"You have paranoid schizophrenia, Lise. Like your uncle."

"No."

"There's a genetic component, you realize—a tendency for the disease to run in families."

(*You and I got a lot in common, Lise.* Uncle Jim with one arm around my shoulders. *We see things differently than other people.*)

"I became a psychiatrist *because* of what happened with Uncle Jim."

"I know that you think so. But look at the symptoms: agitation, social withdrawal, declining personal hygiene, disinterest in pleasurable activities. Complex auditory and visual hallucinations."

"I am . . . Dr. Lise Shields."

"Tasked with a critical mission to save your patient from a radical extremist group receiving information from a mole within the CIA." He looked at me. "*Don't you see?* These are delusions, Lise—delusions of grandeur and persecution. You have disturbances of behavior, thought, and perception—hallmark features of schizophrenia."

(*Sometimes my mind plays tricks on me . . . I'll get an idea in my head that I can't shake, something that isn't right but seems right at the time.*)

"It's your disease that brought you here in the first place,"

Wagner continued. "Five years ago, something horrible happened because of it. You'd been getting sicker, had stopped taking your medication, developed certain delusions about Jason's partner, Amir. You became convinced that you were working for the CIA, that Amir was plotting with terrorists, that he planned to blow up a D.C. subway station. Do you see now how detached from reality you'd become?"

He waited for me to answer. I said nothing.

What brings you to see us tonight? I imagined the way Amir might have smiled, holding the door open and inviting her in. Inviting *me* in.

"I KNOW WHAT you've been planning." The words tasted bitter in my mouth.

"Planning?" The smile had not left his face, but there was something else there as well. Was it puzzlement? Guilt? The face of a liar finally confronted with the truth?

"I know about the meetings with Al-Termir, about the plot to bomb the D.C. subway station. I followed you last week into the District."

"You followed me—"

"Shut up and listen. I am here because of Jason. I've tried to warn him, but he refuses to believe me—loves you too much to think you could be capable of something like that. At one point, maybe I did too. But I've seen the photographs, Amir. I've listened to the tapes of your conversations with them."

"I really don't know what you're talking about," he replied, reaching out with one hand to touch me. I swatted it away.

"Because of who you are to me and my family," I could hear myself saying, "I've decided to warn you—to give you a chance to back away from this thing before it's too late. If you cooperate with helping us catch them, we can put you into a witness protection program—you and Jason both. You'll be safe there, protected from retribution. There's still time. You don't have to go through with this."

"I'm sorry, Lise," he said. "I'm going to have to ask you to leave."

"No."

"Excuse me?"

"I won't go. Not without him. He's not safe here with you any longer."

He put a hand on my shoulder, more forcefully now, and attempted to move me toward the door.

But I'd meant what I said. I wasn't leaving without Jason. I grabbed Amir at the wrist, twisting it in my hand. He yelled out, surprised, tried to pull away. The heel of my right hand flashed out, striking him in the chest. He was shoved backward against the wall, his body bouncing off it and coming back at me. We collided, the force of his momentum toppling us—him forward, and me backward. The back of my head connected with the hardwood floor with a loud crack that filled the hallway. A split second later, he landed on me, the impact snapping ribs, forcing the air from my lungs.

It was like the time I pulled him from his bed—Amir delirious from the fever and influenza, his body landing on top of me on the floor. Only this time he was awake, aware, looming over me with murder in his eyes: for me, for Jason, for the people in the subway station he intended to sacrifice as a political statement against the country in which he was born.

Why did I not anticipate this? After all that I have witnessed, why am I still surprised that he would try to kill me? I reached for my service weapon, slung high in its shoulder holster under my left arm, but for some reason it was not there. Maybe I just couldn't reach it, couldn't bring my right arm across my body with the weight of him on top of me. The world began to blanch, Amir's face floating above me like a balloon tethered to his shoulders.

But the knife was with me. I had brought it just in case.

I arched my lower back, worked my right hand into the space created by the curve of my spine. My fingers closed around the small dark handle and I delivered the knife from its leather casing—a last-ditch effort as I slipped away into the whiteness all around me. *I will be dead soon*, I realized. *We all will.*

I was so far gone that I did not feel my right arm completing its half circle, driving the weapon home between the fifth and sixth ribs.

He grunted. The world began to slide back into focus. He was pushing himself up with his hands, the weight of his body lifting off me. There was a look of surprise in his expression. Bewilderment. He had his knees under him now, moved a hand to the side of his chest, then raised it in front of his face. It hung there—slick with blood—in the air between us, scattered drops cascading onto my forehead.

You baptize me in the name of the Father, I thought, *and of the Son, and of the . . .*

"Why?" he managed, his breathing thick and labored, the hand still dangling in the air between us. Amir looked past it, into my eyes, and for a moment the events that had brought us here were jumbled in my mind. *Is he just awakening from the fever?* I wondered.

The strength in his arms and legs failed, and I guided him to the side as his body went limp on top of me. Air surged into my lungs in deep whooping breaths. The color of the room fell back into place, and with it, the image of Jason looking down on us—the ovals of his eyes wide with horror, his clawed hands filling the slim hollows of his cheeks, the silent scream unable to pass beyond the circle of his lips.

"WHAT HAPPENED THAT night was a tragedy."

I blinked twice, found myself in the hallway of the administration building once again.

"For everyone," Wagner continued. "But you can't change that fact by hiding from it. Amir is gone."

(*No. He's* not *gone. Help me move him to the couch. We've got to—*)

"But you've disappeared, too, Lise. You've chosen to become someone else entirely—a benevolent psychiatrist at a state mental hospital, instead of the guilt-ridden patient who resides here."

I stood with my head lowered, trying to think. *This is how they brainwash you*, I told myself.

"My office was broken into."

"*My* office that *you* trashed," Wagner replied. "I had to move into a new one." He paused, hands clasped in front of him. "Everything has an explanation—an explanation far more plausible than the story you've concocted."

I looked up at Jason, who was watching me from the far end of the hallway.

You've got a visitor, Marjorie advised me from the nurses' station.

Is this going to be one of mine?

She nodded. *I think you should see this one.*

I turned my eyes to Wagner now. "Who is he to me?"

"Pardon?"

"Jason," I said, knowing the answer already, but not believing it—needing to hear it spoken out loud.

"Oh," Wagner replied. "I assumed that much was obvious. It's why he keeps coming here to see you, why—despite everything—he refuses to give up on you. It's why he returned today, in fact, even though I told him he should stay away for a while, that his visits only make you worse." He studied me for a few seconds. The inquisitive look was gone. Now he only seemed sad and a little tired. "Do you really not know who this man is standing behind me? Even when you were growing up, you've always been protective of him."

For a moment, I could picture Jason when he was much younger, could see him sitting up and looking at me from his hospital bed the night after Billy Myers and his fellow bullies beat him into a state of unconsciousness.

This will not happen again, I'd assured him that night, and three weeks later I'd backed that promise up with a Louisville Slugger and a fit of detached violence that almost left all four of those boys dead. Was it any surprise that five years ago I'd stepped in again when I thought his life was in danger, this time with lethal results?

"I don't believe y—" I started to tell Wagner, but Jason was pushing past him now, coming for me down the hall. I met his eyes, and the last of the denial fell away. I was crying now—crying because of what I had done to him and what I was doing to him still. "I'm sorry," I told him, but he didn't stop coming, didn't even hesitate.

"I'm sorry, I'm sorry, I'm so goddamn sorry," I was saying over and over again. He wrapped his arms around me as I buried my face in the side of his neck. He rocked me, told me it was okay, and that he forgave me a long time ago—that all he wanted was to have me back again.

"I will *never* give up on you—*never*," he promised, and I held on to him tighter, unable to let go.

"Thank you for not leaving me here," I whispered. "I'm so alone without y—"

My voice choked up again, the words refusing to come. But it was all right because I wasn't alone anymore. No matter what happened after this, I knew I would be okay—that *we* would be okay. Because the only truly hopeless thing in this world is to be abandoned—forsaken for what you have done—and I could see now that this would never happen. Not between *us*. Not between me and my brother.

Something was gently lifted from my hand. I opened my eyes and saw Wagner standing there, watching me over Jason's shoulder. "I need to take these," he said, giving the thing in my hand a soft tug. I opened my fingers and let go of the shears, or maybe it was the knife that I'd been holding on to these past five years. I wasn't certain, didn't really care. I didn't need either of them any longer.

The past is what imprisons us. There are some things in this world that can never be undone. But they *can* be faced. They can be forgiven. And if we hold on to that, then there is a chance for us. A chance that someday . . . we will be free.

Chapter 51

We spent the rest of the day together, Jason and I. It was good to be with him, to see him for who he really was. For five years he'd been coming here to visit me, trying to break through. *What must that have been like for him?* I wonder— all those years. I could barely imagine. Any attempt to confront me with the truth, he explained, had caused me to disengage completely, to fall into myself for weeks, sometimes months at a time. There had been no choice but to work within the delusion I'd created. It was the only way to interact with me, the only type of relationship I could tolerate.

He and Dr. Wagner had disagreed about his visits. Wagner was convinced that Jason's presence triggered something in me— that on some level I recognized him for who he actually was, and that this made the delusions worse, not better. The attack on Paul and my escape from the facility had brought the disagreement to a head, and Wagner barred Jason from visiting for the indefinite future. I'd spent a week and a half in seclusion following my return to Menaker, and it was more than two months until Wagner finally agreed to meet with Jason to discuss the possibility of resuming visitations. It was what brought Jason here today, that meeting. He'd never stopped trying, never lost hope that one day there would be a breakthrough. And now . . .

I have awakened. But what have I awakened to? I am thirty-three years old and the murderer of my brother's partner—a man he loved and shared his life with. Amir was good to Jason, returned his love as fiercely as it was given. He was kind and gentle, welcomed me into their home, and the way I returned his trust and affection was to drive a knife into his heart. My delusions are a window to my prejudice, feeding on a stereotype I'd accepted blindly, refused to question. If Amir had been a different race, if the color of his skin had looked like mine, would he still be dead? For how many years have I attempted to shield my own brother from such hatred and bigotry, only to find it within myself.

When the killing was over, when there was no taking it back, I retreated into a mental illness that would never leave, would be the dominant force in my life. I have seen it happen with my mother's depression. With my uncle's schizophrenia. The genetic code has found its way to me, condemning me from the point of conception. Is it too much to imagine that Menaker somehow knew—had been waiting for me all these years?

How much of what I experienced as Dr. Shields was real? How much was imagined? What happened during the two days I spent beyond these iron pickets? Was there ever a Haden— someone who drove me to the hospital, sheltered me in his home one night, tried to help me? If so, what became of him? If not, what *really* happened out there?

(*Sometimes my mind plays tricks on me. I hear things, mostly. People talking to me who aren't there. They say . . . They say horrible* things . . . *That's the hell of it, you know: separating out what's real from what's not real. Trying to keep things straight. Knowing when your mind is playing tricks on you.*)

I asked Jason if he remembered the summer Uncle Jim stayed with us. He'd been five then, and memories of those early years are often vague, even absent. He told me that he remembered something of that time, but the details were lost. More so, he remembered my lingering reaction to that summer, how closed off I became in the years that followed.

There were other questions to ask. I wanted to know about Jason's life now, about his career and relationships, about the man he'd become. I interrupted him sometimes, told him over and over how sorry I was for what I'd done. I couldn't escape the guilt, the horror of this thing I did not want to remember. He reminded me that I was ill, that I was delusional and psychotic, not responsible for my actions. It seemed inconceivable that he had forgiven me. I did not deserve it. I do not think that I ever will.

He tried to fill in some of the blanks in my life, told me about the health of our parents. Our father suffered a heart attack two years ago. Since then he'd become a different type of man—scared and frail beyond his years, but also kinder, more accepting. His relationship with my brother was still not a close one—was still strained at times. But it seemed that a truce of sorts had been established—and *that*, Jason said, was a start. In time, maybe something better would come from it.

Our mother's physical health remained strong, but she continued to struggle with a depression that may someday consume her. There were medications, of course, and she took them obediently. But I, more than anyone, realized there were limitations to what medications could conquer.

"Do they ever visit me?" I asked. There was still so much I could not remember, so many darkened rooms in my mind.

"Sometimes," he said. "You don't recognize them. It hurts them to see you."

As NIGHT CLOSED in, Jason asked Dr. Wagner for permission to stay beyond normal visiting hours, to join me for dinner in the hospital's cafeteria. Wagner gave his consent, and we sat at the large wooden table among the other patients as Marj laid out the evening meal.

"The good doctor arrives," Tim Barrens announced through a mouthful of mac and cheese as we joined the group already settled at the table.

"A lady of questionable credentials, blown in from the night wind," Manny Linwood agreed, wiping at his chin with a napkin. It was their nightly repertoire here in Marj's kitchen, but this time I shook my head and told them no, it was only me, Lise Edwards. Dr. Shields died unexpectedly this afternoon—and though I mourned the safety of her company, she would not be missed.

After dinner, Jason and I walked to the front gates of Menaker. Tony Perkins stepped out from the watchman's booth, asked if I needed someone to walk me home. I smiled at that, told him that tonight—for once—I was okay on my own.

"Good night, Jason," I said, brushing his hair back so that I could see the scar, kiss him on the cheek.

"Good night, Lise," he replied, giving me one last hug before he turned to go.

I stood and watched as he walked to his car beyond the fence. He opened his door, turned to wave, and I waved back. The engine started, and he pulled out onto the street, turned right, and disappeared around the corner. I listened until the receding sound of the engine was gobbled up by the night.

Then I turned from the gate and headed back to where I belonged.

Chapter 52

'd hoped that I might be finished with thoughts of Uncle Jim for a while, that with the death of Dr. Shields those memories would retreat to the far recesses of my mind. I didn't need them anymore, didn't want them. What happened with Uncle Jim took place a long time ago, and whether I was to blame for his actions was less important to me now—or at least seemed that way.

AFTER THE POLICE took him away that night, I didn't see him for two and a half months. He was working hard to get better, my mother told me. It was best to let him concentrate on that for a while. Dad scoffed at this. "He's never going to get better," he piped in from the other room. The words sounded a little slurred. "Don't tell the kid her crazy uncle is going to get better when he won't."

My mother and I looked toward the living room's entryway—toward the sound of his voice—then back at each other. "He will," she whispered, and it was a strange thing because I resented *both* of them at that moment—my father for giving voice to what

I suspected to be true, and my mother for promising me something she could never deliver.

"I want to go see him," I told her.

"No way," my father replied from the other room, and my mother just shook her head.

"It's not a good idea, Lise. It's not a place for children."

"I'm almost nine," I said. "I'm not a child anymore."

She gave me a long discerning look, and I stared back at her defiantly.

"We'll see," she said before rising to her feet and heading down the hall and into her bedroom. I watched her close the door behind her, closing me out yet again.

I kept at it, though—didn't give up on the idea. I pestered her about it every chance I got, but I made sure to do it when my father wasn't around. He'd already made his decision on the matter clear.

Children learn early on that there is almost no limit to what can be obtained from a parent through relentless, dogged persistence. I applied that lesson with my mother, and after eight weeks of asking she finally gave in. She drove me and Jason to school that morning but told me to stay in the car while she walked my brother to his classroom. I sat there fiddling with my seat belt, peering through the window as my classmates filed out of the school buses, and waited for her return. When she got back in the car, I looked over at her expectantly.

"You still want to see Uncle Jim?" she asked, and I nodded.

She put the car in gear, drove out of the school's parking lot, and a few minutes later we were merging into traffic on the highway. I didn't ask how long it would take to get there, didn't bother her with an endless stream of chatter. Instead, I sat very quietly in my seat, knowing that at any moment she could change her mind, turn around, and take me back to school. Hadn't my mother said that where we were heading was not a place for children? Hadn't my father forbidden it?

We drove on in silence. Forty minutes later she exited the freeway, and after a few more minutes we pulled into a large parking lot. The place didn't look much like a hospital—at least, not what I'd imagined. In a way, it looked very similar to Menaker: a series of small buildings stretched out across an open campus. I don't remember if there was a fence around the perimeter, but I don't think there was. Back in those days people were less careful, more trusting. My mother turned to me in the car before we got out.

"Not a word of this to your father," she said. "You understand?"

I nodded.

She studied me for a moment, then opened her door and stepped out into the brisk morning air. I did the same.

There was a lot of walking. It seemed to take a long time to get to the Visitors' Building. I moved quickly, concentrating on matching her stride, walking beside her—not behind her like a child—and every once in a while I looked up to read the expression on her face, to see if she was pleased with how I was conducting myself. Her face was stern, her lips drawn together in a tight little circle, and she never looked down at me—not once. But I thought she was pleased anyway, that this was something she and I were doing together and she was proud of me for coming.

At the Visitors' Building, she opened the door and we stepped inside. In front of us was a large reception desk with a bored-looking woman sitting behind it.

"Good morning," my mother said to her. "I'm Carol Edwards

and this is my daughter, Lise. I called yesterday to inquire about visiting Jim Casey."

"Visiting hours don't start until nine thirty," the woman advised her, the expression on her face never changing. A quick glance at a large clock to our left revealed that it was only a little after nine.

"We'll wait," my mother told her.

"No children under ten are allowed in the facility."

"She's ten and a half," my mother responded. It was the first time I ever heard her lie.

The woman gave me an appraising look. "When's your birthday, sweetheart?"

"April fourteenth, 1980," I said. I wasn't nine yet, let alone ten, but it wasn't too difficult to subtract two years from my real birthday.

The woman's eyes remained on my face for a second longer, then she sighed and looked back down at the paperback she was holding. "You can wait over there," she said, meaning the chairs along the wall behind us and to our left. She didn't bother to exert the energy it would've taken to point or nod in their direction.

"Thank you," my mother said.

"Mmm-hmmm," the woman intoned, her eyes scanning the pages in front of her.

We sat in the hard plastic chairs and waited. At 9:25, the woman rose from behind the reception desk. We both looked up expectantly, but she waddled toward the front doors, pushed through them, and stood just outside while she lit up a cigarette. I watched her through the glass pane of the door, remembered how Uncle Jim used to smoke them down to the filter, passing the smooth paper-rolled cylinder over to me every once in a while when he was certain my parents weren't looking. My mother and I sat there, waited for her to finish, the clock's minute hand moving around to eight before she opened the front door again and walked in.

"You can go and see him now," she told us, lowering herself into the receptionist's chair, a little out of breath from her strenuous walk to the desk. "Exit the doors behind me and go to the third building on your right. Tell the security officer at the front desk who you're here to see. Clip these visitor badges to your shirts and make sure you display them at all times."

We did as we were told, walking across the campus until we arrived at the appropriate building.

"He's in the activity room," the security guard advised when we checked in at the front desk. We proceeded down the hall to a large room with many patients. The activities that took place in the activity room, I noticed, mostly revolved around watching daytime television from one of the many tattered chairs and couches. The channel was tuned to a soap opera. On the screen, a woman with big hair and too much makeup was dabbing at her eyes with a handkerchief.

The thing I remember most about him, about the last time I ever saw him, was how much *better* he looked. His face had filled out some, and his body—which had become painfully thin in the weeks leading up to his arrest—looked stronger now, healthier. His hair was shorter and still wet from his morning shower, no longer greasy and in need of a wash like during his final days at our house. And his eyes—turning in our direction as we entered the room and lighting up right away when he saw me—were as clear as they were on the first day he came to stay with us, the brightness there making me think: *This is him. This is Uncle Jim without the disease. This is how he used to be.*

"Lise," he said, getting up from the chair and coming over to us, giving me a hug. "How you been?"

"Good," I said, a little self-consciously, wishing for some cooler reply.

He hugged my mother as well. "What's up, sis? Thanks for coming."

"Lise wanted to see you," she said. "So did I. You"—she smiled, looked him up and down—"look great."

"Sure, sure. How'd you *think* I'd look?" he asked, and we were both silent, not knowing what to say. We'd been prepared for the worst.

"Hey, let's go outside," he suggested. "The day's too nice to be sittin' in here."

"Are you . . ." My mother glanced around, a look of concern on her face.

"Allowed?" he said. "Sure. As long as I don't go running off nowhere."

He meant it as a joke, I suppose, but it was too close to what was on our minds. Neither of us laughed.

"We have an exercise area out back," he said, leading us to a door that opened onto a fenced-in yard. There was a basketball court to our left, an open grassy area to the right. We sat down at a small table adjacent to the building, then got to talking, Uncle Jim filling us in on the place and how he'd been spending his time over the past two months.

"Lately, I've been painting. I've always been good at art," he said, pulling a pack of cigarettes from his pocket, tapping one out and lighting it up. I started to reach for it—out of habit, I guess—then stopped myself, realizing whose company we were in.

"I'm surprised they let you carry a lighter," my mother commented.

"At first they didn't. You have to be responsible. Build trust. Earn privileges," he explained. "Like going outside unattended. When I first got here, I couldn't do that either. It was something to work toward. It's the way they do things here."

He took another pull from the cigarette, turned his head and blew smoke out through the corner of his mouth.

"Say, Lise. How about you and me shootin' some hoops?"

"Okay," I said, getting up from the table and retrieving the ball from where it lay in the grass. My mother excused herself, said she needed to use the restroom. I think she just wanted to give us some time to ourselves.

We shot for a while, played three rounds of horse—two games to one in my favor—then sat on the grass, our backs against the chain-link fence instead of the oak tree in my front yard.

"They treatin' you okay?" I asked. "You like it here?"

"It's all right. Don't have much choice, I guess." He was more serious now, not joking around as much as he was when my mother and I first arrived.

"I'm sorry about what happened," I told him, and somehow it seemed appropriate that *I* should be the one apologizing, that I'd let him down in a way. I couldn't shake the feeling that he was in here because of me.

"No apologies. Didn't have nothin' to do with you." He ran his fingers through the grass, plucked out a dandelion and handed it to me, watched as I blew and its florets dispersed into the air. "I've been sick for a long time," he said. "Long as I can remember. It gets better and worse, but it never goes away. Not completely. It's a part of me, you know? Something I've got to deal with."

I nodded.

"It's important that we take responsibility for who we are," he continued. "We owe it to the people around us."

The door opened and my mother appeared in the yard. Uncle Jim and I both stood up, walked over to where she stood.

"We should get going," she told him.

"Okay, yeah." He dropped down onto one knee, but I'd had a growth spurt over the past two months and he had to look up at me from the position, almost as if he were the child and I the adult, instead of the other way around.

"We'll come back and visit soon," I promised, and he smiled, giving me a hug.

"You take care of your family now," he said. Then, lowering his voice, he spoke only to me: "It's a tough world out there, and they need you. You've always been the strong one. And remember"—he looked me sternly in the eye—"this ain't no dog and pony show."

"Well, I've never seen a dog and pony show," I told him, leaning forward and giving him a hug, my voice a whisper in his ear. "But I really want to."

Chapter 53

The next day was the first of what would turn out to be a five-day stretch of Indian summer. I'd slept poorly the night before, my sleep disturbed by dreams of Uncle Jim and the sound of someone screaming at the end of the hall. I'd pulled the pillow up over my head, tried to get back to sleep. I suppose that when one lives in a psychiatric hospital, such nightly disturbances are not uncommon. Strange how I'd been residing here for the past five years, but was experiencing many of these things as if for the first time.

In the morning, I showered, dressed, and entered the general population room. There was a short line of patients at the window to the nurses' station, and I took my place in line. When I reached the window, there was Amber, my reliable barista, meeting me with a warm smile, a small paper cup of medication—"A few morsels," she said—and a cup of water to wash the pills down. The water found its way to my stomach, but not the pills. It was irresponsible of me to cheek them—reckless after all I'd been through—but the reality of what I'd done five years ago was too fresh, too raw in my memory. My thoughts kept returning to the feel of the knife in my hand, the soft give of flesh as the blade entered his chest, the shock and confusion in Amir's eyes as he looked down at me—bright red blood dripping from his hand, making tracks along my forehead. In a few minutes, the blood would be purple and coagulated. It would take even less time for him to be dead.

There are routines here to be followed, daily rituals to distract us from the wasted passage of our lives. Morning medications are among those rituals, and over the next few weeks I became adept at avoiding those medications when I could. It was not that I wanted to sabotage all that I had worked for, only that I longed to forget, longed for the full protection of this place: an asylum from all that I'd done.

As the weeks passed, I became reacquainted with my brother, who arrived on most mornings around nine and stayed until my group session at eleven. It was mid-November now, and the weather was turning once again, the days growing shorter, tree limbs stretched naked against the vast gray mantle of sky.

"I've been thinking about Uncle Jim," I told him. Jason and I were walking the open grounds, the way we'd done in a different season several months ago. We'd come to Menaker's west end, where the property looked out over the Severn River.

Jason was quiet for a while, considering. "What happened to him doesn't have to happen to you, Lise. The path he chose isn't your path."

I closed my eyes. Ten days after my only visit to see him, they'd found Uncle Jim hanging from the showerhead, legs folded under him, the towel cinched tight around his neck.

I'd cried plenty, hadn't understood it. He'd seemed *so much better* the last time I'd seen him: optimistic and full of life.

"It's when patients are at the greatest risk for suicide," the psychiatrist at Spring Grove had explained to my parents—a conversation my mother conveyed to me later. "Patients typically don't attempt suicide when the symptoms of the disease are at their worst. It's often during recovery, when they have the focus and energy to formulate a plan—to engage in an attempt."

Maybe he finally understood what he had done, I thought, *how close he'd come to killing that child. Maybe he got a good look at how the rest of his life would be and wanted none of it.*

In my mind, when I pictured him hanging naked in the shower, his neck torqued at a severe and fatal angle, I imagined that he'd taken a marker and scrawled "The Dog and Pony Show" across his chest before he died. An apology of sorts. A last message to me that he'd tried but just couldn't stomach the road ahead any longer. There was no evidence for this, of course, and even if he'd done such a thing, they never would've told me. Still, that was the image I pictured. I couldn't help it.

I've been sick for a long time, he'd told me. *Long as I can remember. It gets better and worse, but it never goes away. Not completely. It's a part of me, you know? Something I've got to deal with.*

Jason and I moved on in silence, both of us trapped in our private thoughts. I could still see the river far below us, the earth beyond the fence at this section of the property giving way to that great empty space. For a moment, I was out there, stepping into the abyss—could almost feel myself falling.

We were nearing the front gate at the southern end when I felt something reach out and snatch at my leg. I stopped to look down, noted the tear in my pants. A piece of bramble clung to the fabric. There was no pain—not yet—but when I lifted the leg of my pants to inspect the wound I could see that the thorns had carved a deep gouge in the flesh.

"You're bleeding," Jason noted, but I told him it was nothing—just a scratch, really.

"We're about done for the day, anyway. I'll go inside and clean up," I assured him. "There's a bathroom next to my office."

Jason started to say something, then stopped, his mouth going slack.

"What do you mean 'next to my office'?"

I frowned, not understanding the point of his question. He knew the place I was referring to. We'd held several of our sessions there already.

"Who are you?" he asked, but there was a guarded wariness to his expression, as if the answer he expected might be toxic. I could sense the paranoia radiating from his skin, the product of his disease.

"I'm Lise Shields, your doctor," I told him. It wasn't clear if he was hearing me. The color was quickly draining from his face.

"*Tony,*" I called over to the watchman's booth. "*I need help with this patient.*"

"What is it, Lise?" Tony asked, stepping toward us, radio in hand.

"I don't know," I answered. "Some type of reaction to the medication, maybe. I need you to stay with him for a minute while I get a stretcher."

I turned and walked briskly in the direction of the medical building. I'd increased the dosage of Jason's medications too quickly, I realized. His body had not been able to handle it. It was not the first time I'd witnessed this in a patient, and unfortunately I did not think it would be the last. The human mind is a delicate creature, susceptible to many influences. The stability of the patients I treat here is tenuous. It is important to understand that from the beginning.

Because there are individuals here who will never leave—who will never reside outside of these grounds. Their pathology runs too deep. They will never be restored to sanity, will never return to their former lives. And the danger, I am afraid—and the great tragedy for those who love them—is to cling to the hope that they will.

Acknowledgments

Let's not confuse what is real from what is imagined. *The Forgetting Place* is a work of fiction, and I've taken significant creative liberties in the portrayal of mental illness and the psychiatric institutions in this story. As with most diseases, symptoms vary depending on the individual, and the array of symptoms depicted within these pages are not necessarily representative of those experienced by most patients. It is also important not to lose sight of the human being attached to the disease, and I hope that I've done justice to that principle along the way. Likewise, the men and women who dedicate their lives to the treatment of people with mental illness provide a heroic and invaluable service to both patients and their families, and this story is not intended to suggest otherwise.

Thanks goes to my wife, Lorie, who reads my early drafts, is aware of my many faults, and loves me anyway. Dr. Jay Menaker was kind enough to lend his name to the fictional psychiatric institution depicted in these pages, trusting my assurance that the choice bared no reflection on his own state of mind. My brilliant editor is Jessica Williams, who once again had an unfailing eye for what the story needed throughout its development, and was not shy—thank God—about challenging me to bring everything I had to the table. The publishing team at William Morrow continues to support me with their talent and enthusiasm, and my agent, Paul Lucas, is a Jedi Master in all things literary and provides me with sound advice and enough peace of mind that I can keep my attention focused where it should be.

My usual support group came into play—as they always do—and the list includes so many friends, colleagues, and family members that I dare not even begin to list them for fear of adding another fifty pages to the end of this book. Suffice it to say that I am grateful for every one of you.

This novel is dedicated to my parents, who are the polar opposite of the distant and emotionally absent parents depicted in the story. They've been in my corner since the very beginning, and I've tried to emulate them in many ways. Thanks, guys. For everything.

And thanks to you, reader, for sharing your time and imagination—for joining me in this fictional world for a while. More than anything else, it's your presence that makes it all worthwhile.

John Burley
August 1, 2014